THE BLIGHT OF HARROW HALL

Madeline Quinn

Copyright © 2024 Madeline Quinn

All rights reserved.

For My Husband
thanks for supporting me in all my careers

"Death destroys a man: the idea of Death saves him."
E.M. Forster in *Howards End*

Prologue

Twenty Years Ago

Victor Harrow stood on the edge of the stone balcony, staring out over the vast, dark expanse of the Harrow estate. The wind whipped through his hair as he considered the chilling realities he was about to leave behind. The Hall knew it, too. He felt its fear, its scrambling, as the energy fought to keep him there. The moonlight cast eerie shadows over the grounds, playing tricks on his eyes, but Victor knew better than to trust appearances here. Harrow Hall had always been a place of secrets, a labyrinth of lies and sinister whispers that had haunted his family for generations.

Vic's thoughts were interrupted by the bounce of headlights on the two-track road through the surrounding forest and the crunch of tires as a rusty Volkswagen pulled into the drive. Vic snatched the envelope packed full of cash from his bedside table, shoved it in his back pocket, and strode to the stairs. As he passed his grandmother's apartment on the next floor, she looked up from the book she was reading. "Going somewhere, dear?"

"A friend's here, ma'am. Remember, he was going to bring by those university catalogs."

"Come here, Victor." Grandmother Hyacinth held out her hand, long skeletal fingers reaching toward him. He caught it gently. Her skin was cold and paper thin. "You've had such a distinguished Naval service already. Don't you think that's enough? Maybe it's time to come home permanently." Her gaze was a genuine plea, but he knew the Hall was working on her psyche, too. She'd never fought it.

"There's so much I want to do yet, ma'am, and now that my enlistment is almost up, the Navy will pay for my tuition."

She pursed her lips and increased the strength of her grip with a force that surprised him. "Money never has been nor ever will be an issue for a Harrow. You should be well aware of that."

"I just feel I have earned it and should take advantage of the offer."

"But Florida, Victor? You've already traveled the world. Why do you need to be so far away from me?"

He felt a pang of regret. She truly wanted the best for him, and all she ever asked in return was companionship. It was all she had wanted from his mother, too. He knew the other demands came from the Hall itself. His grandmother was powerless to stop them, and his mother had dealt with them in her own way. After experiencing them for himself, he finally understood what she had been up against, why the drugs had been such a haven for her, and why she'd retreated into them to escape the Hall's grasp.

Maybe…just maybe, Grandmother would listen to the truth. He took a deep breath. "This place—"

"—will be yours before you know it and the fortune along with it." Her pupils dilated slightly, and she tipped her head, focus shifting, as if not seeing him. Vance knew it was too late for the truth. Harrow Hall wouldn't allow her to consider any plot against it.

He stood, releasing her hand. "It's the sun in Florida, ma'am," he offered half-heartedly. "If you could just feel the warmth. We never get anything like it here in Connecticut."

She waved a hand and turned back to the book in her lap.

He didn't linger in his lie, taking the grand staircase two steps at a time. Outside, Oliver Crane, the tech aficionado from New York City who had promised Vic a way out, stood silently next to his car, gazing slack jawed at the Hall.

"Shit man! You weren't kidding. This place is massive. Are you sure you wanna do this?" Oliver's voice was detached, but there was an undercurrent of concern. "Once we start, there's no going back."

Vic cast a glance up to the Hall, repulsion and anger welling. His expression was hard but resolute. "I have to do this, Oliver. There's no other way to save them."

Oliver nodded, his eyes scanning Vic's face as if searching for any hint of hesitation. Finding none, he reached into his bag and pulled out a small, sleek device. "This will wipe every trace of Victor Harrow from the digital world. Your new identity, Vance Miran, will be ready in a few hours. But remember, this isn't just a name change. It's a new life."

Vic took the device, feeling its weight in his hand. It was a small thing, yet it held the power to alter his entire existence. He closed his eyes, taking a deep breath, and thought about the sacrifices he was making. Harrow Hall had been his home, the best one he'd had since his mother's overdose shortly after he turned seven. But it was also a prison. The darkness that lurked within its walls had claimed too many lives already. If he stayed, he would either succumb to it or become a party to it.

"I understand," Vic said, his voice steady as he laid his palm against the screen to trigger the process. "I've been preparing for this. It's the only way to ensure that the truth about Harrow Hall never comes to light and that no one else gets hurt."

Oliver's gaze softened. "It's a heavy burden, living a life of solitude, always on the run, always hiding. Are you ready for that?"

He nodded. "I've made my peace with it. I can't get close to anyone. It's too dangerous. My past... it's something I'll have to carry alone."

On the car's hood, Oliver laid out a stack of documents, all bearing the name Vance Miran. A passport, driver's license, credit cards—everything he needed to start anew. "You're doing a brave thing, Vic. Just remember, your sacrifice won't be in vain. You're saving lives, even if they never know it."

Vic gave a small, sad smile. "That's enough for me."

As Oliver began the process of erasing Victor Harrow from existence, Vic allowed himself a moment of reflection. The darkness of Harrow Hall had always been a part of him, but now he had a chance to escape it. He could leave behind the whispers, the shadows, the fear. As Vance Miran, he could forge a new path, free from the chains of his family's legacy.

But freedom came at a cost. Vic knew he would always have to look over his shoulder, always be one step ahead of those who might discover the truth. He would have to keep his heart guarded, never letting anyone get too close. It would be a lonely existence, but it was a price he was willing to pay to protect the world from the horrors of Harrow Hall.

Oliver cleared his throat, breaking Victor's train of thought. "There's more," he said, his voice tinged with a mix of seriousness and compassion. "I've arranged for all the necessary players to fake your death. We've got a coroner and a funeral home director who owe me favors. The news is going to be routed through your girlfriend first who will no doubt take it to your grandmother. Two weeks later, they'll receive an urn with what looks like your ashes."

Victor's eyes widened slightly, the full weight of his decision pressing down on him. "And Harrowsburg? What will they think?"

"As far as Harrowsburg is concerned," Oliver replied, "Victor Harrow dies a tragic death ten days from now in Florida at the age of 27. The story will be clean, the evidence solid. Your girlfriend, your grandmother, and the people you grew up with—they'll mourn you, but they'll be safe, right?" He gazed at the Hall again.

Vic nodded slowly, absorbing the enormity of the plan. "Thank you, Oliver. I can't imagine this has been easy to arrange."

Oliver shrugged, a small smile playing at the corners of his mouth. "Let's just say it's not every day you get to help someone make a completely fresh start. Use it wisely." The handheld device beeped to indicate the completion of its task, and Oliver took it back.

Vic, now Vance, handed Oliver the envelope jammed with cash from his back pocket and looked out over the estate one last time, the moonlight casting long shadows over the familiar landscape. "I will. For their sake, and for mine."

***

Twelve Years Later

The sun was setting over the beach, casting a warm, golden glow over the sand and Pacific. Vance Miran stood at the edge of a small gathering of friends, watching the waves crash against the shore. He rarely allowed himself to relax, to feel the simple joy of a day at the beach, even here, nearly 3,000 miles from Harrow Hall. But today was different. Today, he felt a strange sense of peace. He sensed the approach of something good in his gut, something that was his reward for all the sacrifices he had made and would continue to make.

As he turned to join the group, his eyes caught sight of someone he hadn't seen before. She was standing a little apart from the others, her dark hair blowing in the breeze, eyes fixed on the horizon. There was something about her that drew him in, a quiet strength and an air of mystery that resonated with him.

He walked over, his heart pounding in a way it hadn't in years. "Hi, I'm Vance," he said, extending a hand.

She turned to him, a smile lighting up her face. "Anita," she replied, shaking his hand. Her touch was warm, and her hair haloed her face in a sudden gust, accentuating kind eyes and full lips. For a moment, Vance felt a spark of something he thought he'd never experience, something he'd tried hard to avoid.

They talked as the sun dipped below the horizon, their conversation flowing effortlessly. Vance found himself captivated by her laughter, her insights, her thoughtfulness. It was as if she could see right through him, past the walls he had built around his heart. He had never believed in love at first sight, but with Anita, he felt something powerful and undeniable.

As the evening wore on, Vance couldn't shake the feeling that he had found something precious that he had thought was beyond his reach. But with that realization came a pang of fear. Anita couldn't know the truth about him, about his past. The secrets of Harrow Hall, the darkness and dark deeds he had fled, were too dangerous to share.

He watched her laugh with their friends, her face illuminated by the glow of the beach bonfire, and he knew he was in deep. He needed her in his life, but he also needed to protect her from the shadows that haunted his past. Vance Miran had been born out of necessity, a new identity to escape the horrors of Harrow Hall. But with Anita, he felt the pull of his real self, a man who longed for connection, for love.

As the night drew to a close and they walked together along the shore, Vance made a silent vow. He would find a way to be with Anita, to build a life with her, even if it meant keeping his secrets buried deep. She couldn't know the truth behind his family history or his real identity.

In the stillness of the night, the waves whispered their secrets to the shore. Vance felt a glimmer of hope. Perhaps, just perhaps, he could find a way to balance the life he had to maintain with the one he now wanted to build. And in Anita's eyes, he saw the promise of a new beginning, a chance to finally find peace.

Chapter One

Memories flooded Anita's mind with each step through the empty rooms of her suburban LA beach front bungalow. The living room, once filled with cozy furniture and vibrant throw pillows, now echoed with the ghosts of laughter and late-night conversations. She remembered how Vance had carried her over the threshold on their wedding day, his eyes full of love and promise for their future together. The walls seemed to whisper stories of their life here—the way he teased her about her baking adventures that often set off the smoke alarms, evenings spent snuggled on the patio sofa watching the sunset colors dance across the waves, movie nights that ended in popcorn fights and retreats to the bedroom—leaving the movie unfinished.

In the kitchen, she traced her fingers on the white quartz counter tops where they had shared countless meals, planning their dreams and soothing worries, or so she had thought. The scent of sea salt lingered faintly in the air, a reminder of their walks along the shore, hand in hand. Stepping onto the small patio, she recalled the peaceful moments spent gazing at the ocean, the rhythmic sound of the waves a comforting backdrop to their quiet conversations. It had been their sanctuary, a place where the stresses of work melted away, and they found solace in each other's presence.

As she approached the bathroom off their bedroom, a shiver ran down her spine. It held the most chilling memory of all—the day she found him sprawled in the bathtub. Throughout her fifteen years as a nurse, she had never seen blood so red or porcelain so white, and she was sure she never would again.

The emptiness of the house now mirrored the void in her heart, a stark reminder of the fragility of happiness and the weight of unspoken pain. She closed her eyes, breathing deeply to steady herself, knowing that though the house was empty, it held within its walls the echoes of a love that had once filled every corner with warmth and hope. She tried, and failed miserably for the moment, to focus on it.

Anita zipped up her jacket against the winter ocean breeze as she stepped onto the front porch. The FOR SALE sign swayed gently, its message a knife to the heart. As she locked the door for what she intended to be the last time, a man in a sharp suit approached her from the sidewalk.

"Mrs. Miran?" he called out as he neared.

Anita turned, her eyes narrowing slightly at the stranger.

The man stopped a few feet away, holding out a business card as a gesture of peace. "My name is Thomas Reddick. I'm a private investigator looking for Vance Miran. I was hoping you could help me with his whereabouts."

Anita's heart skipped a beat at the mention of her late husband's name. Her voice was guarded, tinged with suspicion. "Why are you looking for him?" She stepped off the porch and walked down the short path to her car.

Thomas seemed prepared for the question as he followed her. "I represent a law firm in Harrowsburg, Connecticut. It appears Mr. Miran has inherited a significant property from his grandmother. We need to serve the details of the inheritance on him."

Anita laughed, a short, humorless sound. "You're a bit late, Mr. Reddick. Vance won't be inheriting anything."

The investigator's brow furrowed. "I don't understand."

She shifted her gaze to the quiet street behind him, her voice harsh with resignation. "You can find him at the corner of Hawks Lane and Green View," she said, flipping a hand towards the city.

Thomas nodded, tapping the information into his phone. "Thank you, Mrs. Miran." He turned away and took a few steps as Anita moved around to her car's driver's side. She got in, slamming the door a little more forcefully than necessary. As she started the ignition, Thomas jogged up beside her window. She grit her teeth and punched the button to roll it down.

"Ma'am, that address is, um, a cemetery."

"And?" Anita raised her eyebrows with an irritated look. "That is where you put dead people, isn't it?"

"So, Vance Miran is dead?"

"As a door nail. For the past two months."

The color drained from Thomas' face as he processed the information. "I'm...I'm terribly sorry for your loss, Mrs. Miran. I had no idea."

Anita watched his professional façade waver, a flicker of genuine sympathy crossing his features. "Thank you," she said, though her voice carried little warmth. Anger and irritation shoved their way back to the forefront. "You're not much of a private investigator, are you? A basic Internet search brings up his obituary."

"I'm sure it does." Thomas was unshaken by her insult. "It was only this morning that we tracked down the alias your husband was using.

"That's ridiculous. Vance didn't have an alias." Above and beyond their seven-year marriage, Anita was all to aware of his vital records after submitting his birth certificate, social security card, and driver's license to the funeral home for identification and the filing of his death certificate.

"I assure you, ma'am, he did. It's all in here." He reached into his briefcase and pulled out a thick manila envelope. "I think you'll find that we've done a thorough background. We have the right man. And now, upon his death, the property would legally pass to you. You are now the beneficiary of the Harrow estate. Congratulations."

Skepticism clouded Anita's expression. "I don't know anything about any property. Vance had no connection to Connecticut. This is probably some kind of scam, and I am in no mood—"

"—It's not a scam," Thomas insisted. "Here." He handed her the envelope. "This contains all the legal papers, the last will and testament of the deceased, one Hyacinth Harrow, and the contact information for the lawyers handling the estate. When you reconsider, please give them a call."

Anita took the envelope, her fingers brushing against the cold paper. "I'll look into it," she said noncommittally.

Thomas gave a small nod, stepping back. "Again, I'm sorry to have brought this up at such a difficult time." He turned on his heel and made for the sidewalk.

Anita's gaze lingered on what had been her home. The bungalow had been a place of love and laughter, of dreams and sometimes tears. Now, it was just another tie to sever, another piece of her old life to let go. She tossed the file onto the passenger seat and pulled away from the curb.

The Pacific Ocean glinted in the distance, a vast expanse of blue that seemed unending, shifting and roiling, just like her emotions. As Anita drove toward the bustling heart of the city, the rhythmic hum of the tires on the pavement did little to calm the storm raging within her. Her hands clenched the steering wheel, knuckles turning pale, as a wave of feelings surged through her. She had always relied on driving as a form of escape, a method to clear her cluttered thoughts. But today, the drive served as a harsh reminder of her current turmoil and an unwanted opportunity to confront the deep-seated anger and grief that had festered in the wake of Vance's suicide.

Death had struck like a bolt from the blue, shattering her world into fragments of disbelief and sorrow, just as the bullet had shattered his skull into unrecognizable pieces. In the raw weeks that followed, the initial numbness thawed into a profound emptiness, punctuated by relentless unanswerable questions. She replayed their last conversations, scouring for missed cues or signs of the invisible battle Vance must have fought alone. This persistent script highlighted her own perceived failures, intensifying the guilt that gnawed at her.

Driving in the city, the illuminated skyline blurred before her, distorted by tears that threatened to spill. She tried to blink them back, focusing on the road, each mile a painful roll through the landscape of her grief. She felt betrayed by Vance for leaving her so abruptly, for not seeking her help, for not giving her a chance to alter the ending of their shared story. This resentment towards him was tangled with a furious self-reproach and an overarching anger at the cosmic injustice of it all. Seven years to an abrupt end.

Her thoughts shifted to the unexpected inheritance of some ridiculous property all the way across the country. A fresh wave of anger ignited. It was just an unwanted reminder of the secrets Vance must have kept from her. The bundle of legal documents on the passenger seat felt like a manifestation of his betrayal.

By the time she reached the dense city center and found a spot in the parking garage near her best friend's apartment, resolve hardened within her. The documents would remain unopened; no calls to any Connecticut lawyer would be placed. Anita's path forward would not include delving into the shadows of Vance's unknown past. She sought closure, not through exploration and acceptance, but through severance and distance.

She would move forward alone. With her gaze set firmly on the horizon of her new beginning. Unanchored by the past.

***

Anita sat in a corner booth at Exiles. It was a place Vance had despised—a sanctuary where memories of him shouldn't intrude. The thumping bass of techno music reverberated through the brick walls, adorned with blue and green paint splatters, and made the amber starburst lights above tremble. She sipped her gin and tonic with lime, trying to lose herself in the pulsing rhythm of the music and the vibrant atmosphere.

"Anita, there you are!" Doreen's voice cut through the din as she slid into the booth. Her best friend was a whirlwind of energy, her bright red hair a stark contrast against the dimly lit bar. "I can't believe you're here on a Friday night, amidst all this chaos!"

Anita managed a faint smile, glad for Doreen's irrepressible spirit. "Sometimes chaos is exactly what I need."

Doreen eyed her friend with concern. Anita shifted uncomfortably, all too aware of the circles under her eyes, and the lines that had so recently popped up on once smooth skin.

"How have you been holding up, darling? It's been tough, I know."

Anita nodded, swirling her drink absently. "Yeah, it hasn't been a picnic."

"Is it done?"

"Yep. All the furniture is being sold on consignment, and the house is in the hands of the realtor now."

"Then let's celebrate!" Doreen's phone buzzed as an area code 959 number flashed across the screen. She grabbed it off the table. "Oh," she said. "I've got to take this. I'll be right back."

Doreen shimmied away through the crowd. After a few minutes of watching the lights swirl and couples dance, Anita decided she needed to use the restroom. As she pushed through the door, she was surprised to find Doreen on the phone in front of the mirror. "—I'll take care of it, Vanessa. Don't worry…Yes, I—" She spotted Anita heading to a stall. "Look, I'm not on call tonight. Bother someone else." Doreen hung up and mouthed "Sorry" to Anita. Doreen pointed out back out toward the floor.

Anita nodded. As she used the bathroom, she worried about her friend. Doreen was a recovered drug addict. She made an amazing nurse and friend because she understood pain so deeply. Anita wondered if she had been thinking too much of herself lately. She resolved to do better.

When Anita slid back into their booth, she found two more of each of their drinks waiting for her. "So, what exactly are we supposed to be celebrating?"

"The last week of your bereavement leave, and to your oh-so-comfortable spot on my sofa for the foreseeable future!"

Anita laughed despite herself. "You will find a way to celebrate anything."

"Damn right!"

"Okay, but how about to our friendship as well, and to you, the best damn floor nurse in all of LA."

Doreen grinned.

"I mean it Doreen. You'd tell me if I could help with anything right? I know I've been caught up in everything with Vance, but we still need to take care of each other, and that means helping you out too."

"I know you've got my back, girl."

And as they raised their glasses amidst the pulsating music and the splattered walls of Exiles, Anita felt a flicker of excitement ignite within her—a flicker of hope for a future where all the doors to the past were shut and locked and those to the future all opened up as planned.

***

Anita and Doreen had spent the night dancing away their cares in the vibrant heart of downtown LA. The pulsing music beat had merged with the rhythm of their laughter, creating a temporary bubble that grief and reality couldn't pop. As they stumbled out of the club in the early morning hours, arms linked and hearts light, the city seemed to wrap around them in a warm embrace.

The rideshare to Doreen's apartment was filled with giggles and nonsensical conversation, the type that only made perfect sense to those involved. They leaned on each other, literally and metaphorically, as they navigated the steep stairwell of Doreen's sleeping building. By the time they reached the apartment, the sky was beginning to lighten, painting the smoggy horizon in shades of pink and orange.

Doreen collapsed onto her bed, barely managing to kick off her shoes, while Anita made an even less graceful descent onto the sofa. Exhaustion quickly took hold, and she was asleep within moments, the cushions enveloping her in the scratchy embrace of wool blend.

Anita woke with the sun streaming through the windows, casting harsh lines across her face. Her head was pounding—a fierce reminder of the night's careless celebrations—and the sight that greeted her did nothing to ease her irritation. Doreen was sitting at the kitchen table, completely engrossed in the contents of the manila envelope from the investigator. A pile of papers spread across the tabletop like some sort of treasure map.

"What the hell, Doreen?" Anita grumbled, pushing herself up into a sitting position, her voice thick with frustration and hangover. "Why did you open that? I meant to throw it away." She eased herself back down to the sofa as her head spun.

Doreen looked up, her expression one of earnest excitement undimmed by Anita's tone. "Anita, you've got to see this. It's gorgeous. Look at this photo," she insisted, rushing over to the sofa with an 8x10 and shoving it in her friend's face.

Anita glanced at the photograph only briefly, her eyes hardening as they took in the image of the sprawling estate. "I don't care how pretty it is," she snapped, her anger flaring up. "It's just Vance dumping his unresolved crap on me from beyond the grave." She grabbed the photo and flung it like a frisbee across the living room.

Doreen didn't flinch at Anita's harsh words. "Anita, come on. This could be something good—a new start. It says right here that if the heir apparent—ooh, so official—is unable to take possession, the inheritance moves to the surviving spouse. Maybe it's a chance for you to—"

"—Don't," Anita cut her off sharply. "Don't make this into some kind of sentimental journey where I find myself in the ruins of Vance's secrets. He's gone, Doreen. He *chose* to leave. Now I'm supposed to uproot my life because some obscure relative of his kicked the bucket in Connecticut? I'm already uprooting things, selling *my* ocean-side bungalow—that I bought before I even met him—to pay for his funeral and debts."

Doreen's voice softened, trying to pierce the armor of Anita's resentment. "You couldn't go back there even if you didn't have bills to pay," she said softly, leaving the elephant in the room unnamed. Anita rolled over on the sofa to face the back cushions, refusing to think about the scene in the bathroom.

"Even his name—" Anita threw a punch against the couch back. "The investigator said he was going by an alias! WTF?"

"Yes, it's all here." Doreen dug in the pile of documents. "People change their names all the time, hon."

Anita growled and paused for a moment before asking the question on her mind. "So, who the hell was he really?"

Doreen understood her query despite the muffling of her voice against the sofa. "Victor Clifton Harrow. Ew. I would have changed it, too."

Anita rolled back over. "Why is all this coming out now? Why didn't he tell me about his rich grandmother? Why didn't he tell me about *anything*?"

"I know you're hurt but think about it, 'Nita. You could sell the property, at least, and if you want to come back here and buy a different house, you'd definitely have enough. It could be a huge opportunity for you. And who knows, maybe you'll even like it there. Connecticut needs good nurses, too."

Anita sighed heavily, a mix of exhaustion and irritation lingering in her voice. "I have a job I love here, Doreen. I have a life here. Why would I leave that for some guilt-ridden inheritance and some snooty East Coast city? It's probably snowing there! Why would Vance do this to me?"

Doreen came over and sat down on the coffee table, laying her hand on Anita's elbow. "Maybe it's not about what he did anymore, Anita. Maybe it's about what you can do for yourself now. Give it a chance, for your own sake. Go see it. If you hate it, fine. Sell it. Come back. My sofa is always open. But what if it's a chance for something better?" Doreen held her other hand over Anita, and an antique brass key on a lavender ribbon slipped from her palm, swinging like a pendulum. Anita turned away.

The room fell silent except for the faint ticking of the kitchen clock. Anita side-eyed the document spread and key Doreen had tossed on the coffee table, her mind racing with conflicting emotions. Doreen moved around the apartment, getting ready for her shift at the hospital, giving her friend space. Finally, Anita's shoulders slumped under the weight of unresolved grief and a future she had never asked for, and she let the hangover spin her back to sleep on the scratchy sofa.

Chapter Two

Six Months Later

Feeling the weariness of the entire expanse of the United States etched into her bones, Anita rolled up to one of two lone gas pumps at a station with an attached diner in Harrowsburg, Connecticut. Her little green sedan, a faithful companion through miles of uncertain roads, sat quietly as it guzzled down much-needed fuel. Eyeing the buggy headlights, she wondered if she would ever get the goo, wings, and leg bits off or if they were now a permanent fixture of her cross-country journey.

The town itself seemed to be frozen in time by its quaint charm. A sign nearby boasted a population barely above 4,000. The end of August lingered in the air, teasing at the promise of autumn with just a hint of crimson touching the edges of the leaves.

Anita gazed down the sleepy New England town's Main Street. It was untouched by the hustle and bustle of modernity. The buildings, predominantly constructed from weathered stone and aged brick, served as stoic witnesses to generations gone by. The post office, with its wooden sign creaking gently in the breeze, held steadfast at one end of the street, while the grade school, its red brick facade softened by ivy creeping up the walls, stood at the other. Between them, the pharmacy, clinic, and veterinarian's office catered to the needs of the townsfolk, their storefronts offering glimpses into a simpler era.

Despite the late summer sun casting a warm glow upon the cobblestone sidewalks, there was an undeniable aura of fatigue that permeated the air. The occasional resident shuffled along, their steps measured and unhurried, out for an evening stroll, adding to the town's tired rhythm.

At the heart of it all, the town square lay shaded by ancient oak trees whose broad branches would provide sanctuary from midday heat. Here, weathered stone benches offered respite for those inclined to linger. A fountain, perhaps once proud and mighty, sputtered intermittently, its water trickling lazily into a shallow basin adorned with pennies tossed in by hopefuls. The atmosphere was one of serene resignation, where time moved slowly and each day unfolded with the same unhurried cadence that had characterized the town for generations.

"What the hell have I gotten myself in to?" Anita muttered.

The gas station, worn like a forgotten relic of the past, greeted her with a sense of familiarity that only weary travelers understand. As she stepped away from her car, she could feel the curious eyes of the locals—two elderly men, their weathered faces telling tales of a lifetime spent here, glancing up with mild interest. Behind the counter stood a slightly younger man, eyeing her arrival with the cautious reserve of someone accustomed to the ebb and flow of transient visitors.

Ignoring the gazes that followed her, Anita stretched her tired limbs. The relentless drive from Los Angeles had taken its toll, but there was a steely determination in her eyes. Doreen ensured that the proceeds from the consignment sales of Anita's furniture back home awaited her in her bank account, though it wasn't generating as much as she'd hoped. Her connection with Doreen was a lifeline, a tangible reminder that she was not alone.

The ancient gas pump clicked softly as it filled her tank, a mechanical heartbeat in the stillness of the evening. With a sigh of relief, Anita hung up the nozzle and took a slow stroll around the parking lot, gravel crunching underfoot. The air was crisp with the promise of a changing season, a subtle shift from the relentless heat she had experienced through the west and midwest to the gentler embrace of an East Coast late summer.

Completing her circuit around the lot, Anita walked slowly to the station entrance. The elderly men had resumed their conversation, their interest in her fleeting as they returned to the comfort of their routine. Shelves of candy, automotive cleaning supplies, and oil stood to the right. The smell of coffee and fried food meandered its way from the diner attached to the back of the station. The man behind the front counter offered her a brief nod of acknowledgment as Anita swiped her card to pay for the gas.

"Thanks," she said.

"Sure thing, Ms. Miran," the man said peering over his glasses at the small print on her receipt. He handed it over and she nodded, thinking it a tad creepy. But then again in a town this size, everyone probably knew everyone else. She'd never experienced small town life, but she'd heard the stories from coworkers who transplanted themselves to LA and from patients searching for specialized medical treatment not available in their rural communities.

Anita glanced at the man's embroidered work shirt and decided to give one-for-one. "Take care, Chuck."

Returning to her car, she started the ignition, and the engine purred to life, a reassuring sound amidst the quiet of the town. Glancing once more at old men in the gas station who were once again focused on her, she checked her map app. It showed an error, so she closed and restarted it, punching in the Hall's address. The search crawled along but finally gave her a route. She breathed a sigh of relief at not having to ask the men at the gas station for directions.

Anita drove out of the lot, marveling at the lack of traffic. She was sure to follow the 20 mph speed limit. The last thing she needed was a ticket to start her time here. The subtle details of Harrowsburg unfolded before her: modest houses with neatly trimmed lawns, an occasional passerby whose friendly nod spoke of a community bound by more than mere geography. Here, amidst the quiet rustling of leaves and the distant hum of a tractor working a field, Anita felt a flicker of possibility. She squashed it. Hardcore. She was here to sell, collect the money, and go home.

The route took her through town and then merged onto a quiet country road. The sun dipped lower, a warm glow radiating over the changing leaves. The town dwindled behind her, a speck in her rearview mirror.

She had driven about three miles when the road came to a dead end. The route continued on her phone, on a nonexistent road. "Shit," she muttered. There was nothing ahead of her but a tangle of weeds and a ROAD CLOSED sign, the once red paint faded to pink and the white tarnished with dirt and peeling. Across gulleys to her right and left, well-tended fields stood, blanketed by five-foot tall broad leaf plants of a crop she couldn't identify. Rolling hills and trees beyond obscured the view of any buildings. Anita zoomed in on the map. There were no identifiable routes circumnavigating the field.

With a frustrated sigh, she decided to return to the gas station and ask for directions.

***

Anita pulled back into the dusty gravel lot. She glanced at the old neon sign flickering above the entrance, which had come to life in the lowering evening light. A sense of uncertainty hovered over her.

Stepping out of her car, Anita straightened her jacket and pushed open the gas station's glass door for the second time that evening. The bell above tinkled softly, announcing her re-entrance. The soft hum of a 60s song she hadn't noticed before played over speakers behind the counter.

"Hey, Chuck." She approached the man at the counter who had moved very little from where he stood a half hour ago. "I'm trying to find Harrow Hall, and—" she clicked her tongue and waved her phone "—the map seems a bit off. Could you give me some directions?"

"Harrow Hall, you say?" Chuck shot a glance at the old men still seated along the wall. "Some might argue that the Hall's what's a bit off."

"What business you got there?" One of the seated men piped in a high rasp. The skin folds on his scrawny neck jiggled with the words.

Anita forced a smile. "I just need to find it, guys. Can you help?"

They shared a loaded glance again. "Best go talk to Logan," Chuck said. "He's in the diner."

"Thanks." Anita stalked down the narrow hallway. Red booths and a young woman in an honest-to-goodness pink and white waitress uniform carrying trays emerged.

Anita approached a counter off to the side. A middle-aged woman with a greying bun and identical—if a few sizes larger and a bit less crisp—uniform stood rolling silverware into napkins. The woman offered a friendly but tired smile. "Hey, there. What can I get you?" She wiped her hands on a rag.

"Actually, I'm looking for someone named Logan?" Anita inquired, motioning with her head back toward the gas counter. "Chuck sent me."

"Oh sure." She pointed to a booth near the window where a man in flannel sat opposite a striking blond woman. "Logan!" the woman called out. "Someone's looking for you."

"Thanks," Anita said through gritted teeth as all the diner guests turned to stare at her. She walked over to the booth, feeling the weight of their eyes on her. As she approached, Logan looked up, his expression curious. Anita stopped in her tracks about six feet from the table, dread punching her in the stomach.

"Can I help you?" he asked, his tone friendly.

At first glance, she thought she'd been looking at a more robust version of Vance. Even though the build was bolder on this man, they shared the same angular jaw, dark eyes, and golden-brown skin. Anita blinked a few times. The resemblance faded a bit with the man's movement, but not entirely.

"Logan Emmerich," he introduced himself and stood, extending his hand. His smile held an intrinsic warmth that Vance's never had, and it helped to dispel the similarity—as did the pure northeastern accent. Anita felt another internal punch as she realized she'd never hear her husband's quiet southern drawl again.

"Hi…" She drew out the word unintentionally, took a few steps forward, and shook his hand. "I'm Anita Miran. I'm trying to find my way to Harrow Hall," she explained, noting how the gorgeous blonde next to him startled, microbladed brows arching, at the mention of the property.

"Anita, huh?" Logan said with surprise. "We expected you quite a while ago."

"We?"

"Mr. Charleton at the law office. He said you'd be coming to take possession." He looped a finger through his belt loop. "I manage the grounds there."

"I, uh, I live in California. There were some things I needed to take care of first."

"Sure. I can show you the way out there."

The blonde, still seated, did not mask her displeasure. Her lips thinned into a tight line, and her eyes darted between Logan and Anita with undisguised irritation. Logan, seemingly oblivious to the reaction, grabbed his jacket from a hook on the booth's frame.

"I don't want to interrupt your meal," Anita said, scanning their plates. Logan's was empty. The woman's boasted the remnants of a salad with dressing on the side.

"We're finished up. Right, Vanessa?"

The blonde gave a forced smile, but her eyes still held daggers for Anita.

Logan bent and gave Vanessa, still seated, a quick kiss. Anita noticed neither wore a ring. He pulled his billfold out of the back pocket of his jeans and laid a couple of bills on the table next to the condiment and napkin tray. He smiled at Anita. "We can head over now if you're ready."

Anita nodded, feeling a surge of relief mixed with a new wave of anxiety about following this stranger. She returned to her car, watching as Logan strode over to a vintage turquoise and white pickup parked near the entrance.

They pulled out of the gas station, and he led her down the same route she had tried to take but then suddenly veered off onto a narrow, almost hidden two-track trail that Anita would have certainly missed on her own. Her heart thudded loudly in her chest as they drove deeper into the woods, the canopy of trees above making the twilight seem like full-on night.

Anita's grip on the steering wheel tightened as her car bumped and jostled over the uneven path. She questioned her decision to follow this near-stranger into such isolation, her mind racing with every possible worst-case scenario.

After what felt like an eternity but was likely only fifteen minutes, the trees began to thin, and the dense forest opened up to reveal the sprawling grounds of the Harrow Hall estate. They triggered a mixed sense of awe and foreboding, grandeur and decay, its walls holding secrets of generations.

Logan parked his pickup near what looked like a gardener's shed, and Anita pulled up beside him. They got out of their vehicles, and Logan turned to her with a smile that fully reached his eyes, perhaps sensing her unease. Anita wondered if serial killers were able to smile like that. If so, it was part of their success. She shook herself out of such musings, trying to convince her over-tired mind that this was just an easy-going, kind man. They did exist—didn't they?

"There she is, Harrow Hall. I can give you a quick tour of the nearby grounds if you'd like," he offered, his voice a blend of pride, as if he were custodian to its stories as much as to its land.

Anita nodded, taking a deep breath as she looked around her at the array of outbuildings and variety of landscaped spaces. "Yes, I'd like that very much." She tried to sound more confident than she felt, her mind still reeling from the surrealness of her journey and the stark reality of her new inheritance. "Why is the road so primitive? You'd expect a place like this to have its own highway or something."

"Well, Mrs. Harrow—" he glanced at her "—the last Mrs. Harrow that is, Hyacinth, she valued her privacy. Didn't want any uninvited guests, I guess. Shortly after her husband died, she had the main road—

where you probably found a ROAD CLOSED sign?" Anita nodded, and he continued, "She had that plowed over and fields planted. Ever since I was a kid, this little two-track has been the only way onto the property. Hyacinth's room on the second floor," Logan gestured toward the Hall, a good hundred yards away, "had a clear view of this road."

Anita marveled at the sights around her as Logan spoke. To the west, a lush green meadow rolled gently towards a dense forest of ancient oaks and maples. Their massive trunks stood tall and proud, their branches reaching out like arms of wise sentinels guarding the estate. The forest floor was carpeted with wildflowers, their vibrant colors a stark contrast to the somber shades of the old Hall.

To the east, manicured gardens sprawled in intricate patterns of symmetry and grace. Flower beds burst with riot colors – crimson roses, azure delphiniums, and heavy clusters of blue and pink hydrangeas swayed gently in the breeze.

A winding gravel path meandered through the gardens, bordered by neatly trimmed hedges and fragrant lavender bushes. Stone benches were strategically placed along the route with an invitation to pause and soak in the surrounding beauty.

Near the gardens, an orchard stretched out in orderly rows, laden with fruit trees heavy with apples, pears, and plums. Anita could almost taste the sweetness of the ripe fruit, imagining the joy of harvesting and sharing the bounty with others.

As she walked along the path, she marveled at the contrast between the vibrant, thriving natural world and the aging, weathered facade of Harrow Hall itself. Ivy clung to the timeworn stones. The Hall seemed to loom over the landscape like a shadow, its once-grand columns and portico now weathered and worn, the immense windows dull and dusty, frames warped with age.

The grounds seemed to pour their vitality toward the house, as if trying to breathe life back into its weary bones. Yet, the more they gave, the more the Hall seemed to absorb, like a black hole sucking in all the goodness and light, leaving the boundary between the two muted and subdued.

Anita approached a large oak tree near the edge of the gardens, its gnarled branches reaching skyward in defiance of time. She sat down momentarily on the stone bench beneath it, running her fingers over the cool, smooth surface. From this vantage point, she could see the entire estate before her: the gardens, the orchard, the meadow, and beyond.

Despite the stark contrast between the natural beauty and the declining Hall, Anita suddenly felt a deep sense of peace and belonging in this place, and she fought against it.

She surged to her feet. Logan, a few strides up the path caught her gaze after the sharp, unexpected movement. His silhouette was illuminated in soft rays of the dying sun's golden kiss. Profiled as such, he looked less like Vance. She breathed a sigh of relief, but then her breath caught in her throat as he walked farther down the path. The man was gorgeous. Anita cussed in a quiet mumble under her breath.

He glanced back her way, a quizzical look on his swarthy Adonis face, and she shook her head. "Just, uh, talking to myself," she mumbled, shoving her hair behind her ear and overtaking him on the path so she wouldn't have to watch him ahead of her anymore.

The stars burgeoning now above seemed to whisper of old sorrows and secrets, and the nearer they came to the house, the sense of peace flowed quickly out of reach. She noticed the intricate detailing of the architecture, the carved trim around the windows, the sweeping lines of the staircase leading to the front door, and the faded but still elegant charm of the porch swing.

Vines snaked their way up weathered columns, clinging desperately to the cracked facade. Drawing closer, she could see the intricate woodwork that adorned the porch railing, now chipped and weather-worn, its former elegance a mere memory. Once solid and imposing, the front door now appeared warped, with a gap underneath she could throw a cat through. Anita swallowed hard, her imagination conjuring whispers of stories long forgotten, voices of bygone residents echoing faintly in the empty spaces.

"Why are the grounds so pristine, but the house so…" She searched for the right word. "So neglected?"

"The estate funds for the house improvements and maintenance can only be touched by the current beneficiary. The grounds are funded through a separate trust that the caretaker uses with the law firm's oversight. Hyacinth died nearly a decade ago."

"Seems a strange setup for the funds."

Logan shrugged. "The mechanics of the whole thing were put into place even before Hyacinth was born. Who knows what they were thinking back then."

The gravel crunched under their shoes as they came to the front steps. "Well, you do a magnificent job as grounds manager. It looks like it probably takes a lot of time. Is it a full-time?"

"Yes. I'm usually here five or six times a week. I also do a little carpentry work on the side." He tugged at his ear lobe, and his similarity to Vance again struck Anita.

She looked away, taking in the peeling paint, missing shutters, and the sagging roofline of a side porch, its once-graceful arch now bowed downward. "Well, I imagine the new owners will keep you on and maybe give you some extra work fixing the house up."

He gave her a confused look, and she ignored it. She was beginning to enjoy his company, so she felt a strong need to end the tour. "Are the water and electricity on?"

"Electricity should be good to go, though you might find quite a few bulbs that need replacing. I just need to turn on the main valve for the water supply."

Anita nodded. "If you could do that before you go, I'd appreciate it."

"Are you planning on staying here tonight?" He seemed surprised.

"I've spent every night of the last week in a different motel in a different state. I really don't think I have it in me to check in to another."

Logan nodded, and a strange look of concern crossed his face. "Sure. Well, let me give you my number if you need help. I'll be by tomorrow morning also to do a few things on the grounds."

"Thanks." She opened a new text message and handed her phone to him. He typed in his number and hit send.

"Did the lawyers get you a key already?"

She nodded. "I'll just grab my stuff if you want to turn on the water before you leave." She strode back in the direction of her car, only paying half attention to the small utility shed into which Logan disappeared. Cash on the barrel head—she was selling this place. She didn't need to learn its specifics.

Anita heaved her overnight bag out of the trunk, followed by a sleeping bag and a backpack filled with essentials: a flashlight, snacks, electronics, and chargers. She hesitated momentarily, a fleeting urge to jump back in her car and hit the road to return to California, then squared her shoulders and grabbed a couple bottles of water before shutting the trunk. She decided to leave her large suitcase for tomorrow. Even so, the weight of her partial luggage made her steps hesitant.

Logan appeared at her side, deftly tugging the straps of the heavier bags from her bicep where they had slipped and tossing them effortlessly over his shoulder. "Oh no," she started to protest. "I don't need—"

"It's no problem."

Anita rolled her eyes toward his back as he took the lead, approaching the towering main door of the colonial manor. Freed from the bulk of the bags, she dug in the cargo pocket of her pants for the key. A few yardlights, either through motion detection or timing she wasn't sure, switched on.

She took a deep breath. "Here goes nothing," she muttered. Out of the corner of her eye, she caught another smile on Logan's face. As she inserted the key into the oversized lock, she considered again that there had to be something wrong with a man who was both so seemingly happy and good-looking.

The door creaked open reluctantly, revealing a cavernous foyer beyond. Her slender fingers brushed the antique wood, feeling insignificant against its weathered grandeur. The foyer stretched before her, dominated by a sweeping staircase that ascended gracefully to the upper floors, mirroring the imposing scale of the entrance itself. "Whoa," she breathed.

"Mmmhmm," Logan replied. "It's been years since I was inside."

Anita's eyes were drawn to a chandelier that still hung from the high ceiling, though now dim and dusty, its once twinkling lights long extinguished. She couldn't help but wonder about the light fixture's structural integrity after so many years of neglect. She stepped cautiously onto the carpet below it. The woven pattern was obscured by years of grime, dirt, and dead leaves that crunched softly underfoot in the low light.

The echoes of their slow footsteps mingled with the musty, forgotten air that filled the massive room. The glow from the yard light outside filtered through the stained glass above the entryway, casting colorful patterns on the floor and highlighting Logan's features—features Anita found uncomfortably compelling.

Logan glanced around the foyer with a sigh that seemed to carry a mixture of respect and reluctance. He set her bags down gently and walked over to a push-button light switch. Several of the wall sconces illuminated with a soft orange glow. "Well, here you are. Harrow Hall in all its... splendor."

Anita crossed her arms, her gaze drifting over the grand staircase and the portraits of long-gone Harrows staring down at them. "It's a lot," she admitted, her voice echoing in the vast space.

Logan nodded, his hands sliding into his pockets as he stepped toward the door. He paused, turning back to look at her. There was a curiosity there, held back by a polite restraint. "It's a big place for one person. If you need something, or if there's anything you want to know about the house or the estate—give me a call or text."

There was a kindness in his offer, a protective edge that Anita found both sweet and suffocating. "I think I can manage," she replied, her tone sharper than she intended as she bent down to nab her flashlight out of her backpack. "I'm not completely helpless."

Logan's expression faltered momentarily, but he quickly masked it with a polite nod. "Of course, I didn't mean to imply—"

"It's just a house," Anita cut in, her words brisk. "A big, old, dirty house."

He studied her for a moment, his eyes thoughtful. Then, with a slight smile, he said, "Well, then, Mrs. Harrow, I'll leave you to it."

Anita's brow furrowed at the name. "It's Miran. Anita Miran, I told you that."

Logan's handsome smile didn't waver. "Around here, anyone in your position is Mrs. Harrow. But, noted." His tone was gentle, almost teasing. He opened the door, the nearest yard light casting his silhouette in a long shadow across the floor. "Remember, I'm just a phone call away if you need anything. Anything at all."

With that, he stepped out, closing the door softly behind him, leaving Anita alone in the echoing silence of the foyer. She stood there for a moment, torn between irritation and loneliness. Logan's charm was undeniable, and his departure left a surprising chill in the air.

Turning away from the door, she sighed deeply, the weight of everything pressing down on her. "Just a big, old, dirty house," she muttered again, unsure if she was trying to convince herself or the ghosts of Harrows past.

Curiosity pulled her deeper into the shadows, and Anita loaded her bags onto her shoulders. She peered into the first room off the foyer, sweeping the beam of her flashlight. It was dark and musty, the furnishings barely discernible in the dim light filtering through grimy windows. A movement caught her eye—a mouse darting across the floor and disappearing into a crack in the wall. She shuddered involuntarily and moved on to the next room, finding it similarly cloaked in shadows and neglect, the air thick with dust motes dancing in the faint light.

Headlights skimmed the windows, and she heard the crunch of Logan's pickup tires turning around in the gravel drive. The bright white was replaced with the dim red of tail lights, and she knew she was now truly alone.

Deciding to explore further, Anita ascended the staircase, her hand trailing along the banister, which left streaks of dust and grime on her fingertips. She wiped her hand absently on her thigh. Each step felt like an echo of time past, resonating through the silent corridors and abandoned rooms that whispered of forgotten stories.

At the top of the grand staircase, Anita turned slowly, her breath catching as she took in the panorama of the mansion's rundown first floor below. The vast foyer stretched before her, its once-elegant features now marred by neglect and decay. Moths and other insects danced in the shafts of muted light filtering through cracked windows, casting eerie shadows on the worn carpet. The chandelier now at eye level hung like a silent sentinel, its crystals dulled with age, starkly contrasting the opulence it once exuded.

The weight of thousands of miles driven to reach this place pressed upon Anita's shoulders and mingled with the overwhelming reality of her unexpected inheritance. Tears welled up in her eyes, unchecked emotions spilling over as she stood alone in the silence of the mansion. It was a mixture of disbelief, grief, and a yearning ache for Vance. A profound sense of solitude engulfed her in that moment.

Turning away from the staircase, Anita sought refuge in the first bedroom she came across. Pushing open the heavy door more fully, she entered a room enveloped in a nostalgic charm that momentarily eased her troubled mind. A quick fumble of fingers found the button for the lights which brought to life the wallpaper—a tapestry of green ferns and vines, faded but still retaining a hint of its former vibrancy. Against one wall stood a deep mahogany four-poster bed, its intricately carved posts adorned with dusty peacocks, their feathers frozen in perpetual splendor.

Matching bookcases flanked the bed, their shelves filled with musty volumes that spoke of another era. A small round table occupied a corner, its surface adorned with a delicate lace doily and an empty porcelain vase. Anita thought of the varieties of flowers outside. A different bloom could occupy the vase for weeks on end without repeating. A bureau and vanity gleamed dully in the dim light, their surfaces enhanced with fine etchings and aged silver-backed mirrors that reflected ghostly images of a bygone elegance.

Anita unrolled her sleeping bag atop the bed. She lay down fully clothed, staring at the empty half of the mattress beside her. A pang of loss stabbed her heart as she thought of Vance. Tears trickled down her cheeks, mingling with memories of his gentle humor, his deep creativity, and the enigmatic part of him that would remain forever shrouded.

She thought back to their honeymoon in Oregon's Cascade Mountains, during a simpler time when they had explored each other's body and soul within the cozy confines of a room a quarter the size of this one. It had been more than enough for them then, their love blossoming amidst the mountain vistas and whispered promises of forever. Now, in this cavernous mansion that reverberated with emptiness and secrets, Anita clung to those memories like lifelines, seeking solace in the echoes of love.

How could she have missed the pieces that sat so poorly in her husband's soul? How could she not have known that he couldn't go forward?

As dusk deepened into night outside the windows, Anita's tears and breathing gradually slowed, the weight of exhaustion pulling her into a fitful sleep. Dreams mingled with reality, memories intertwined with hopes for what lay ahead in this forgotten mansion that now held the key to her uncertain future.

***

Logan's hands tightened on the steering wheel of his restored pickup as he navigated the winding road away from the Harrow estate. The moon cast a pale glow over the landscape, the ancient trees casting long shadows that danced in the night breeze. The pickup's engine purred smoothly, a testament to the hours he had spent under its hood, coaxing life back into the old machine. Tonight, the familiar hum of the motor and the rhythmic crunch of gravel under the tires were not enough to quiet his thoughts.

Anita. The name repeated itself in his mind, mingling with the image of her standing in the dimly lit foyer, her eyes wide with wonder and something else he couldn't quite place. Sadness? Uncertainty? It was only their first meeting, and yet he felt a pull towards her, a desire to understand the layers beneath her calm exterior.

Logan wondered if she was the type to stay. The Harrow estate had a way of enveloping people, making them a part of its history, but it could also be an isolating place, its grandeur suffocating to those unprepared for its silent demands.

Anita didn't seem like the kind to be easily overwhelmed. There was a strength in her, a resilience that shone through despite her evident sorrow. But there was also a softness. Logan thought it seemed to be a broken kindness that set her apart. He found himself comparing her to Vanessa.

Vanessa. Polished, high-class, and high-maintenance. Their relationship had always been a roller coaster, thrilling at times but more often exhausting. She had a way of commanding attention, of demanding the best, and Logan had always fallen a step behind, trying to keep up with her relentless pace. She was beautiful, sophisticated, and, when she wanted to be, incredibly charming. But there was a hardness to her, a layer of impenetrability that had always left him feeling a little cold. Kindness, broken or not, was never a description he would have equated with her.

Anita seemed different, even after a short introduction. She was more down-to-earth, definitely a bit more scattered, but it added to her charm. There was a genuineness about her, a warmth that drew him in. He remembered the way she had looked at him when she complimented his work on the grounds. It had been a long time since someone had looked at him like that, with such openness and sweetness.

He was attracted to her, no doubt about it. But he and Vanessa were trying to make it work again, after years of being off and on. She had seemed more committed this time, more willing to put in the effort. He didn't know why. Maybe she had realized that there was no one else who would tolerate her whims and moods as he did. Or maybe she genuinely wanted to make it work. Logan really wasn't sure.

The road stretched out before him, a dark ribbon leading him back to the small cottage he called home. It was modest compared to Harrow Hall of course, but it was his. The nights were quiet there, and he often found solace in the simplicity of his surroundings. But tonight, the thought of going home filled him with a strange sense of restlessness.

He wanted to know more about Anita. There was something about her that intrigued him, a complexity that he wanted to unravel. She would technically be his boss, the new Mrs. Harrow, overseeing the estate grounds, but he couldn't help but feel that their relationship could be more than just professional. He wanted to hear her laugh, to see her eyes light up with joy instead of shadowed by grief. He wanted to know what she loved, what she feared, what dreams she held close to her heart.

Logan shook his head to clear his thoughts. He had to remind himself that he was with Vanessa, that they were trying to make it work. But as the pickup rumbled down the lonely road, he couldn't shake the feeling that meeting Anita had changed something in him. She had stirred a longing that he hadn't felt in a long time, a desire for connection that went beyond the physical.

What did he really want? A life with Vanessa, filled with its familiar ups and downs? Or something new, something uncertain but potentially beautiful?

Logan pulled into his driveway and turned off the engine. He sat for a moment in the silence. The night was still, the only sound the distant hoot of an owl. He leaned back in his seat and let the memories of the evening wash over him. Anita's voice, soft and melodic, her eyes, so full of emotion, and the hint of her smile, with such potential warmth.

He didn't know what the future held, but for the first time in a long while, he felt a spark of hope. Hope that Anita would find a reason to stay. Hope that he would get the chance to know her better. Hope that, maybe, this was the beginning of something new and wonderful.

With a deep breath, Logan opened the door and stepped out into the cool night air. The journey home had given him much to think about, and he knew that the days ahead would be filled with decisions and discoveries. But as he made his way to his front door, he couldn't help but smile.

***

Anita

Hey, Doreen! Just wanted to let you know I've finally arrived at Harrow Hall.

Doreen

How did it go? How's the house?

Anita

It's beyond anything we imagined. Huge, old, full of character... and dust. Lots and lots of dust.

Doreen

Wow, sounds amazing! And a bit of a nightmare? How much work does it need?

Anita

A ton. Seriously, it's going to need a lot of cleaning and fixing up. But I'm hopeful it'll sell fast, so not all of it will be on me.

Doreen

Houses like that have a certain charm that people love. You might even enjoy working on it a bit.

Anita

I guess. But honestly, I just want to get it done and get home as fast as possible. How are you doing-REALLY?

Doreen

Great. Honestly. You don't need to worry about me.

Anita

Are you keeping in contact with your sponsor? She called me as I was going through Illinois.

Doreen

Oh yeah, I caught up with her. It was just phone tag.

Anita

She said you missed two meetings.

Doreen

I just took on a couple of extra shifts in ED is all.

Anita

Really?

Doreen

Really. I'm going to pay you back.

Anita

I told you that's not necessary. But you have to make rehab stick this time. Not because of the cost but for your own good.

Doreen

Stop worrying. You're in New England during fall! You should take some time to enjoy it. There are so many new things to find and experiences to have.

Anita

Yeah, yeah. I'll see. Maybe if I get some free time. But right now, it's all about getting this house in shape.

Doreen

Don't work yourself too hard. Try to enjoy it a little, okay? This could be a really good experience for you.

Anita

I'll try.

Doreen

Seriously. Like if you go apple picking or syrup catching, you never know what kind of hottie you might stumble on.

Anita
Syrup catching??? LOL
Doreen
You know what I mean…some sexy lumberjack in flannel.
Anita
I'm not ready for that.
Doreen
You'll never know unless you try.
Anita
We'll see. Thanks for the suggestions.
Doreen
Always here for you. Goodnight and good luck with everything. Check in again soon, okay?
Anita
Will do. Goodnight!

***

Anita drifted through the corridors of Harrow Hall, the air around her tinged with a soft, ethereal glow. The walls and floors seemed more like wisps of cloud than wood and plaster. The Hall, so imposing and shadowy, now felt airy and almost insubstantial, as if built fully from the stuff of dreams.

A woman dressed in an elegant gown of brocade blue silk met Anita on the landing of the grand staircase. Golden leaves, shapes reminiscent of those in the nearby fields, flowed freely over the gown's sumptuous fabric, lifted and rounded by a hoop skirt. Her dark hair was styled in a graceful updo that framed her delicate features. There was something familiar about the woman, a warmth that drew Anita closer.

"Come with me." The woman's voice was as wispy as the air around them. She led Anita up to the attic. Gentle, warm light streamed through the windows, casting lacy shadows on the wooden floor.

In the center of the room stood a dress form, draped with a stunning antique bridal gown. The fabric shimmered with a subtle radiance. Its intricate lace and delicate beading glimmered. "Try it on," the woman encouraged, her smile gentle and inviting.

Anita approached the gown, her fingers tracing the fine details. Despite the surreal quality of the dream, the material felt incredibly real under her touch—the coolness of the pearls and the lace's flat filigree.

With a sense of wonder, she slipped out of her cargo pants and t-shirt. The woman lifted the dress over Anita's head, the fabric falling perfectly around her, as if it had been made just for her. The woman fastened the tiny buttons along the back, and then gathered silk stockings, lace garters and white kid boots to match from a nearby chest.

Once dressed, Anita followed the woman back down the attic stairs. As they reached the ground floor, the front door of the Hall swung open on its own, revealing a landscape transformed. The gardens and orchards of Harrow Hall burst with vibrant colors and lush greenery, more vivid and alive than should have been possible on the cusp of autumn. A dark blue mist with luminescent edges, curled around the steps leading down into the gardens.

The woman nodded, encouraging Anita to step into the mist. "Go on," she whispered. "See where it leads you."

Anita stepped forward and the mist enveloped her like a cool, gentle shroud. It guided her down a path that began to darken. Huge charter oaks formed an archway above. Anita squinted into the mist as she walked. Suddenly, the shapes of headstones bordered by a fence coalesced ahead.

She paused and caught a movement to the right. A younger woman in a sequined flapper dress eased her way out from behind an oak tree's broad trunk. "Psst," she said with a wink. The feathers and pearls on her headband moved in the breeze. She smiled sadly with haunted dark eyes. "Follow me," she whispered.

Anita looked toward the cemetery where the mist was leading her and then back to the woman. A warm light glowed behind her, and Anita chose to follow her. The woman led her quickly over fallen branches and through the thick growth of the forest floor, all the while tossing glances behind them where slow tendrils of mist sought to catch up to them.

She led Anita deep into the apple orchard, twisting and turning until stepping out in a small clearing. In the center stood a man, his back to her. As he turned around, Anita's heart leaped. For a moment in the dream's soft light, she thought it was Vance. But as he stepped closer, the features defined, and she realized it was Logan, hair askance as if woken from a deep sleep, shirt buttons incorrectly fastened, his jeans barely on his hips, belt unfastened. He even lacked a shoe.

The woman beside her gave Anita a gentle shove forward and then disappeared in a quiet shimmer. Logan looked as dazed and enchanted as she felt, his eyes wide with the same mix of confusion and awe.

"Anita, what..." His voice trailed off as he took her in, the wedding dress swirling around her. The mist suddenly caught up, encircling her. Anita and Logan moved toward each other almost magnetically, and the mist shied away.

Logan reached out, his fingers skimming her cheek, and Anita felt a jolt of electricity, a connection so profound it seemed to transcend the dream. They stared into each other's eyes, the world around them fading into a backdrop of roiling blue mist and whispering leaves.

The dream massaged their connection, molding it into a deeper bond between them, crafted in the surreal tapestry of the unconscious. The blue mist danced and twirled, a visual echo of burgeoning emotions swirling within them. In this moment, in this dream, nothing else existed but the two of them, connected by an inexplicable force that felt both new and as old as time itself.

Logan's strong arms slid around her waist, holding her tightly. His voice was hoarse when he spoke, as if on the cusp of sleep and wake. "I can't stop thinking about you."

"Why is this so real?" She breathed the words out through a sigh of intense pleasure at the touch of his lips on the curve of her neck. Anita felt her whole body flush at his touch. She slid her fingers under the hem of his shirt, skimming the warm flesh of his muscled abdomen.

"Thank God for dreams," Logan murmured against her earlobe as he nipped it. Anita threaded her fingers through his thick, dark hair. They lay down in a rolling dreamscape, soft as velvet.

No self-effacement, anxiety, or embarrassment touched either of them. They gave in fully to their attraction. Every touch, caress, and taste was fair game, empty of reality's judgment.

Each time they took one another, the sweeter their connection became, until finally they both collapsed, compellingly sated, fully exhausted. They held one another in a tangle of naked limbs and sweet apple blossoms.

As the dream began to fade, Anita sought the look in Logan's rich brown eyes, clear and deep—a reflection of her own feelings, the realization of something profound and shifting between them. The blue mist thickened, obscuring everything until all that was left was the feeling of Logan's hand in hers, grounding her, as the dream dissolved into the ether.

Chapter Three

Anita stepped out onto the country road, her breath forming small clouds of vapor in the crisp morning air. Her water bottle swung lightly from her fingers as she set off towards the quaint town of Harrowsburg. The path stretched ahead, lined with ancient oak trees whose gnarled branches arched overhead, casting dappled shadows on the two-track road below. Birds chirped in the distance, their songs a soothing backdrop to the morning solitude. Her face warmed with a blush when she thought of the outrageous dream that had filled her night. Her thoughts were still tangled with the remnants of it—so vivid, so unsettlingly real.

Guilt ate at her. What was the designated time frame for attraction to be appropriate after a spouse's death? Vance had been gone from her life for eight months, and she'd fought against coming to Connecticut for six. The only reason she was here was because the proceeds from the sale of her California house had not gone as far as she'd hoped to pay their bills, especially after the cash she'd paid for Doreen's month in rehab. She realized after Vance's death that they really had lived above their means, and cutting two professional salaries down to one took a toll. The life insurance they'd always assumed would suffice was null and void due to the suicide. If she wanted to get off Doreen's couch anytime soon, she needed to knock those bills out. After seeing the Hall and grounds, she believed its sale would easily do so and allow her to buy a new house outright. She should also be able to put away a nice cushion for the future.

That's why she was here. That and only that. Logan was a nice guy, but he seemed to have a relationship with that blonde from the diner. Anita would stay as far away from him as possible during this process and get back to California as soon as the sale allowed. Then, she could figure out the attraction time frame. Doreen would help her to understand what was normal, if there was such a thing in these situations. Her subconscious and her body had pushed her there with Logan. It was just a dream and nothing to feel guilty about.

Huffing a sigh and shaking her arms and legs out, she shoved her ear buds in, gripped her water bottle more tightly, and started off at a brisk jog down the two-track road toward town. As she ran, lost in her thoughts, music volume raging, she missed the sound of the approaching vehicle. Only when the sun's glare bounced off its windshield did Anita notice Logan's pickup rounding the bend in the road towards her. She moved off to the side of the track as he slowed to a stop beside her, the engine rumbling softly.

Logan rolled down the window. Anita had never been so grateful for the vintage of vehicle that truly required rolling as it gave her time to catch her huffing breath and set her expression to one she hoped was sufficiently neutral. Logan's expression, on the contrary, was a mix of concern and something else that Anita couldn't quite place. He seemed to hesitate for a moment before speaking. "Morning. How'd your first night go?"

Anita shifted uncomfortably, tearing her focus from the water bottle in her hands before meeting his gaze. "It was... fine," she said, the word feeling inadequate for the delicious storm of emotions she had experienced. She was aware of the awkwardness seeping into the space between them, a stark contrast to the profound connection of their shared dream. *Not real*, Anita reminded herself, as she tugged at the sleeves of her activewear jacket. But even their interaction the evening before when he showed her to the estate had been warmer than this.

Logan searched her eyes and chuckled softly. "I half expected you to change your mind and book a hotel room in town instead."

The comment stung. She straightened, her voice sharper than she intended. "I'm tougher than I look, you know."

He caught her edginess, and his eyes widened slightly. "Hey, I didn't mean it like that," he said quickly, his gaze intense. "I just meant—" He paused, searching for the right words, his focus flickering over her face with what looked like a mix of admiration and something deeper. "I was just worried, is all."

Anita felt a flush rise to her cheeks at the intensity of his look—a hungry, lingering glance that spoke volumes.

Logan seemed to realize how he'd come across and cleared his throat, looking away. "I'm sorry, that came out wrong." He fumbled through his next words, his usual ease buried under a sudden and inexplicable awkwardness. "Can I offer you a lift into town? Maybe grab some coffee?"

It was tempting, not just for the promise of coffee but for the chance to understand what this tension between them meant. Yet, her body felt oddly weary, her muscles more fatigued than a simple night's sleep should warrant. "Thanks, but I think I need to run. Clear my head a bit, stretch my legs." she said, forcing a smile.

Logan nodded, his expression understanding yet filled with a hint of disappointment. She caught him glancing down the slender, long line of her yoga pants from hip to ankle. He coughed and looked away, out the windshield again. "Sure thing. If you're looking for coffee, though, try The Steaming Bean down on Main. Can't miss it."

"Thanks, I will," Anita said, her mind still racing with thoughts of their dream. Logan hesitated, as if wanting to say more but unsure of himself.

They parted with a lingering, awkward silence that spoke louder than words. Anita watched as Logan's pickup disappeared down the road toward the estate, her heart a confusing mix of disappointment and relief. As she fell into her jog again, the dream replayed in her mind, the surreal meeting with Logan beneath the swirling blue mist feeling more like a memory than a figment of her imagination.

It was madness, she thought, to feel such a connection so quickly, especially based on a dream. But as she ran, the fatigue in her muscles kept pulling her back to the reality of that experience. The dream had felt so real, so tangible. Was it just a product of her anxious mind, or had something truly inexplicable happened between them? *No. Ridiculous.*

Her rational mind battled the part of her that yearned to understand the mysterious bond that seemed to have formed between her and Logan. The line separating reality and dreams blurred a little more, leaving Anita to wonder where this path would ultimately lead.

***

Anita emerged out of the forest, leaving the two-track behind and continued her run on the main road for a few miles more, winding beside fields dotted with wildflowers and bordered by wooden fences that leaned slightly askew. Harrowsburg appeared ahead, its small collection of buildings nestled cozily against the backdrop of rolling hills. She quickened her pace, now eager for a coffee shop's warmth and some caffeine.

Entering the town square, she spotted the coffee shop Logan had mentioned, its sign swinging gently in the breeze. She gave herself a quick cool-down walk around the block and then pushed open the door. Coffee and the sweetness of baked goods met her head-on. The interior was cozy, with cleverly mismatched tables and chairs that still somehow made sense together. A few were occupied by locals chatting over their morning cups.

An elderly couple behind the counter smiled warmly at Anita as she approached. "Morning, dear," a woman with salt and pepper hair in her mid-60s greeted her cheerfully. "What can we get for you today?"

"An americano," Anita replied with a grateful smile. "And one of those cinnamon rolls, please."

The woman nodded, bustling about to fill Anita's order while her husband struck up conversation. "You must be the one who inherited the Hall. Quite a sight, isn't it?"

Anita nodded, realizing news traveled fast in a small town. She wondered if he'd heard about her from the old men at the gas station or someone else. "Yes, that's me. It's certainly... impressive."

"Well, you'll find the best coffee in town right here," the elderly man chuckled, handing her a steaming mug and a bright blue plate with the thick roll, dripping with icing. With fluffy gray muttonchops that continued right into a remarkable mustache, he looked like a Union Civil War general. The tan apron with cutesy illustrations of pastries just did not fit. Anita hid a smile as he rang her order up, and she tapped her phone on the payment tower. "If you need anything else," the man said, "just give a holler."

Settling into a small corner table, Anita watched the townsfolk come and go. She made mental notes of things she needed to do. First up was finding the law office to prepare for the sale of the estate. With such a huge property, she was sure there were a million documents to sign. From what Logan said the previous evening, there was an extensive history of litigation surrounding the estate. She hoped the process wouldn't take too long.

Before she returned to the Hall, she was definitely getting some rodent traps and cleaning products. This morning, she'd heard nothing but scurrying and scuffling above her as she changed clothes and brushed her teeth. The clawfoot bathtub in her room needed a good scrubbing before it or the shower could be used.

Anita pulled out her phone and placed a video call to Doreen, who took her sweet time picking up. Her face filled the screen sans makeup and hair in tangles.

"Time zones, girl," Doreen growled, rubbing a fist against her eyes.

"Sorry! I wasn't thinking." Anita quickly did the math—her phone showed 8:27 am which meant 5:27 am on the west coast.

"Fah-get-ah-bout-it," Doreen mimicked. "Isn't that how they say it out there?" She yawned widely.

Anita laughed. "Not so far, no. But I haven't talked with too many people yet."

"Any opportunities for syrup catching?" They both laughed. "I have no idea what they really call it."

"No not yet." Anita felt her thoughts drift to her dream with Logan and she fought to change the subject. "Harrow Hall is huge and old, just like I expected. It's got a lot of features that will definitely interest buyers—original woodwork, a grand staircase, fruit orchards, and a botanical garden. The grounds are pristine. The house needs work though."

Doreen's face grew thoughtful. "What does it feel like living there? Has it grown on you at all? And, more importantly, have you met anyone interesting?"

"Jeez. It's only been one night. You're expecting a lot." Anita hesitated, her gaze flickering away for a moment before returning to the screen. "It's...overwhelming, honestly. The house is massive and full of all this amazing furniture. I feel more like an intruder than anything." She paused, taking a sip of her coffee before continuing, "And, well, there's Logan."

Doreen's eyebrows shot up. "Logan? Who's this now?"

"He manages the estate grounds. He's been...helpful," Anita said, the corners of her mouth turning up slightly despite her attempts to remain neutral.

"Spill the tea, girl." Doreen teased, bringing the camera up close and personal to her nose. "There's something there. I can smell it."

Before Anita could formulate a response, the bell above the coffee shop door jingled. She glanced over and saw the blond woman from the diner, Vanessa. She was dressed impeccably in a designer suit and high heels—utterly out of place in the casual atmosphere of the shop.

'"Listen, Doreen, I've got to go," Anita said abruptly, her attention still partly on the new arrival.

"Ooh, got more important things to do? Go on then. But check a damn clock before you call next time." Doreen winked. "JK. Love you."

"Love you, too." Anita ended the call.

She sipped her drink and observed as Vanessa ordered her coffee. Her poised demeanor, perfect makeup and hair didn't escape Anita's notice nor did the deferential treatment she received from the elderly couple behind the counter. Leaning back, Anita picked up snippets of conversation.

In response to something Vanessa said, the woman responded, "I wouldn't worry. He already left this morning."

The set of Vanessa's shoulders indicated a certain amount of irritation.

"He's just doing his job," the man behind the counter responded, his tone slightly abrupt as Vanessa swiped a rewards card and then a debit card.

Vanessa turned on her heel. "Well, it's not right, is all I'm saying." She stopped in her tracks when she spotted Anita in the corner. Anita gave a small wave. Vanessa heaved a frustrated sigh, shoving sunglasses onto her nose, and stomped out of the coffee shop.

Anita noticed the couple behind the counter exchanging a look that mixed embarrassment with a touch of exasperation.

The man caught Anita's eye and offered a warm, apologetic smile. His voice gentled from the tone he had used with Vanessa. "She's got strong opinions about things. Especially before she's had her morning coffee." He laughed.

The woman, her hair a soft halo of curls, nodded in agreement. "Yes, dear, we're so sorry if she seemed a bit rude. She's very protective of Logan, you see. They grew up together, and they…well, I guess, as you youngsters say, they go together now."

"I met them together at the diner last night," Anita replied, her curiosity piqued. "So, you must be related to Logan then?"

"I s'pose we'll claim him," the man said with a proud nod.

"He's the youngest of our five." The woman bustled over and sat herself down on the chair across from Anita. "Do you have any?"

It took Anita a moment to realize the woman was asking about children. The question from a complete stranger left her a little flustered.

"Uh, no. We didn't really plan to—nursing schedules and—What I mean is I'm a nurse, and Vance worked in the tech sector. We just never found the time."

"Women in today's world do get the chance for the career thing first, now don't they? In my day we did it backwards. Kids first, and now this little shop here. I love it though. If I knew then what I know now, I might have done things differently." The woman's kind tone boasted no judgment, just a genuineness that Anita found welcoming. "George, there," she gestured to the man in the apron, "could have been home with a baby on his hip and a spoon in his hand. I'd have been out in the work world."

The man came over to the table. "You'll have to excuse my wife. She's a born talker. We're the Emmerichs. This is my wife, Martha. And you're Anita, aren't you? Logan mentioned you."

So that was how they'd recognized her as connected to Harrow Hall. Anita wondered what else he might have mentioned, but she responded with a polite smile. "Yes, that's me."

Martha leaned forward, her eyes twinkling with interest. "And how do you find it here? It must be a big change from where you came from."

Caught off guard again by the boldness, Anita found herself sharing more than she had intended. "It's beautiful, but quite overwhelming. I'm from LA actually. The quiet in Harrowsburg is... different."

George chuckled. "I can imagine it's quite the adjustment. But you'll find we have our own charm once you get to know us, Mrs. Harrow."

Anita bristled and downed the last of her americano. "It's Miran, Anita Miran, and I don't really plan to be here for that long."

"Did any other family make the trip with you?" Martha removed Anita's empty plate and fork and bustled away as Anita stood. She quickly worked up a second americano, this time in a to-go cup, handing it to Anita as she passed the counter.

Anita fished her phone from her pocket intending to pay, but Martha waved it off.

"No, it's just me," Anita said. "My husband... he passed away, so I'm sort of figuring things out on my own now."

"Goodness, yes! Let me tell you, the news that Victor Harrow was still alive after all these years and then all of sudden gone again—it sure set Harrowsburg abuzz! But you poor thing. So young," Martha said, her voice laced with genuine sympathy. "Well, you're not alone here. If you ever need anything, George and I are always around."

Appreciating their kindness but wary of divulging too much to Logan's parents, Anita quickly steered the conversation away. "Thank you, that's kind of you. Actually, I'm trying to find the law office that handles the estate. Do you know where it is?"

George pointed down the street. "It's just a few of blocks away. Only one in town. Charlton and Dodd's, can't miss it. Take a left after the post office."

"Thank you both so much," Anita said. She offered a smile, feeling grateful for their kindness but a little relieved to be moving on. "It was nice meeting you."

"Have a good day, Mrs. Harrow," Martha called, busy behind the counter. Anita couldn't imagine she meant offense by the name, but it aggravated her nonetheless.

As she left The Steaming Bean, Anita felt a mix of emotions. George and Martha were undeniably warm and welcoming, and yet she hoped her personal details wouldn't find their way around town through Logan's well-meaning parents. Her life, still wrapped in the shadow of grief and change, felt too fragile to share fully, even with the friendliest of faces.

***

Logan parked his pickup in front of the bank and caught sight of Anita leaving The Steaming Bean in his rearview mirror. Her expression was a blend of warmth and hesitation. His parents were always good at making people feel welcome, but he understood any reservations Anita might have. Her life had been upended, and she was still grappling with the aftershocks of her husband's death. The last thing she needed was for her personal struggles to become the town's latest gossip.

He sighed. Logan felt a sense of urgency pulling him away from the familiar comfort of the café. He needed to talk to Vanessa.

Their relationship had been a roller coaster for years, filled with euphoric highs and lows that left him questioning everything. But after that strange dream last night, Logan had felt a shift within himself. His heart was obviously no longer in his relationship with Vanessa at all. He'd felt it coming on for a long time. Few would put the same stock he did in the dream he'd had, but only a handful of people would understand the power the Harrow estate held. He was wary enough to know that his attraction to Anita was most likely not mutual, but he wasn't going to ignore it completely. He was a patient man, and he would see what developed.

Logan's mind switched to the conversation ahead. The buzzer sounded to mark his entry into the bank. He threw a wave at Jedadiah Atkins, the security guard. Atkins tossed him a chin lift and returned to scrolling on his phone. The placard on Vanessa's doorframe denoting her status as vice president gleamed as usual. Logan knew she had a habit of buffing the brass every morning. As he approached, he steeled himself for the confrontation, knowing it wouldn't be easy.

Vanessa looked up from behind her laptop, her perfectly manicured nails tapping away on the keyboard. She smiled when she saw him, but it didn't reach her eyes.

"Logan, what a surprise," she said, her voice dripping with a mix of charm and annoyance.

"Hey, Vanessa," he replied, his tone steady. "Can we talk?"

"Sure, what's on your mind?" She raised an eyebrow as he slowly closed the door.

He took a deep breath. "I think we both know this isn't working anymore. We've been trying to force something that's just not there."

Her eyes narrowed. "What are you saying?"

"I'm saying we should break up. It's not fair to either of us to keep pretending this is going somewhere."

For a moment, there was silence. Then Vanessa's expression shifted from confusion to anger. "You're breaking up with me? Just like that?"

He nodded. "It's better for both of us. We want different things."

Her face twisted with fury. "Different things? What do you even want, Logan? To be a gardener for the rest of your life?"

He held her gaze, refusing to let her words sting. "I love what I do. It makes me happy."

"Happy?" she scoffed. "You think happiness pays the bills? You think it gives you a future? You're delusional."

He remained calm, his voice steady. "I don't need a lot to be happy, Vanessa. I just need to be true to myself."

"True to yourself?" she mocked. "You're pathetic. You're never going to be more than a small-town loser. I'm going places, and you could never keep up with me."

He felt a sense of relief wash over him, her words confirming what he had known deep down. "Maybe you're right. Maybe I can't keep up with you. But I don't want to. I want a life that's meaningful to me, not one where I'm constantly trying to prove myself to someone else."

Her eyes blazed with anger. "You'll regret this. You'll see."

He shook his head. "No, Vanessa. I won't."

He left the office door open as he exited, leaving her fuming behind him. As he stepped outside the bank into the fresh air, a weight lifted from his shoulders. Breaking up with Vanessa had been long overdue, and now that it was done, he felt a newfound sense of freedom.

He wandered down Main Street, his thoughts drifting to Anita. She had come into his life unexpectedly. He knew she was still healing, still finding her way, but he couldn't help but feel a connection to her.

He decided to take a walk through the park before making his hardware store supply run, hoping the tranquility would help clear his mind. The park was a haven of peace, with its winding paths and blooming flowers. He found a metal bench under a large oak tree and sat down, letting the serenity of the surroundings wash over him.

As he sat there, Logan thought about the future. For the first time in a long while, it didn't feel uncertain or scary. Instead, it felt like a blank canvas, ready for him to paint his own story. He knew it wouldn't be easy, and there would be challenges along the way, but he felt ready to face them.

***

Anita let herself walk casually along the quiet, cobblestone streets of the small New England town, sipping her coffee refill and enjoying the fresh air, even if it was a little chilly. She spotted the Charlton and Dodd Law Office. Stately, wrought iron lettering identified the weathered brick building. She took a deep breath and pushed open the door.

Inside, the office was dimly lit and smelled faintly of old books and polished wood. A receptionist's desk sat empty, but the sounds of shuffling papers and file cabinet drawers closing came from a room beyond. Anita approached the desk and tapped the small bell sitting on its edge.

"Just a moment," called a pinched voice from the back. A man emerged. His hair, a distinguished shade of silver, framed his face in gentle waves that suggested a life seasoned with wisdom and experience. His light complexion bore the lines of age.

He was impeccably dressed, exuding an air of dignified professionalism. His suit, tailored to perfection, spoke of a man who took pride in his appearance. The patterned vest he wore added a touch of elegance to his ensemble, complementing the crisp white shirt beneath. A black bow tie, fashioned with precision, completed his attire, emphasizing the meticulous attention he paid to even the smallest of details. Anita felt extremely out of place in her sweaty lavender activewear.

"Mr. Charlton?" Anita asked, trying to mask her discomfort.

"Yes, indeed. And you must be Mrs. Harrow," he replied, a polite smile stretching his lips though there was a flicker of something in his beady eyes beneath his thick glasses—disdain, perhaps, or at the very least apprehension.

"Actually, my last name is Miran, not Harrow. I was just out looking for coffee and thought I'd stop by. I apologize for not making an appointment."

"That's quite all right, Mrs. Harrow." He blatantly ignored her correction. "Thank you for coming in. I'm always happy to get files in order." He motioned her through the doorway into his office. "Right this way, please."

They entered a small, cluttered space filled with stacks of papers and old leather-bound books. Mr. Charlton settled behind his desk and gestured for Anita to sit.

"Now, you've inherited Harrow Hall and the grounds," he began, shuffling through a stack of papers until he found the right file. "In addition—"

"Maybe I can save you some time, Mr. Charlton. I want to sell it."

He blinked his beady eyes.

"All of it," she added to fill the ensuing silence.

He burst out laughing. "Oh, you westerners. Such a sense of humor. Now, in addition—"

"—I assure you, I'm quite serious. I want to sell and go home."

He regarded her with a puzzled expression and picked his glasses off his face. "You can't, Mrs. Harrow."

"It's Anita, and what do you mean I can't."

"The property cannot be sold. If you don't take ownership as beneficiary, it will be held in line for the next Harrow. To the best of our knowledge, your late husband was the last blooded Harrow remaining, and you, ma'am are the last Harrow spouse."

"There must be something that can be done."

"God Himself could not break the bonds of this estate, Mrs. Harrow."

He returned his glasses back to his face and continued on as if the exchange hadn't even occurred. "Now in addition to the property, you have full access to the spouse's portion of the estate's legacy account, which Mrs. Hyacinth Harrow built to quite a tidy sum. It's more than enough to maintain the estate and its operations comfortably. Here," he said, handing her a bank statement, "this will give you a detailed overview."

She set the paper on her lap without looking at it. "But I don't want it. My husband—"

"My condolences to you, ma'am. The private investigative firm informed me of the details."

"Thank you."

"As you and Mr. Harrow had no children, after you pass, the estate will go—"

"—You're not hearing me. I don't want it. I don't want any of it." Anita sat back against the chair, crossing her arms over her chest.

In the twilight of his years in such a position, Anita was sure Mr. Charlton remained a figure of respect and admiration in the community. His presence was a reminder of a bygone era, where integrity and honor were the cornerstones of a man's character. Though time had etched its mark upon him, it had only served to enhance the aura of venerable wisdom that surrounded him. As it was, she meant to meet the measure of his wisdom with the measure of her bullheadedness.

"Look, Mr. Charlton. I am not a Harrow. My husband was not a Harrow. He apparently went to great lengths to ensure that, or so your private investigator indicated. We were married for seven years, and I know nothing about his parents—"

"His mother was Collette, the late Mrs. Hyacinth Harrow's only daughter. She never disclosed his paternity to our knowledge and his mother's maiden name was used on his birth certificate. He was born in New Orleans and lived there until his mother died of a narcotics overdose when he was seven. After that, he came to reside at the Hall with his grandmother until the age of 18, when he joined the Navy. His grandmother was in regular communication with him for the next six years, but then he was reported to have died of an overdose. She believed him to be plagued by the same addictions as his mother, and despite her best efforts, she was unable to help him. It was, I would venture to say, her greatest regret."

Anita was speechless. It took her more than a moment to respond, during which the lawyer shuffled his papers on the desk, sliding out a folder and handing it across to her. "That wasn't Vance," she insisted. "He did not have a drug problem. I'm a nurse in LA, for heaven's sake. I know what that looks like."

"Regardless, that was Mrs. Harrow's conclusion at the time."

Anita shook her head as she opened the file folder. "This is all just a case of mistaken identity. Vance did not—" Anita caught her breath. There he was. Her husband, younger but definitely him, in a sailor's uniform, the cap at a jaunty angle that was just like him. She flipped through the pictures, and they were all him—graduation, a red and gold cap and gown with honor braids; a picture at the beach playing volleyball, broad smile on his teenage face, muscles developing, limbs still gangly on the cusp of manhood; as a child of eight or nine, in a professional photograph, forced smile, despite boyish roundness of his face, eyes and hair distinctive; in a suit as a young man with a distinguishably dressed seventy-something woman next to him, neither smiling.

And more, so many more. Hidden parts of Vance's life that he never shared with her. That for some reason he completely left behind. That he attempted to erase before starting over with her, on the opposite end of the country.

At the very back of the file was a recent printout of Vance's obituary from the funeral home, with a favorite picture Anita had chosen. It was one she had snapped during a lazy morning with coffee on the back patio. In the photograph, his hair was slightly tousled, a carefree hint of rebellion that contrasted with the composed man she knew. His smile was subtle, just enough to suggest a secret he was unwilling to share with the world, but it was his eyes that had captured her. They were dark and deep, like the midnight sky, hinting at mysteries and depths she could never fully uncover but felt irresistibly drawn to.

She remembered teasing him lightheartedly about that enigmatic gaze, a teasing that ended with his charm enveloping her like a warm blanket. His response had been swift and effortless, his voice a velvet caress that left her weak in the knees. They had laughed, hearts light and free, and the day had melted away as they explored each other with an intimacy that needed no words. In those moments, everything else faded to black save for the crash of the ocean surf outside their bedroom window, a constant rhythm that mirrored the beating of their hearts.

Nothing else had ever mattered when she'd been in Vance's arms. She hadn't needed to know about his past to understand the essence of his being. His confidence was a silent testament to his strength, his empathy a gentle whisper of his soul's kindness. He loved her with a quiet intensity that spoke louder than any proclamation. She knew it, inside and out, a truth as unshakeable as the tides that marked the passage of their days together. In his embrace, she had found a sanctuary, a place where the world ceased to exist and only their love remained.

Anita could not stop the tears streaming down her face. "Vance was here." She felt it as a confession and as a failure of her defenses. "He really lived here, at Harrow Hall?"

Mr. Charlton, unshaken by her emotion, fished a handkerchief from his pocket and handed it to her. Anita laughed breathlessly at the anachronism and wiped the tears from her face with the pressed, monogrammed square. "We knew him as Victor," the lawyer said.

"You *knew* him?"

"You'll find most of the residents here did. He was a steady part of Harrowsburg and the Hall for more than a decade."

Anita closed the folder and shuffled it under the paper on her lap. She hadn't meant to read it, but just a glance revealed seven-figure columns. "This—" her voice squeaked. "This is the money I would have access to?"

"Indeed, Mrs. Harrow. The spouse's portion of the legacy account has just shy of 17.8 million dollars in it. The grounds, of course, are funded separately. You needn't worry about those financials. If you're interested, though, I do have the—"

Anita held up her hand. "Seven—" she was breathless "—seventeen million dollars?"

"Seventeen point eight."

"And what's the catch?"

"As the current Mrs. Harrow, it is your duty to maintain the Hall for future generations."

"So, this money can only be spent on the house?"

"It is at your discretion, ma'am. A woman must live after all, but I am sure, just as the caretakers in generations before you, you will do all you can to maintain the Harrow legacy for the future."

The weight of the decision to be made pressed down on her. The Hall, with its imposing structure and the seventeen million dollars tied to it, was an unexpected inheritance that held the promise of a secure future. But more than the monetary value, it was the history and memories intertwined with Vance's childhood that tugged at her heart. The townspeople would have stories of him as a boy, clues to paint vivid details of the man she loved in a place she never knew.

Would it also give her the answers to understand why he made the decision to take his own life? Wracking her brain repeatedly over every conversation they'd had before it happened, over every action they had taken, every person they'd come in contact with those weeks beforehand—none of it led to even a hint. There were bills, yes, some she didn't know about, but mostly debts that they had shared. Together though, they were making it.

After two months had passed, she'd set a boundary for her own sanity. She called it her veil line. The things on the other side—the reason behind Vance's suicide, why he'd changed his name, and why he never liked to talk about his past—the edges were there, but they would never be seen clearly. She would never know.

Slowly, this strategy had been working. She'd returned to work, kept on living with Doreen, waiting for her house to sell to pay their debts.

"Now, Mrs. Harrow, it seems you have quite a few things to consider before making a decision. I respect that. Perhaps you should take some of this information with you, and when you are ready to define your beneficiary status, please return to see me."

He picked up an expandable file and handed it to her. Anita stood, accepting the packet and adding it to what she already held, feeling the weight of it all in her hands and on her mind.

The lawyer extended a hand, and Anita slid the bundle into the crook of her elbow, so that she could shake it. "Thank you, Mr. Charlton."

"If you have any questions, don't hesitate to contact me. You'll find my information enclosed."

In a daze, Anita turned to leave, but she couldn't shake the feeling that Mr. Charlton's eyes were following her every step as he escorted her to the front door. It seemed to shut behind her more forcefully than necessary.

***

Hyacinth Harrow's Diary

March 15, 1943
Today has been another tumultuous day in a string of many, and I find myself seeking solace in these pages once more. I am but a young

woman, yet the burdens and suspicions cast upon my family weigh heavily on my heart. Harrowsburg, our quiet little town, has turned cold and hostile towards us, and the atmosphere within Harrow Hall is strained beyond measure.

The trouble began a fortnight ago when Mrs. Eliza Whitmore, a young widow, and her son, Timothy, vanished without a trace. The townsfolk, ever ready to point fingers and whisper behind closed doors, have turned their suspicions towards us. The Harrows have long been subjects of town gossip, and our reclusive nature and the privacy of our home make us convenient targets. But this time, the accusations are more pointed, more venomous.

I walked through the town square today, feeling the eyes of every passerby on me. Their gazes were hard and accusatory, their whispers like knives cutting through the air. Children whom I used to play with shunned me, and old friends turned their backs. The disappearance of Mrs. Whitmore and Timothy has ignited a fire of fear and mistrust, and we are caught in the flames.

I overheard Mrs. Lawrence at the market, her voice loud and shrill, proclaiming that Harrow Hall is a place of dark secrets and that no good could come from our family. Her words stung, not because they were new, but because they were believed so readily by those around her. I wanted to shout, to defend us, but what good would it do? The townsfolk have already made up their minds, and nothing I say will change that.

But what troubles me most is not the town's judgment, but the rift it has caused within our family. Aunt Melusine, who has always been an enigma, has taken the side of the town. She has been vocal in her belief that something is amiss at Harrow Hall, that our family is hiding something. This has led to fierce arguments with my parents, the likes of which I have never seen before.

Last night, the shouting echoed through the halls, a cacophony of anger and betrayal. I stood outside the drawing-room, my heart pounding, as Aunt Melusine and my parents hurled accusations at each other.

"You must see reason, Melusine!" my father bellowed. "We have done nothing wrong! That poor widow had no future and her son, even less. Her cad of a husband was shot for desertion!"

Aunt Melusine's voice was cold and sharp. "It's not ours to judge them or their futures. You cannot ignore the truth forever, Charles. The Harrow name is tainted, and the town has every right to be suspicious.

You have secrets, and those secrets will destroy us all."

My mother, usually so calm and composed, was in tears. "Please, Melusine, you are tearing this family apart. We need to stand together, not fight amongst ourselves."

But Aunt Melusine was unmoved. "I will not be complicit in your lies, Rose. The truth must come out, whatever the cost."

The argument raged on, and I could bear it no longer. I fled to my room, my mind a whirlwind of confusion and sorrow. How could Aunt Melusine betray us like this? What did she mean by secrets? I have always known there were things unspoken in our family, shadows that lurked just out of sight, but I never imagined they could lead to this.

Today, the house is eerily quiet, the calm after the storm. Aunt Melusine has retreated to her rooms, and my parents are withdrawn, their faces pale and haggard. I feel like I am caught in the middle of a nightmare, unable to wake up.

Hyacinth Harrow

Chapter Four

Anita stepped out of Charlton and Dodd's Law Office feeling as though she were floating in a strange, disorienting fog. The revelations of the morning had been overwhelming. She clutched the thick files of documents to her chest, her mind racing with the implications of what she'd just learned.

Lost in her thoughts, she wandered down the main street of Harrowsburg, barely noticing the creative storefronts and the gentle hum of the small-town morning. It wasn't until she nearly bumped into Logan, who was exiting the hardware store, that she snapped back to reality.

"Oh, it's you." Her disappointed tone struck him, and he flinched, adjusting the paper bag in his hands. "I'm sorry. I didn't mean that like it came out. I've just been to the law office and…"

He nodded, surveying the stack of folders. "A lot to take in, I imagine."

"I… yes, I'm more than a bit overwhelmed," she admitted, managing a weak smile.

He nodded, his eyes softening. "I had to come in for a few things and am just heading back to the Hall now. I can give you a ride."

She hesitated for a moment, then remembered another errand she had meant to run. "Actually, I wanted to get some mouse traps before I go back. I could hear them scurrying around last night and…" She shuddered.

He grinned at her grimace, and it lightened her mood. "No problem," Logan replied with a reassuring smile. "I'll grab them for you."

"I wanted some cleaning products too."

"Sure." He set his paper bag on the wooden planks of the pickup's bed and walked around to the passenger door and opened it for her. She pushed back hard at the response in her gut, and instead took note of the vehicle. After finally coming to the end of her long journey last night and then their awkward meet-up this morning after the dream, she'd paid little attention to it before. The pickup stood out like a gem against the mundane backdrop of the parking lot. Its body was painted a vibrant, eye-catching turquoise, reminiscent of a summer sky, flawlessly maintained with a glossy sheen that caught the sunlight and made the whole vehicle gleam. The white roof provided a striking contrast, giving it a classic, yet timeless appeal. The chrome accents on the front grill and bumpers shone with a mirror-like finish, while the wide, polished wheels added a touch of ruggedness to the otherwise elegant demeanor of the truck.

Inside, the cabin was a seamless continuation of the exterior's color scheme, bathing the interior in a calming sea of turquoise and white. The bench seat, upholstered in a pristine combination of the two colors, was inviting with the promise of comfort and style. The dashboard, an homage to mid-century design, was equally divided between function and form. Simple, yet sophisticated, it boasted clean lines and an array of meticulously restored dials and switches that seemed to whisper stories of the open road. With its classic, unadorned design, the steering wheel hinted at a time when driving was an unhurried pleasure, a dance between man and machine.

"Logan, this is gorgeous," she said, sliding onto the bench seat of the immaculate interior.

She regretted casting a glance his way as she said it. The ruddiness of his chiseled features increased as he actually blushed. Again, she shoved hard against the stirring inside of her.

"Just a project to keep me busy," he said.

"You did all this?" She traced the ridges of the glove box, everything polished so much, it glowed.

He nodded. She was aware that the smile on his face was due to his enjoyment of her enjoyment, and she meant to put a stop to it. "Mouse traps?"

"Yes," he said, "I'll be right back." He closed her door and Anita refused to allow herself to watch him walk into the store.

The air inside the cab carried a hint of nostalgia, blending the scents of well-maintained leather and the faint aroma of gasoline—a reminder of the truck's storied past and the adventures it had seen. The manual gear shift stood tall between the seats, a silent invitation to take control and feel the road beneath. Every detail, from the gleaming radio to the polished air vents, spoke of a vehicle loved and cared for, ready to offer its owner and passenger not just a mode of transportation, but a piece of automotive history.

Anita felt unwelcome gratitude and curiosity about the man who seemed so entwined with her new circumstances. When Logan returned, he set the bag with the mouse traps and cleaning products on top of her stack of files as he slid into the driver's seat. She was happy for the barrier between them.

As they drove toward Harrow Hall, the engine hummed softly, and Anita's thoughts tumbled. Finally, she broke their silence. "Logan, did you know Vance?"

His grip on the steering wheel tightened slightly. "I knew him as Vic," he corrected gently. "Yeah, he was four or five years ahead of me in school. It's a small town…we all knew each other one way or another."

Anita absorbed this information, her heart aching a little. "What was he like as a kid?" she asked, her voice barely above a whisper.

"He was…reserved, even back then. Smart, definitely. But he kept to himself a lot," Logan replied, his tone reflective. "I always got the sense that he was waiting to get out of Harrowsburg. Never quite fit in, you know?"

Anita nodded, her eyes staring out the window at the passing scenery. It was strange to think of Vance, the man she had loved and mourned, as a boy in this small town, dreaming of escape.

"Oh!" she said, recalling the events of the morning that felt so long already. "I took your advice and visited The Steaming Bean. Your parents make a mean americano."

"That shop is their pride and joy. I never figured they'd own anything like that as a kid. Dad worked as an electrician, and Mom was home with us, but when retirement hit, they wanted something new."

"Strange how you hear of that happening. Just the phases of life, I guess."

"What did your folks do once you flew the coop?"

She shoved a lock of hair behind her ear that had escaped her ponytail and gazed out the window. "My parents died in a boating accident when I was 17."

"Wow. I am so sorry, Anita."

She closed her eyes and refused to look at him. Her name in his voice sounded so agreeable, and she could feel the sincerity in his sentiment.

"Would you say my name again?"

"Anita."

"Everyone here keeps calling me Mrs. Harrow, and I find it aggravating. From that lawyer in particular."

"Mr. Charlton is a bit of a stickler for formality. I doubt you'll get him to stop." Their gazes met briefly. His focus returned the two-track in front of them, and she stared down at her hands. "But I won't use it again, okay?"

She nodded. "Thank you."

The road now bordered a field of the same tall, broad leaf plants that Anita had seen blocking her route the evening before. "What is this crop?" she asked.

"It's tobacco. Once it's harvested in a few weeks, it will dry up to a golden brown and be sent off to a cigar factory in Windsor."

Anita's breath caught, imagining the broad leaves as golden foliage—just like on the woman's gown in her dream last night. Her heart began to race, and she switched to a topic that would be sure to get her mind off that dream.

"So, Vanessa…your parents said you two have a thing."

He swallowed hard. "You talked to my parents about a lot, huh?"

"Not really. She came in for a coffee while I was there."

"Oh. On her way to work. She's the vice president of the bank."

"Mmm. I see." *That explains the clothing and hair,* I suppose. "On the road to president, probably?"

"That's her plan."

"Have you been together long?"

He seemed to hesitate and finally replied, "Off and on for the last few years."

"She really didn't seem too happy about you helping me last night or that you had already gone out to the Hall this morning."

He pulled up to park next to her car on the estate grounds. "Well for Vanessa, it's personal, I guess."

Anita opened the door and then gathered her hardware store bag and the files into her arms. "In what way?"

Logan came around and held the door as she got out. She mumbled a thanks as he scrubbed a hand over his clean-shaven chin, apparently trying to formulate an answer to her question.

"It's complicated."

"More complicated than a dead husband with an alias and hidden relations with millions? Because I doubt you'll beat that."

"Unfortunately, I think I will."

"Oh." Anita wasn't so sure she wanted to hear it. She moved over to her car and popped the trunk, pulling out her suitcase with her free hand.

"Here, let me." Logan took it from her, and she closed the trunk.

They walked toward the Hall. "Look," he said, "why don't we get this stuff put away, and then we can sit down somewhere and talk. There are some things you need to know about Harrowsburg, and it looks like I'm going to be the one to tell you."

The grimace on his face made Anita's stomach drop. It must have shown because he caught her elbow, as if to reassure her or support her, she wasn't sure which he intended. But the moment their flesh touched, they both shied away from one another. Anita quickened her pace.

"Okay, sure, that'd be fine," she babbled. "You know what?" She took her suitcase back from Logan. "I'm a sweaty mess from my run this morning. Why don't you give me 20 minutes to freshen up, and we'll have some coffee or something?" She glanced behind her. Logan nodded and headed in the direction of the largest shop building a few hundred yards away.

***

Vanessa gripped the steering wheel so tightly that her knuckles turned white, making the polish of her gel nails seem even more blood red than usual. The road stretched out before her, a narrow ribbon of asphalt winding through the dense New England woods, but she barely noticed it. Her mind was a storm of fury, resentment, and bitter disappointment. Logan had ended it, just like that, with scarcely a word of explanation. He had the nerve to look almost relieved when he did it, as if he had been freed from some great burden. That thought only fueled her anger more.

She had invested too much time and effort into Logan to just let him go without a fight. But this wasn't just about him—no, this was about her plan. Her meticulous, carefully laid-out plan to claim Harrow Hall, the sprawling estate that had captivated her imagination since she was a child. She had been so close, so damned close, to getting her hands on it, and now it felt like everything was slipping through her fingers.

Vanessa's foot pressed harder on the accelerator as she sped along the winding road, the Viper's engine growling in response. She needed to clear her head, to think, to get away from Harrowsburg, away from the mess Logan had made. She'd drive the fifty miles out to the coast, to that desolate strip of shoreline where she had spent so many summer afternoons as a teenager, planning her future with Vic.

Victor Harrow. Just thinking his name made her jaw clench. The abandoned lighthouse would be there, standing tall and weather-beaten against the relentless Atlantic wind. She'd spun so many dreams in its shadows, and it still held a magnetic pull over her. She hadn't been there in decades, but today, it seemed like the only place she could go.

The drive was a blur. Vanessa barely registered the passing of time until the scent of salt and seaweed began to permeate the air, pulling her back to reality. She turned off the main road and onto a gravel path that led down to the beach. The lighthouse loomed in the distance, its stone tower battered by decades of harsh weather, yet still standing defiant against the sky.

Vanessa parked the car and stepped out, the cool ocean breeze pulling her blond hair from her bun and whipping it around her face. The rhythmic crashing of the waves on the shore was a familiar sound, but today it did little to soothe her turbulent thoughts. She started walking toward the lighthouse, the heels of her shoes sinking so far into the sand that, with a shriek, she reached down and plucked them off.

The door to the lighthouse was unlocked, as she knew it would be. It creaked on its hinges as she pushed it open, the sound echoing eerily in the empty tower. Inside, the air was damp and smelled of salt and decay. Dust motes danced in the dim light that filtered through the grimy windows. Vanessa made her way up the narrow spiral staircase in her stockinged feet.

When she reached the top, she paused, leaning against the wall as she caught her breath. The small room was just as she remembered it—bare, cold, and uninviting. But it was the wooden beam in the center of the room that drew her attention. She walked over to it and ran her fingers over the rough surface, tracing the double *V* carving she and Victor had made so many years ago.

She could still remember the day they had whittled their names into the beam. They had been so young, so full of dreams. Back then, it had all seemed so simple. She would marry Vic after college, and together, they would claim Harrow Hall and all the power and prestige that came with it. He had been everything she had ever desired—handsome, charming, with that air of mystery that kept her on her toes. He had a natural knack for manipulating people and getting them to do what he wanted, and she had loved him for it. He didn't have the heart to get the full use out of his charisma, though. That she would have helped him with. They had been perfect for each other.

But then, Vic had died—at least, that's what she had been led to believe. Vanessa clenched her fists as she recalled the shock of seeing him last October at the tech convention in Las Vegas. She had been certain it was him, even though he was going by the name Vance Miran. When she finally caught up to him and cornered him, the way he had looked at her with such cold detachment had left her reeling. He had told her off, demanded she leave him alone and forget she saw him, and then he had disappeared again, leaving her more enraged and confused than ever.

Victor had lied to her, lied about his death to escape the responsibilities of Harrow Hall. How dare he? She had been counting on him, planning on him. And then all of a sudden, he was just gone, living some new life while she was left to pick up the pieces of her shattered dreams.

She turned away from the beam, her anger boiling over. The lighthouse, once a symbol of her dreams, now felt like a tomb, a monument to everything she had lost. Control was slipping through her fingers like handfuls of sand.

Logan had been a poor substitute for Vic, but he was all she had left. As the grounds manager of Harrow Hall, he was the closest she could get to the information she needed about the strange power that fueled the Harrow legacy. She had been so sure that she was on the verge of uncovering the secret. But then this Anita woman had shown up, and everything had gone to hell.

Vanessa felt a surge of frustration and rage. How had everything gone so wrong? She had thought she had it all figured out, but now it seemed like every move she made was being thwarted. Anita was just another roadblock in her path, another obstacle to overcome. She should have had Doreen take care of both Anita and Vic when she had the chance. But no, Vanessa had been too cautious, too afraid that Doreen wouldn't have the guts to go through with it, no matter how much money or coke she waved in her face.

She kicked at the base of the wooden beam, her bare foot connecting with a dull thud. The pain that shot through her toes only fueled her anger. Vanessa stood there, breathing heavily, as the reality of her situation settled over her. She had nothing left. No plan, no backup, no way to salvage what she had lost.

But Vanessa wasn't one to give up easily. She hadn't come this far to be defeated now. She would find a way to turn things around. Harrow Hall was more than just an estate; it was power, prestige, a legacy. And she would stop at nothing to make it hers. She would find a way to claim it, no matter what it took.

***

Anita hurried up the front steps and into the house. She set the paperwork and mousetraps on a half-moon table in the foyer. The weight of her luggage seemed to mirror the day's revelations as she ascended the grand staircase of Harrow Hall. Each step creaked under her burden, the echo bouncing off the ornate walls, reminding her just how alone she felt in the vast Hall. She maneuvered her way through the corridors, her pace quickening with a mix of eagerness and anxiety to freshen up after the morning's hard run.

Once inside her room—which she now saw in the full light of morning had a spectacular view of the gardens—Anita set her belongings down with a huff. She wasted no time unpacking the cleaning supplies and heading straight for the bathroom. The state of disrepair that the estate had fallen into was evident even here, but she was determined to make the best of it. Scrubbing the tub and shower head vigorously, she managed to erase layers of grime, her actions fueled by a mix of determination and the need to stop thinking about all the decisions that she had to make. The task gave her a brief, satisfying sense of control, something she had felt steadily slipping away ever since Vance's death.

The shower she took afterward was less rejuvenating than she had hoped; the water was lukewarm, teasing the edge of comfort. Still, it felt good to wash away the sweat and dust. Anita's next challenge was finding something suitable to wear. She rummaged through her suitcase, which seemed to contain nothing but wrinkled clothes that screamed of long days and thousands of miles. Her frustration grew along with irritation at herself for caring so much. She finally settled on a gray summer halter dress with a few peach stripes across the middle. It was definitely better suited to a California afternoon, but its polyester fabric made it one of the most presentable options. She found a white shrug that she would normally wear outside by the beach and threw that on over her shoulders and then pulled floppy sandals on her feet. They wouldn't work well outside, but the carpets and floors all needed some serious cleaning.

All the while, her mind raced with thoughts of Logan and Vanessa and what the dynamics between them could mean. How could Anita's situation be "personal" to Vanessa? She tried to shove these thoughts aside, focusing instead on the tangible—her clothes, the cleanliness of her space, the simple act of getting dressed. But as hard as she tried, the questions about Logan's serious information about Harrowsburg lingered in the back of her mind, casting a shadow over her.

Finally ready, Anita took a deep breath and opened her bedroom door, stepping out into the corridor. Her footsteps were soft on the carpet runner as she descended the stairs to the foyer. There, she saw Logan waiting for her, looking unexpectedly vulnerable. He sat on one of the antique chairs, his leg bouncing with nervous energy, his fingers running through his hair, and occasionally checking the time on his phone. As Anita approached, the reality of their impending conversation settled in, filling her with a mix of anticipation and apprehension.

Logan surged to his feet when he saw her coming down the stairs. She pretended very much not to notice a hungry look in his eyes. He tore his gaze off of her and strode to the side table. "I brought the coffee and coffee maker from the shop. I figured anything you found in the kitchen would be pretty out of date."

"Great." Anita gathered up the files from the law office. "Um, where is the kitchen?" she asked with a laugh. "I haven't explored that far yet."

Logan smiled. "Follow me."

They curved around the north end of the foyer. Anita couldn't believe all the rooms that spread off of their route.

She dropped all of the files with a sudden scream.

"What?!" Logan whirled around, baubling the coffee maker and canister of grounds.

Anita stared transfixed into the open door of a study. On the far wall above a fireplace mantle, hung a full-length painting of a woman. Not just any woman, but the first woman from her dream—the one in the blue silk gown with the brocade golden tobacco leaves. Anita walked cautiously into the study.

Logan stared from Anita to the painting. "That's Victoria Harrow. Oswald Harrow's wife. They built this place."

Anita shook her head. "No, that's the woman from my dream last night." The smile and gaze of the woman in the painting was an exact likeness.

"Maybe you saw the painting before you went to sleep and—"

"—No. I never came in this direction. I only looked into the rooms directly off the foyer and then went upstairs. I've never seen this painting before. I met her in the dream last night before…"

"Before what?" Logan's tone was cautious.

Anita couldn't keep her eyes off the painting. Despite the airy enchantment of her dream, the connection to the woman was so strong, her likeness so true.

"Anita, you need to see this." Logan sounded apprehensive despite the positive affirmation of his word choice. He had set down the coffee maker and canister on a sofa table and was peering closely at a shelf on a half-empty bookcase. A collection of small, framed pictures arranged by size filled it, layers of dust creating a film over the daguerreotypes.

She approached the shelf and recognized what concerned him without the need for an explanation. In the third photograph from the left stood a young woman in a wedding dress…waist cinched tight…pearls…lace…and Anita would wager a guess that she also wore the silk stockings, lace garters, and kid boots beneath the full skirt. The same gown that Victoria Harrow had dressed Anita in during her dream last night…and from the shocked look on Logan's face, the same gown he had eagerly removed from her body.

It hadn't been a dream.

**

Anita sat on the edge of the chair, Logan on the sofa. The furniture still held the dust covers with years of grime, but neither one felt steady enough to stand. She rubbed her thumb over the detailed silver frame containing the picture in her hands. Victoria Harrow and an elderly man stood behind the unidentified bride.

"Logan, what does this mean?"

"I think it means that you and I…"

"We couldn't have."

"In the apple orchard?" He sounded stunned.

Anita felt her cheeks flame. The sweet smell of blossoms would forever be linked to him for her. She shook her head with the incredulity of it all. "Maybe there's a logical explanation." She dug for it, trying to convince herself and him as he held his head in his hands. "How about this?" She realized she was gesturing needlessly with her hands and arms, and she quieted them down in her lap. "We had just met. There was a little bit of attraction, maybe, —" she chanced a glance at him for confirmation. He was looking at her over his fingertips, his hands rubbing the lower half of his face with frustration. He gave her a nod. "Okay," she continued. "The attraction just kind of got into our subconsciouses, and it mixed with this crazy house. I'm sure you may have seen this picture before, being from Harrowsburg and working here, and this dress…Maybe I saw something online…or maybe in the file the PI gave me…maybe…"

Logan groaned with frustration and shoved his fisted hands against his thighs. "Anita, you have a tattoo of a raven on your lower left ribcage, and a birthmark on the inside of your right thigh…uh…very high up… that looks like a broken heart."

Anita froze, her breath caught. He was right.

"It was real." He shoved to his feet and began to pace in front of the fireplace. "Damn," he muttered, "It was too good not to be real."

"Oh God. Don't say things like that."

"Why? Wasn't it for you?"

"Well, of course, but—" She sighed angrily "—I don't even know you, Logan."

He crossed his arms over his chest and stared out the window. His voice was speculative as if testing a theory. "Look, people supposedly have one-night stands all the time with someone they don't know, and it all seems to work out fine for them."

"Is that how this feels to you?" she asked cautiously.

He shook his head, casting a glance her way.

"Me neither. But I don't know what to *do* with this. I don't know how to act around you. I don't know what this means. I just don't know!" She stood, brushing the dust off the back of her dress.

"I feel the same way." Logan turned to face her.

"At least it's out in the open now. We can figure it out."

He nodded but still looked shaken.

"I don't know about you, but I would really like a strong cup of coffee and maybe something else with it." Anita strode out of the room and continued down the hall, looking for the kitchen and leaving the strewn legal files for now. She muttered to herself. "Alcohol only gets better with age, right? Maybe old Hyacinth was a lush."

The room took her breath away like the rest of the Hall. The kitchen was a harmonious blend of elegance and rustic charm, bathed in soft, natural light that poured in through the tall paned windows. The walls were adorned with white subway tiles that when cleaned of the grime of time would create a pristine backdrop that accentuated the darker, richer hues of the furnishings. At the heart of the kitchen stood a grand island with a wooden butcherblock countertop, a testament to craftsmanship and utility. Surrounding the island were high-backed black chairs that invited one to sit and partake in delicious culinary creations that surely emerged from this space for generations.

Logan turned on the lights and made his way over to a counter to plug in the coffee pot. Anita started looking through the cabinetry. She couldn't help but appreciate the sophisticated mix of white and gray. The brass fixtures and hardware, though needing buffing, added a touch of vintage elegance, completing the look with a subtle, yet unmistakable, nod to the past.

Anita shoved one of the island chairs over to a set of high cabinets and climbed up on it, next to the farmhouse sink where Logan was filling the coffee pot. "Ah ha! I knew it." She pulled a dusty green bottle of scotch from the back of a cupboard. "There's a few open ones in here, but this one's still sealed."

As she attempted to climb down, the seat of the rusty chair twisted. Logan caught her as she came down, the coffee pot clattering into the deep sink. She clutched the bottle to her chest just as he clutched her to his. He was so close, hands and arms wrapped across the open back of her sundress. Her heartbeat sped to a gallop as her breathing increased, lips parting. Gazing into each other's eyes, something changed in his face, and a pleasurable grin replaced the earlier apprehension.

"I saved the scotch," she breathed. The sound of the running faucet was loud in her ears.

"That's the important thing," he said, shifting focus from her eyes to her lips.

Suddenly, he righted them from their jumbled stance against the chair and counter and let go of her. "I'll get the coffee going." She stared after him and leaned against the cupboard, weak-kneed.

He grabbed two glasses from a shelf and rinsed them thoroughly, shaking the majority of the water off. "Will this do?"

She opened the scotch, poured a heavy splash into each with a shaky hand, and took hers like a shot. The liquor burned a hot trail down her throat but lent some strength to her knees. Logan picked up his glass and swirled the warm honey-colored liquor. "Here's to dreams," he said quietly, a frank gaze meeting hers. He lifted his glass to her before he downed it.

"Another?" she asked.

"I'll wait for the coffee."

She poured herself two fingers but drank more slowly this time.

Above the island hung a trio of pendant lights, their warm glow casting a welcoming ambiance across the room. Beneath a giant wrought iron clock that would have dwarfed any other place, an array of grimy pots and pans hung neatly from tarnished brass rails.

Opposite the island, a series of open shelves showcased an eclectic collection of crockery and kitchenware, each piece seemingly chosen with care. Above white marble countertops, tall windows offered a picturesque view of the flourishing herb and vegetable garden beyond. The growth must have been a labor of love for Logan. She would have a hard time keeping a cactus alive in a desert.

Anita brushed a swath of counter off with her hand and lifted herself up onto it, her sandaled feet swinging. She grabbed her glass and sipped. After a swallow, she said, "So what is it about Vanessa and Harrowsburg that you need to tell me?"

Logan perched on one of the old high-back chairs, watching the coffee brew. His face once again serious. "It involves Vic, uh, your Vance."

She nodded.

"Vic and Vanessa were high school sweethearts."

"Of course they were," Anita growled. She took another sip. Her stomach was doing flips. She couldn't believe she had shared not just one but two men with that woman.

"After they graduated, Vic joined the Navy, and Vanessa went to Yale, but they still kept in touch. To hear Vanessa tell it, she was all about Vic."

Anita rolled her eyes. "I'm sure."

"After she graduated, she moved to Charleston to be closer to him at the naval base. She would come back home for holidays, but he rarely did. Vanessa always said they were still going strong. Mrs. Harrow—Hyacinth—she was still in touch with him at that time, and she never spoke much about their relationship. I know she and Vic wrote to one another pretty regular, but maybe he didn't talk about Vanessa. I do know that his grandmother was not a fan of her, even back in high school."

"How do you know that?" The coffee pot had reached about half, and

Anita hopped down off the counter to get it. She filled Logan's cup and then hers, mixing it with the remnants of her scotch. Logan took the bottle and poured a splash into his while Anita returned the pot to the warmer.

"I worked summers out here through high school and college. That's how I ended up with the full-time position before she died. Sometimes, toward the last years of her life, Mrs. Harrow would make me lunch. I think she was just lonely, but in conversation before Vic died—or before we thought he'd died—she would say she wished Vic had made another choice. She called Vanessa a weak-willed woman, and she always said she'd find any way she could to stop Vanessa from becoming the next Mrs. Harrow."

Chalk one up for Hyacinth, Anita thought.

"I was three years out of college, I think, when Vanessa showed up here at the Hall unannounced one afternoon. She marched her way in and told Mrs. Harrow that Vic was dead. Just bluntly, cruelly. I thought Mrs. Harrow was going to collapse. Vanessa said he'd died of a drug overdose on leave in Florida."

"But he hadn't."

"It sure seemed real. I helped Mrs. Harrow with the phone calls to the funeral home in Florida. We even called the medical examiner once because Mrs. Harrow insisted it couldn't have been him. The doctor took a lot of time to review the report with her over the phone, and by the end, she finally acknowledged that it was him."

Anita leaned against the counter, warming her hands around the cup. "Why?"

"He apparently had gotten a tattoo of a snake down one arm during high school. There was something special about it that really struck Mrs. Harrow, something the doctor said to prove it was Vic."

"Do you remember which arm?"

"The right one, I think."

"It was a phoenix when I...when I knew him." She pictured it—intricate details etched in shades of black and grey that imbued a haunting elegance. The bird spread its wings wide across Vance's upper arm and shoulder, feathers drawn with painstaking precision. Each plume seemed to ripple with an otherworldly energy, as if caught in an eternal gust of wind. The body curved gracefully, head proud, eyes glinting with a fierce determination. The flames that surrounded the creature were subtly suggested through the fluidity of the lines, merging seamlessly into the skin, creating a dynamic and deeply rooted image.

The curving body of a snake would have been the perfect canvas for it. The bird's wings would have extended over the areas where the snake's scales were most prominent, the intricate feather work effectively masking the underlying reptilian pattern. The swirling feathers and smoke at the base of the phoenix would have enveloped the snake's coiling form, using the dark shading to obscure the first tattoo's outline. The natural curvature of the phoenix's body, along with the fluid lines of its feathers, would blend seamlessly over the snake's shape, transforming the previous design into a symbol of rebirth and transformation.

"Well, the tattoo was the integral piece for Mrs. Harrow. She finally believed. According to the funeral home, he—" Logan stopped. "Anita, I don't want to say this to you. Mr. Charlton briefed me about your situation when you were located, and I don't want to—"

She knew what was coming. She'd lived it. She'd seen what they called "not viewable." She wiped tears away with her palm and took a long swallow of her coffee. "Say it."

"He shouldn't be seen, they said. It was summertime in Florida, and it was a few days before anyone found him in the hotel room."

"Bastard," Anita mumbled through a sob she tried to hold back. "Why would he do that? Why would he put his own grandmother through that? Through those thoughts? Why did he put me—"

Before she knew it, Logan's arms were around her, holding her close. She gave up strength and leaned into him. A wave of conflicting emotions washed over her, and her body trembled with mixed relief and sorrow. Logan's presence offered a sense of stability in the swirling chaos of her grief, and for the first time since her husband's death, she felt a glimmer of safety, a momentary reprieve from the relentless storm of her emotions. Anita was profoundly grateful for Logan's kindness; it was a balm to her aching soul, soothing her in ways she hadn't realized she needed. His understanding and patience seemed boundless, and in that moment, his support was an anchor she desperately clung to.

Still, a deep-seated anger simmered, directed at Vance for leaving her so abruptly, without warning, without a chance for a final goodbye or an explanation. Each kind gesture from Logan, each moment of understanding, only highlighted the void Vance had left behind. How could he have departed without considering the shattered world he would leave her to navigate alone? The pain of his absence was a constant ache, exacerbated by the responsibilities and revelations his death had thrust upon her. Anita wrestled with these tumultuous feelings, entangled, torn between the warmth of Logan's kindness and the cold, lingering resentment toward her husband, outlined in a hard, sour shell of guilt.

Anita lifted her head. She wiped ineffectually at the wet patches her tears had soaked into Logan's shirt. He chuckled lightly. "It's alright."

"What happened next?" Anita asked through sniffles, resting her hands against his chest.

"Mrs. Harrow gave permission for him to be cremated, and then she and I buried his urn in their family cemetery here on the grounds. Vanessa wanted to hold a memorial service in town, but Mrs. Harrow put a stop to that. More than anything, I think she was upset because there was no one left to take over the estate. Vic was the last. This property was everything to her."

"How would he have pulled that off? The funeral home? The medical examiner? How would he have gotten all of them involved?"

"After the law office got the tip last year that Vic was still alive, I tried to figure that out. If Vic was anything, he was resourceful. Maybe the Navy or government had something to do with it. I never figured it out. Neither did Charlton."

"But to whose benefit would that have been?" Anita eased back out of Logan's embrace, and he released her. They sat down at the island on the high back chairs next to one another with their drinks. Their knees brushed beneath the overhang.

Logan shrugged. "Who knows? The government might have used him for some top-secret job. That would have been right up his alley." He swigged the last of his coffee.

"Vance worked in the tech sector in LA. He didn't…I would have known if…" Anita thought back. Seven years. Wouldn't she have known if her husband was doing some top-secret or covert work? They each had their careers. She taken on a variety of nursing shifts over the years that overlapped and coincided with his workdays. They spent their time off together as couples do. Sometimes at home, sometimes with friends. Their vacations were spent traveling to new places. She had met a few of his coworkers over the years, but he'd never associated with them as friends. Anita's best friend Doreen was also a nurse, but the rest of her social circle was composed of people in all different types of careers.

She had spoken of the events of her day in vague terms due to the medical privacy of the patients, and while Vance talked a little about some of his projects, it was in a vague sense as well. The tech sector was competitive, and she didn't understand most of the development processes he worked with anyway. She really had had no interest in it, just as he had no interest in the medical procedures she assisted with or the diseases and conditions she helped to treat. He went on business trips, but that was nothing out of the ordinary for his industry.

"Did I know him at all?" Anita asked rhetorically, and Logan let her process her thoughts, pouring himself another cup of coffee.

But she *had* known Vance. In the quiet corners of their shared existence, they had woven a tapestry of love that was as delicate as it was profound. Their work lives ran on parallel tracks, seldom intersecting, each immersed in their own professional worlds.

When they were alone together, it was as if the universe conspired to carve out moments of pure, unfiltered connection. Vance's eyes would soften from the intensity of his usual character, any guarded demeanor melting away in the warmth of Anita's presence. They would sit on their back patio, the stars above bearing silent witness to whispered confessions and dreams shared over cups of coffee during lazy mornings or wine for late nights. The mundane and the extraordinary blurred in those times, and the weight of unspoken truths momentarily lifted by the simple act of being together. In those precious hours, they were not just two individuals, but a singular entity bound by a timeless and unassailable love.

Yet, Anita would sometimes glimpse a faraway look in Vance's eyes, a silent echo of a past she could never fully reach. He didn't want to talk of it, and she respected that. She knew what it felt like to have to talk of difficult times. She avoided conversations about her parents and their deadly boating accident as often as she could, and so it was within their variety of normal to not touch on the subjects of the past.

"Who gave Mr. Charlton the tip that he was alive? Why did they start looking for him?"

Logan shrugged. "It came in anonymously through the mail, but with multiple photos of Vic and proof of the time, date, and location the photos had been taken. Even so, it took a while to track him down. But by then it was too late. The only one left…"

"Was me." Anita finished for him. She stood, running her fingers along the butcher block. She thought of the woodwork that adorned the walls and the sweeping grand staircase that spiraled upward with timeless grace. The Hall exuded a sense of history, its craftsmanship a testament to an era where artisans poured their souls into every detail. Each room seemed to whisper stories of the past, of grand gatherings and quiet moments alike. The weight of its legacy pressed upon her; this wasn't just a house, but a cornerstone of Harrowsburg's history and a crucial chapter in Vance's family saga. The Harrows had built this place with care and intention, and now, with Vance gone, it rested on her shoulders to decide its fate. Could she really leave it to rot if there was truly no one else to take it? Why would Vance have gone to such lengths to cut ties with his family and their legacy? Was that his intention or was he forced to do it?

Anita's thoughts and gaze drifted to Logan, the caretaker who had become an unexpected anchor in this storm of uncertainty. The thought of being so close to him, day in and day out, filled her with a mix of anticipation and apprehension. What was this thing between them? How could they ever explain what had happened the previous night? Their undeniable attraction could either blossom into something beautiful or become an awkward tension that complicated their interactions.

And then there was the Vanessa of it all. Why did she have to connect on both sides, to Vance and to Logan? What was it about the woman that set Anita's teeth on edge and her skin crawling? She'd not spoken a word directly to her, and yet, it was just something about her that made Anita want to be on full guard at all times.

As Anita stood there, caught between the allure of the Hall, the mysterious history of Vance and the complexity of her feelings for Logan, she knew she wasn't ready to make any decision yet. She could only ponder the possibilities, allowing the grandeur of the hall and the potential of her new life to weigh against the uncertainty of what the future might hold.

***

While Logan went to retrieve the rodent traps from the foyer, Anita placed the bottle of scotch in a lower cabinet than its previous home. The buzz she was feeling would have to do. Despite an urge to get sloppy and check out, she knew she needed to keep a semi-clear head about her. Surveying the kitchen, she couldn't help but think about how the combination of updated appliances with the existing classic design elements would create a kitchen that was both functional and beautiful, a true heart of the home where memories could be made and cherished.

Still though there was something about this place. A void that the life outside didn't quite touch. Something she felt not all the cleaning and scrubbing in the world would wash out.

"Ready to tackle this together?" Logan asked when he returned, with a friendly smile that didn't quite hide his concern for her.

Anita nodded, grateful not just for the help, but for the company. As they walked through the expansive hallways of the Hall, each room they entered seemed to echo with the whispers of the past. Logan pointed out the peculiarities and histories of each space as they set up traps—a narrative thread that wove itself through the fabric of the Hall's grandeur and mystery.

In the lounge, with its grand fireplace and portraits of stern-looking ancestors, Anita felt a chill that wasn't from the drafty windows. Logan noticed and quickly joked about the family's severe expressions, making her laugh and momentarily lightening the atmosphere. The dining room was a grand affair, with a table long enough to seat thirty guests and intricate tapestries that told tales of the Harrow family's exploits both in Europe and after they immigrated to America.

On the second floor, the series of guest bedrooms each decorated in the styles of different eras, showcased the evolution of interior design over the decades. Logan shared anecdotes about the notable guests who had once slept there, while carefully placing traps in inconspicuous corners. The library was next, a room lined with towering bookshelves filled with leather-bound books, some as old as the Hall itself. Anita ran her fingers over the spines, feeling the weight of knowledge and time in her hands, while Logan secured the area against the less literary types of visitors.

As they ventured up to the third floor and into the servants' quarters, Anita saw the stark contrast between the luxury of the family areas and the simplicity of the spaces where the staff had lived and worked. It was a humbling insight, and she appreciated Logan's respectful tone as he shared stories of the people who had kept the Hall running through the years.

Finally, they climbed the narrow stairs to the attic. The air grew cooler as they ascended, and the space was a treasure trove of forgotten items: trunks, clothes, toys, and countless documents. While a few empty dress forms dotted the space, she was relieved to see none contained the wedding gown.

As Logan set a trap near an old chest, Anita peered inside and found a stack of letters tied with a ribbon, faded by time. She wondered if they might include correspondence between Vance and his grandmother. The musty scent of paper and wood filled the air, a reminder of all that had passed under this roof.

"It would be a lot, wouldn't it?" Logan said softly, watching her as she carefully thumbed the edges of the letters. "Taking on this place."

Anita nodded, feeling overwhelmed yet strangely connected to the history around her. "But seeing all of this... I feel like it's worth preserving. Worth the effort, but I don't know if I'm the person for it."

Logan smiled, his expression gentle. "I'd be here to help. Not just with the mice."

They made their way back down to the main floor. It was mid-afternoon now, and the sunlight streamed through the stained glass, casting colorful patterns on the carpet. "I think I'll rest for a bit," Anita said, feeling the weight of the day pressing down on her shoulders.

Logan nodded. "I have some work to do on the grounds. But before I go," he paused, hesitating as he looked at her. "I know there's a lot on your plate right now. Whatever happened between us last night, we can set it aside. You don't need that kind of distraction. There may never be an explanation for it anyway. This place..." He looked around slowly. "...It has more than just history. Things I'm not sure we'll ever understand."

Anita was touched by his consideration, but suddenly, she frowned. She didn't want to put aside the one thing that had brought her some comfort. As if reading her thoughts, Logan turned back to face her, stepping closer. His hands gently framed her face, and he leaned in, their lips meeting in a kiss that was both a promise and a pause, filled with all the tension and tenderness of unspoken feelings.

Pulling back slightly, Logan looked into her eyes. "Please don't make any hasty decisions where I'm concerned, Anita. I'll keep."

The words hung between them, heavy yet hopeful, as Logan left her standing in the foyer, the echo of his steps a counterpoint to the rapid beating of her heart. Alone, Anita touched her lips, the kiss lingering like a warm imprint. Maybe, just maybe, she could navigate the complexities of Harrow Hall and what it meant to be a Mrs. Harrow—with Logan nearby.

***

Vanessa
You were supposed to convince her to stay in LA.
Doreen
I did my best. You had six months before she showed up. Why didn't you do something?
Vanessa
These things take time, idiot. Find some way to make her leave Connecticut or else.
Doreen
Or else what?
Vanessa
You don't want to find out.

Chapter Five

Anita stood in the corner of a dimly lit room at Harrow Hall. The flickering light from candle wall sconces cast eerie shadows that danced across the room, stressing the dark hollows of antique furniture and mysterious artifacts that filled the space. The air was thick with a sense of foreboding, and Anita could feel her heart racing as she took in the scene before her.

At the center of the room stood a circular table made of dark mahogany, its surface adorned with intricate carvings of arcane symbols and sinister creatures. The table seemed almost alive, the designs shifting and changing in the flickering candlelight. Around the table, two men and two women, dressed in expensive suits and gowns, the women draped in jewels, sat with solemn expressions as they chanted words that Anita could not understand. Their layers of clothing and hairstyles spoke of epochs gone by. She recognized the trio from the bride's daguerreotype as the two women and one of the men, but the second man was unknown to her.

Victoria Harrow, though dressed differently but equally exquisitely as her first dream, had a face with a mask of dignity and calm. Her eyes were cold and unfeeling. The young girl who had worn the bride gown in the photo was completely the opposite. The men chanted along with the women but had their gazes anxiously focused on four strange dolls that also each held a place at the table, one person seated in between each.

Even small as the dolls were—the tallest being perhaps 30 inches—the table and the gathering in general seemed to belong to them rather than to the humans. Anita noticed the dolls' intense gazes all settled on her, and her heart beat faster under their constant focus.

Each antique doll seemed to be of a different era. With hollow eyes and matted hair, a tattered straw doll slumped slightly, as if burdened by the weight of forgotten years. It seemed to be the oldest. Next, a porcelain beauty with a tarnished gown exuded a ghostly grace, its unblinking eyes loaded with chilling intent. A cherubic doll, pristine in a lace dress, stared blankly ahead, its unsettlingly large face with parted lips dominating its body. Completing the sinister circle, a Victorian doll, cloaked in black, sat with an air of quiet menace, its dark eyes reflecting the flickering candle flames like portals to some unfathomable abyss. Together, they created a tableau of frozen dread, an assembly of nightmares forever trapped in an eerie, silent communion.

Anita's focus shifted from the table and landed on a woman in a maid's uniform, gagged and tied to an intricately carved chair poised at the opposite end of the room. The wood was so dark that it appeared to fade in and out of the shadows, adding to the surreal nature of the scene. The woman's shoulders shook with silent sobs, eyes wide, her body trembling with panic and dread. It seemed not just her life at stake as the apron of her uniform bulged with the roundness of a pregnant belly. Her muffled cries were heart-wrenching, filled with a desperation that tore at Anita's soul.

The people around the table, however, paid no attention to the woman's pleas. Their chanting grew louder and more intense, drowning out her cries. The words they spoke were foreign and haunting, echoing through the room with a malevolent energy. The air around the table seemed to thrum with power, and Anita could feel it pressing down on her, suffocating her.

Anita's eyes were drawn to the maid's face, soaked with tears. Her screaming, diminished by the gag, fell on deaf ears in the cacophony of chanting. She threw her head back, obviously seeking the intercession of a higher power to save her. Anita wanted to reach out, to tear her from her bindings, to save her, but she found herself frozen in place, unable to move or speak. The pain in her chest grew more intense, mirroring the agony that the maid was experiencing.

The chanting continued to rise in volume, a relentless crescendo that seemed to vibrate through Anita's very bones. The room began to spin, the shadows lengthening and twisting around her. The faces of the people at the table blurred and shifted, their features becoming monstrous and grotesque. The dolls' eyes glowed with an eerie light, their expressions shifting disproportionately to reflect a sinister glee.

Anita's head throbbed with pain, her vision darkening at the edges. She could feel herself being pulled into the darkness, the chanting growing louder and louder until it was all she could hear. The maid's cries were lost in the roar, and Anita felt a surge of helplessness and despair wash over her.

***

With a rush of pain, Anita jolted awake. She sat up in bed, drenched in sweat, her heart pounding in her chest. The room around her was dark and silent, but the echoes of the nightmare still lingered. She took in deep, shuddering breaths, trying to calm herself, but the fear and pain from the dream were slow to fade.

She grabbed for the side lamp, wrenching the pull chain and gawked around the room, half-expecting to see the eerie table and its occupants, but there was nothing there. She was alone in her bedroom. The nightmare had been so vivid, so real, that it took her several minutes to fully convince herself that it had been just a dream.

Anita swung her legs over the side of the bed and stood up, her knees weak and trembling. She walked to the window and looked out at the grounds of Harrow Hall. The moonlight cast long shadows across the garden. The night was still and quiet, but the sense of unease from the dream lingered, making her feel as if she were being watched.

She took a deep breath and tried to shake off the remnants of the nightmare. Images replayed in her mind: the chanting, the crying maid, the sinister dolls. She couldn't shake the feeling that there was something deeply wrong with the house, something that went beyond the realm of nightmares.

Anita returned to bed, but sleep was elusive. She lay awake, staring at the ceiling, her mind racing with thoughts of the nightmare. The fear and pain she had experienced were unlike anything she had ever felt before, and the maid's despairing cries haunted her.

***

Logan arrived at Susan and Brad's house just as the sun began to rise, casting a warm, golden hue over the sleepy town. He parked his pickup in the driveway and walked up to the front door, feeling a sense of excitement. He had always enjoyed these early morning breakfasts with his sister's family. It was a time to connect, share stories, and enjoy the simple pleasures of life.

As he opened the door, he was greeted by the smell of fresh coffee and the sound of Grace's laughter. Susan was bustling around the kitchen, flipping pancakes, in slippers and a robe while Brad was helping Grace with her homework at the dining table.

"Uncle Logan!" Grace squealed, hopping off her chair and running to him. He scooped her up in a big hug, her infectious energy brightening his morning even more.

"Hey there, munchkin!" Logan said, giving her a playful squeeze. Gracie giggled.

He set her down, ruffling her hair.

Susan turned from the stove, her face lighting up when she saw Logan. "Morning, Logan! Coffee's ready, and pancakes are almost done. Sit down and make yourself comfortable."

"Thanks," Logan said, grabbing a mug and pouring himself a cup of coffee. He took a seat at the table next to Brad and Grace. He watched his sister rub at the small of her back, her pregnant belly dwarfing her short stature. "Can I help with the breakfast."

"Nope. Just about done."

Brad looked up from the homework sheet. "Morning. How's everything going?"

Logan took a sip of his coffee, savoring the rich flavor. "Things are good, Brad. Really good, actually."

Susan raised an eyebrow as she flipped the last pancake onto a plate. "You sound different today. Happier."

Logan smiled, a sense of contentment washing over him. "I guess I am. I broke up with Vanessa yesterday."

There was a brief moment of silence as Susan and Brad processed the news, exchanging a glance. Susan was the first to speak, her voice filled with a mix of surprise and curiosity. "Really? What happened?"

Logan shrugged, leaning back in his chair. "It was time. We've been going in circles for too long, and it wasn't fair to either of us. She didn't take it well, but it needed to be done."

Susan set the plate of pancakes on the table and sat down, her eyes searching Logan's face.

"You seem... lighter. Like a weight's been lifted."

Logan nodded. "That's exactly how I feel. And there's something else. We've got a new Mrs. Harrow at the estate."

Susan's eyes widened. "A new Mrs. Harrow? Tell me more."

Logan took another sip of his coffee. "Her name's Anita Miran. She inherited the estate from Vic. She's been through a lot, though. His death was unexpected, and it wasn't pretty. It's been tough on her."

Susan frowned, her brow furrowing in concern. "Victor Harrow... That was such a strange drama. And it must have been hard for Vanessa, too, this past fall. Dealing with all of that. Finding out he'd been alive all these years."

Logan nodded. "Vanessa wouldn't talk about it much. I think more than anything it hurt her pride. Remember when we were growing up how much she wanted to be a Harrow?"

"Yeah. The Hall creeped most kids out, but it was a fairytale castle to her." I still don't know how you work there every day."

Logan grinned. "But Anita... she's different. Strong. Resilient. I'm hoping she decides to stay."

"Why wouldn't she?" Susan asked.

"The Hall holds a lot of memories, and not all of them are good. The whole estate is wrapped up so tight legally, I don't think there's a snowball's chance in Egypt of it being sold, but it would have to move on to some other long lost relative."

Susan reached across the table and squeezed Logan's hand. "Well, I hope she finds some peace here. It sounds like she could use a fresh start."

Logan smiled, appreciating his sister's empathy. "Yeah, me too."

Grace, who had been listening quietly, looked up at Logan with wide eyes. "Is Mrs. Harrow nice?"

Logan chuckled, ruffling her hair again. "She is. I think you'll like her."

Brad cleared his throat, drawing everyone's attention. "Well, whatever happens, we'll support her. That estate is a huge part of Harrowsburg. The town has felt the loss of Hyacinth for years."

The rest of breakfast was filled with light-hearted conversation and laughter. Grace chattered excitedly about her school projects, while Susan and Brad shared stories from their week. Logan felt a sense of belonging, a comfort that he hadn't realized he had been missing.

After breakfast, it was a flurry of activity as they got Grace ready for school. Logan helped her pack her backpack while Susan made sure she had everything she needed. Brad loaded the dishwasher, humming a tune under his breath.

"Can you walk me to the bus stop?" Grace asked, her eyes shining with hope.

"Of course, munchkin," Logan replied, smiling.

They all walked out together, the crisp morning air invigorating. At the bus stop, Grace gave Logan a big hug. "Thanks for coming to breakfast, Uncle Logan. I love you."

Logan's heart melted. "I love you too, Gracie. Have a great day at school."

As the bus pulled away, Susan turned to Logan. "Take care of yourself, Logan. And keep us posted about the new Mrs. Harrow."

Logan nodded. "I will. Thanks, sir. Try to take a load off."

"Ugh. January can't come fast enough."

They exchanged hugs, and Logan got into his pickup, waving as he drove off. The drive to Harrow Hall was peaceful, the morning sun casting long shadows over the road. Logan felt a sense of optimism about the day ahead. There was work to be done, but for the first time in a long while, he felt ready to face it with a clear mind and a hopeful heart.

***

Anita sat on the dilapidated porch swing of Harrow Hall, a cup of coffee warming her hands against the brisk morning chill. The rich blue sky above promised a sunny day ahead, but the air still held a bite. Wrapped in multiple layers, Anita contemplated her surroundings—the grandeur of the estate and the massive responsibility it represented. Her thoughts were interrupted by the familiar rumble of Logan's pickup as it pulled up alongside her car.

Logan stepped out dressed in his usual work attire—jeans, a flannel shirt, and sturdy boots, looking every bit the part of the estate's caretaker. His broad smile beamed in her direction as he approached the porch. Anita, feeling the weight of her sleepless night, offered a weary smile in return and shuffled over on the swing to make room for him.

"Morning," Logan greeted, his voice carrying a cheerful note as he placed a shopping bag on the porch. Anita, stifling a yawn, wrapped her sweater-clad arms tighter around herself.

"Rough night?" Logan inquired.

"You could say that," Anita responded, managing a small laugh.

Logan's expression softened with concern. "Anyone wander into your apple orchard?" he joked, trying to lighten the mood.

She chuckled, appreciating the attempt. "No. That's definitely not the kind of dream I had last night, though Victoria Harrow was there."

"Really?" Logan's interest piqued, his brow furrowing slightly. "What happened?"

"Let's just say I think I watched one too many horror movies as a kid," Anita replied, dismissing her discomfort with a wave of her hand.

"Did you get any sleep at all?" Logan asked, his voice laced with worry.

"Not much. And still going on very little from my trip across the country. I'm sure that's all the nightmare was. I've decided to spend the next two days like I'm at a one-of-a-kind vacation rental. I'm going to relax and nap and explore, and on Thursday, I'll go visit Mr. Charlton's office again with whatever decision I've made," Anita explained, hoping to convey a sense of control she didn't quite feel.

She gave a slight kick, setting the porch swing into a gentle motion.

"Do you want to take a full tour of the estate today?" he ventured.

"Mmhmm," Anita nodded, pulling her sweater closer. "But maybe this afternoon if it works with your schedule? It's freezing this morning."

Logan laughed, a warm, hearty sound that made Anita smile despite herself. "Now you're going to tell me you've never seen snow."

"Oh no, I have. Two times," she confessed.

He gave her a side-eyed glance, still smiling, and kicked their swinging up a notch. "Twice? That's it?"

"Let's see. I had an airport layover in Minneapolis one winter on the way to a nursing convention in Atlanta, and Vance and I stayed in a hotel in Denver once that had a view of the Rockies," Anita recounted.

"What? An airport view and hotel view? That's it?" Logan teased.

She nodded.

"You've never had a snowball fight or made a snow angel?" he continued, disbelief coloring his tone.

"Nope."

"Never cut down your own Christmas tree?"

"People do that in real life? I thought it was just a thing for the movies."

Logan laughed again. "Well, you are in for a treat this winter. We will find you a perfect tree for the foyer, and I will personally see to it that you receive a proper lesson in making snowballs," he promised, his eyes twinkling with amusement.

Anita shivered. "My temp's dropping just at the thought of it," she laughed.

"Nah. You have to get out of those California clothes is all." He surveyed her layers. "Speaking of which." He grabbed the shopping bag at her feet and plopped it onto her lap.

"What's this?" Anita inquired, curiosity piqued.

"Well, those sandals and clogs you've been wearing won't do for our tour of the grounds at all," Logan stated matter-of-factly.

Anita dug into the bag and brought out a pair of hiking boots with distressed leather and pink camo edging. They were the perfect size. "Logan, I can't accept these."

"Consider them a welcome-to-the-neighborhood gift," he insisted.

She slipped out of her clogs and put one foot into the boots. "They're surprisingly light," she noted, "and comfortable." She then slipped the other foot in. Logan reached down, scooped her feet into his lap, and began lacing them up. She laughed at his actions.

"You California girls probably don't know how these work." He grinned at her. Anita couldn't help but wonder how a simple touch, even through layers of cloth, leather, and canvas, could send such exhilarating shivers through her.

"That actually does sound nice," she said thoughtfully. "The Christmas tree, I mean, I've never had a real one."

Logan's eyes widened in genuine surprise. "Never?" he echoed.

She shook her head. "Did Hyacinth put one in the foyer?"

"I've only seen pictures of it from her younger days when they had a house full of servants to do the dirty work. She told me once that the maid staff would decorate it," he shared.

"Where's the fun in that?" Anita asked, her tone playful.

"Exactly," Logan agreed, finishing up the lacing but keeping a hold of her feet.

They swung in silence for a few minutes before Logan cleared his throat. "For what it's worth, Anita, I really hope you decide to stay."

Anita gave him a smile, but she felt it didn't quite reach her eyes. "I know, and it is worth something."

"Good," he responded warmly, gently setting her feet down. "Well, I'll go get some work done and pick you up after lunch. How does that sound?"

"That sounds great," Anita agreed, watching him walk away toward one of the outbuildings. As she turned back into the house, her heart was a tangle of emotions—anticipation, fear, and a burgeoning hope that maybe, just maybe, she could find a home here, not just in Harrow Hall, but someday with Logan by her side.

***

Anita
Hey, Doreen. Got some news and it's not great.
Doreen
Oh no, what's up?
Anita
So, the estate can't just be sold. It's all wrapped up in legal mumbo jumbo. Basically, I either take it on or they find some long-lost relation of Vance's and give it to them.
Doreen
Seriously? That's a lot to dump on you. What are you going to do?
Anita
I'm not sure yet. I was hoping this would be a quick in-and-out job, but it looks like it's going to be more complicated.
Doreen
You could just come back to Cali.
Anita
What happened to the fall leaves and syrup catching?
Doreen
Well, I don't want you to get mixed up in anything dangerous.
Anita
Dangerous? What do you mean?
Doreen
Well, there's a lot of money at stake, isn't there? Someone else always wants it.
Anita
Yeah, I suppose. But I would be set for life. It's just…
Doreen
What?
Anita
This place doesn't always seem right. It just has a weird vibe.
Doreen
Then come home.
Anita
I don't know. I think I just need a few more days to figure things out.

***

Logan's proposal for a dirt bike ride around the Harrow estate caught Anita by surprise, her eyes widening as she processed the suggestion. "You're serious?" she asked, a hint of trepidation lacing her voice. Logan's grin was infectious, his excitement evident as he nodded. "Absolutely. It's the best way to really see the place," he insisted, leading her to where two dirt bikes stood, ready for adventure.

At first, Anita was hesitant at the unfamiliar feel of the bike under her. The roar of the engine made her heart race with a mix of fear and excitement. But as Logan showed her the basics, her confidence slowly began to build. "Just hold on tight, and trust the bike," he advised, his tone reassuring. With a deep breath, Anita gave a tentative twist of the throttle, and they were off.

The wind whipped past her as they sped along the rugged trails of the estate. The initial fear that gripped her heart gave way to exhilaration as the landscape blurred past them—rolling hills, dense woodlands, and sprawling fields stretched as far as the eye could see. Logan led with ease, occasionally looking back to make sure she was keeping up, his smile wide whenever their eyes met. Anita, feeling the thrill of the ride, began to relax and enjoy the freedom that came with speeding along the dirt paths.

They zoomed up and down country roads and across section lines, the estate seemingly unending. Logan pointed out landmarks as they passed—a hidden pond that was a favorite spot for deer, old stone walls that marked colonial property lines, and wildflower meadows that erupted in color during the spring. Every so often, they would stop, and Logan would share stories about the estate, his knowledge deep and his pride in the land evident.

The ride took them over two exhilarating hours, during which Anita's apprehension melted away completely, replaced by a budding love for the untamed beauty of the land. As they returned to the Hall grounds, Logan shifted the tour to a more leisurely pace, showing Anita the various outbuildings. Each structure had its own story—a weathered barn that had once housed prized thoroughbreds, a stone outbuilding that served as a seasonal cider press, and a charming cook's cottage shrouded in ivy.

When they returned to the gardens near the house, they dismounted and walked. The well-tended plots were a testament to generations of care, with rows of meticulously planned flowers and shrubs. Logan talked about the ideas he had for the space, and his vision for bringing parts of it back to its former glory. Anita listened, deeply moved by his connection to the place.

As they strolled through the apple orchard, the late afternoon sun filtered through the branches, casting dappled shadows on the ground. The air was sweet with the scent of ripening fruit, and the peaceful ambiance starkly contrasted with the adrenaline of their earlier ride. "I never realized how much history and life could be packed into a place like this," Anita confessed, her voice soft, reflective.

Logan stopped and looked at her, his expression earnest. "There's a lot here worth preserving." His tone was gentle yet hopeful.

The tour, filled with speed, stories, and the serene beauty of nature, had not just shown Anita the breadth of the estate but had also subtly woven her into its tapestry. As the shadows lengthened and the day drew to a close, she felt a profound connection to Harrowsburg and its history—a sense of belonging that she hadn't anticipated. The adventure of the day, Logan's companionship, and the undeniable beauty of the land had sparked something within her, a desire to stay and become a part of the estate's ongoing story.

Logan's presence, both reassuring and exciting, had shown her that Harrow Hall was not just a relic of the past but a place brimming with potential for the future. As they walked back to the Hall, Anita's mind was abuzz with possibilities, and she allowed herself a limited hour that night to pretend she had chosen to stay.

She explored the Hall's interior with fresh eyes, imagining possible restoration work. The grand staircase, the opulent but dusty ballroom, the numerous bedrooms and sitting rooms—all would need attention. She took notes, her mind buzzing with ideas and a cautious optimism. She prayed for a quiet night with neither dreams nor nightmares.

***

Hyacinth Harrow's Diary

June 2, 19__

The ink on this page feels heavier tonight, as if the weight of my thoughts makes the pen harder to lift. I am engaged to Roger Wainwright, a man I find entirely repugnant. Yet, here I am, writing about a future that seems inevitable, a future where I will be Mrs. Hyacinth Wainwright, by law, and bestowed as Mrs. Harrow to all, bound by duty and legacy rather than love.

My parents are elated by this arrangement, their faces glowing with the satisfaction of securing the future of Harrow Hall. Roger comes from an old family, one with almost as many secrets and shadows as our own. The Wainwrights have been intertwined with the Harrows for generations, their fates linked by more than just proximity and wealth. It is The Covenant of Shadows that binds us most tightly, the ancient pact that dictates our actions and our alliances.

When my father informed me of the engagement, I could see the gleam of triumph in his eyes. "Hyacinth," he said, his voice rich with the gravitas of tradition, "this union will fortify our family's position and ensure the continuation of our legacy. You understand the importance of this, don't you?"

I nodded, the words caught in my throat. How could I express my dismay when I knew it would fall on deaf ears? My mother embraced me, her touch cold and perfunctory. "You are making us so proud, my dear. This is the path you were meant to walk."

Roger arrived at the Hall the following evening, his presence as unwelcome as a storm cloud on a clear day. He is handsome in a way that seems almost artificial, his features too perfect, his smile too calculated. His eyes, though, betray his true nature—cold, scheming, and devoid of genuine warmth.

"Hyacinth," he greeted me with a smirk, bowing slightly as if he were a knight and I, his queen. "It is a pleasure to finally call you my fiancée."

I forced a smile, the corners of my mouth aching with the effort. "The pleasure is mine, Roger."

We spent the evening together, the four of us—Roger, my parents, and I—dining in the grand hall. The conversation was stilted, filled with hollow pleasantries and forced laughter. Roger spoke of his family's illustrious history, of their role in The Covenant of Shadows, and how our union would be a powerful symbol of our families' continued alliance.

As he spoke, I felt a chill run down my spine. The Covenant of Shadows, that ancient pact, has always been a source of fear and fascination for me. It is said to be a bond forged in blood, a contract with dark forces that ensure our family's prosperity in exchange for unwavering loyalty and the occasional, mysterious sacrifice. I know little of the details, but I have seen enough to understand its power and its danger.

Roger is as complicit as my parents in this dark alliance. He spoke with an ease and familiarity that made my skin crawl, recounting tales of rituals and ceremonies that sent shivers through my soul. I felt trapped, a pawn in a game played by forces far greater than myself.

After dinner, Roger and I walked through the gardens, the air thick with the scent of blooming roses. He took my hand, and I resisted the urge to pull away. "Hyacinth," he said, his voice softer now, almost tender, "I know this arrangement may not have been what you wanted, but it is what is best for our families."

I looked into his eyes, searching for any sign of sincerity. "And what of love, Roger? What place does it have in this?"

He chuckled, a low, mocking sound. "Love is a luxury we cannot afford, my dear. We are bound by duty, by honor. The Covenant of Shadows demands our loyalty above all else."

His words stung, but they also clarified my purpose. Love, it seems, is a frivolity for those not bound by ancient pacts and familial expectations. My role is to ensure the continuation of the Harrow legacy, to keep Harrow Hall strong and its secrets safe.

I must marry Roger. To do so will please my parents and cement our family's position within The Covenant of Shadows. The weight of this responsibility is crushing, but I must bear it. There is no other choice.

Returning to my room, I sat by the window, gazing out at the darkened landscape. The moon cast long shadows across the grounds, and I could almost hear the whispers of my ancestors urging me to accept my fate. The legacy of Harrow Hall is a heavy burden, but it is mine to carry.

As I write these words, I feel a mixture of resignation and resolve. Roger Wainwright is not the man of my dreams, but he is the man who will help me uphold the traditions and expectations of our families. Together, we will continue the work of The Covenant of Shadows, ensuring that our legacy endures for generations to come.

I have always known that my life would be dictated by forces beyond my control. This engagement is merely another step on that path. I must find strength in the knowledge that I am fulfilling my duty, even if it means sacrificing my own desires.

In the stillness of the night, I can hear the echoes of the past, the voices of those who came before me. They remind me that I am not alone in this struggle, that I am part of a lineage that has endured much and will *continue to endure. Harrow Hall stands as a testament to our resilience, our power, and our unwavering commitment to The Covenant of Shadows.*

I will marry Roger. I will do my duty.

Hyacinth Harrow

Chapter Six

Anita found herself once again in the dimly lit room within Harrow Hall. She could feel her heart racing as she took in the scene before her.

At the center of the room stood the same circular table made of dark mahogany, its surface adorned with intricate carvings of mythical creatures and arcane symbols. The table seemed almost alive, the carvings shifting and changing in the flickering candlelight. Around the table sat multiple members of the Harrow family, dressed in expensive 19th-century clothing and draped in jewels. Their faces were masks of concentration and fear as they engaged in a sinister ritual.

Anita's gaze swept over the table, noting the four eerie dolls seated again at the north, south, east, and west positions. The dolls' delicate porcelain faces and finely detailed clothing gave them an unsettling realism. Their glassy eyes seemed to follow her every move, and she felt a chill run down her spine as she looked at them.

This time, instead of the pregnant maid tied to the chair, there were two children in grubby clothing, blindfolded and sitting together in the intricately carved highbacked chair. The children's shoulders shook with silent sobs, their bodies trembling with fear as they sat helplessly in the chair.

Anita's attention was drawn to a middle-aged man who suddenly stood from his seat at the table, his face etched with a look of terror. She recognized him as Aldous Harrow from one of the portraits along the grand staircase. He picked up two bone dice from the table, his hands shaking as he prepared to roll them. The tension in the room was palpable, and Anita could feel the fear and desperation emanating from Aldous.

Seated at the table was Aldous's mother, Victoria Harrow, her expression cool and composed. Next to her sat her teenage granddaughter, Emmiline, who watched the proceedings with a mix of curiosity and dread. Aldous's hands trembled as he rolled the dice, and the room fell silent as they clattered across the table's surface. They came to a stop, revealing two opposing symbols.

A collective gasp went through the room, and the oldest doll at the table spoke in a voice that sent chills down Anita's spine. "Shadows meet light, and the stakes have now doubled."

Aldous ran his hands through his hair, thoroughly terrified and glancing repeatedly at the crying children in the chair. The fear in his eyes was unmistakable, and it was clear that he did not want to continue.

Victoria, however, remained calm and authoritative. "Roll again," she commanded, her voice cold and unyielding.

Aldous hesitated, his reluctance evident, but he eventually complied. With trembling hands, he picked up the dice and rolled them once more. The room held its breath as the dice came to a stop, revealing two identical symbols.

A collective sigh went through the dolls, and the oldest doll spoke again. "Shadow meets shadow. Emmiline Marguerite, you will be the recipient of the years when it is your time."

"Emmiline?" Victoria's voice was sharp with surprise and anger.

One of the younger dolls turned its porcelain head toward her. "The Harrow has chosen," it said, its voice mechanical and emotionless.

The dolls began chanting, their voices rising in a haunting melody. A smoky blue light began to run through the carvings on the table, illuminating the intricate designs. The light pulsed and shifted, casting an eerie glow over the room. The dolls all turned their focus to Victoria, and she began chanting as well. The other Harrow family members followed suit, their voices blending with those of the dolls in a chilling harmony.

The smoky blue light crept across the table, snaking its way toward the children. The light wrapped around them, and they breathed it in through their sobs. Their cries grew louder and more desperate as the light enveloped them, their bodies trembling with fear and pain.

Anita watched in horror, unable to move or speak. The chanting grew louder and more intense, the air thick with a malevolent energy. The children's cries were drowned out by the chanting, their bodies writhing in agony as the ritual continued. The light pulsed and throbbed, its eerie *glow filling the room.*

***

Vanessa
Is she going back to LA?
Doreen
She said she needs some time to figure things out. But it doesn't sound like she will soon.
Vanessa
Have you *blown* thru all the $ I gave you?
Doreen
No.
Vanessa
Good. Use some of it to get a flight out here. ASAP
Doreen
Why?
Vanessa
You find out when you get here.
Vanessa
Book it tonight. Tell her you're coming.
Doreen
I have to put in for the time off work. I'm already on thin ice as it is.
Vanessa
A coke problem will do that to a person.
Doreen
I don't want to do this anymore.
Vanessa
You should have thought of that before you stole the drugs to inject Vic. You should be smart enough to know that was the point of no return.
Doreen
Fine.
Vanessa
In my pocket or behind bars. Your choice.

***

Anita woke before dawn, the remnants of her nightmare still clinging to her consciousness like a dense fog. It was the same as the previous night—the mahogany table, the dolls, Victoria and others chanting, and this time, two poor children in such desperation. Anita sat up in bed, her heart pounding in the pre-dawn silence of the Hall. Sleep was out of the question now, so she decided to get up and make herself useful.

She slipped into a pair of old jeans, a sweatshirt, and her clogs, the creaky wooden floors sending shivers up her spine as she made her way to the kitchen. The Hall, vast and grand, seemed to breathe with its own life, every squeak and groan a testament to its age. The kitchen was her target for the morning. Anita knew that if she were to make a go of living here, she'd need to understand just how much work it would take to get the rooms to livable and clean states.

The first light of dawn filtered through the tall, narrow windows, casting long shadows across the room. Anita took a deep breath and set to work. She began by clearing away the dust and grime that had accumulated over the years. The task was monumental, but she found a rhythm in the repetitive motions. She scrubbed the counters, swept the floors, and polished the old, tarnished fixtures until they gleamed. The physical exertion was cathartic, a way to channel her restless energy.

By the time she finished, the kitchen looked almost new. Anita stepped back to admire her work, wiping sweat from her forehead. The room had transformed from a dusty relic to a warm, inviting space. A sense of accomplishment filled her as she imagined the possibilities this kitchen held. She could almost hear the clatter of pots and pans, smell the rich aromas of homemade meals.

Feeling a spark of excitement, Anita decided she wanted to experience cooking in such a place. But first, she needed ingredients. Logan's pickup was parked in its usual spot outside, indicating he had already arrived for work. She didn't see him as she made her way to her car, but after experiencing the vastness of the grounds yesterday, she figured he might not even be within sight of the Hall.

The drive into town was a peaceful one, a morning sun casting a clean, warm light over the landscape. The map app showed a single grocery store that served the entire community. As she parked her car and walked inside, the familiar scent of fresh produce and baked goods greeted her.

Anita moved through the aisles, filling her cart with essentials. She was determined to make a gourmet lunch to christen her newly cleaned kitchen. Maybe, she thought optimistically, Logan would be around at just the right time, and she'd ask him to join her. If not, she tried to convince herself, she'd enjoy it just as much alone. Butter, meat, asparagus, parmesan, salt and pepper, lettuce—she ticked off the items on her mental checklist.

The butcher, a burly man with a grizzled beard, was behind his counter, busily chopping meat.

"Morning," she said, trying to sound cheerful.

He looked up, his eyes narrowing. "What can I get you?" he asked gruffly.

"I'd like two filet mignon and half a pound of bacon," Anita replied.

"You're one of them Harrows, aren't you?" he said, his voice laced with disdain.

She felt a flush creep up her neck. "My husband was." she said quietly.

The butcher snorted. "That's what I thought. Stick out like a sore thumb."

Anita shifted uncomfortably and shoved a lock of hair behind her ear.

"Harrows look out for no one but themselves. You think they're doing some good, but in the end, it only benefits the precious estate. And you ain't no different."

Her stomach tightened. "Excuse me?" she said, her voice shaking slightly.

The butcher slammed a cleaver into the cutting board, making her jump. "I've seen it time and again," he growled. "You Harrows are all the same. High and mighty. Anything you choose to do hurts the people of this town. Always has. You ought just go back where you come from and let that damned place rot."

Feeling a mix of anger and embarrassment, she watched as the butcher wrapped her order and shoved it across the counter. She took the packages and turned to leave, but then thought better of it. "You know," she said, more grit in her voice than she felt, drawing on the well of knowledge Logan had instilled in her yesterday, "It seems like most of the cropland around here belongs to the Harrow estate and is on lease to local farmers. The opportunity for planting, raising, and harvesting gives a lot of families a good income and a good life. And the grants Hyacinth created the last 30 years made a difference for locals to open a new variety of business here."

"Just collecting people to put in your pocket is all you Harrows are doing." The butcher raised his voice. "That's all you ever want—control over us! You can package it nice and call it whatever you want, but in the end, all you want is us to be indebted to you. You start poking around in that Hall and before you know it, people will start disappearing again. And won't nothing touch you. Just like before!"

Anita turned on her heel and strode away. She could feel the eyes of the other shoppers on her, all aware of the butcher's accusations which had been voiced at full volume. In the produce section, two old women whispered to each other, their gazes fixed on her. A mother with two kids in the cereal aisle gave her a cold look, pulling her children closer as if to shield them. The old man in the checkout line behind her mumbled something about "a Harrow having nothing better to do with the day" when she offered to let him go ahead of her.

Anita kept her head down, paid for her groceries, and rushed out of the store. Her eyes stung with tears, and her cheeks burned with shame for things she didn't even understand. The drive back to the Hall was a somber one. The sun was high in the sky now, casting a bright light on the picturesque countryside and even some decent warmth, but Anita couldn't enjoy either. Her thoughts were clouded with doubt and unease. Would she be making a mistake by staying in Harrowsburg? It seemed like the town itself was against her.

How many others shared the butcher's opinion? Was it just the have and have-not attitude? What about the disappearances he spoke of? That sounded important. Logan would know. As she bumped along the two-track, she hoped he'd be nearby so that she could ask him about it. She felt very alone after the experience in the grocery store.

***

Doreen
Guess who's coming to Connecticut?
Anita
No way!
Doreen
I'm going to make it work sometime in the next couple weeks. If you decide to step away from the craziness there, we can drive home together.
Anita
OMG, Doreen, that's amazing! I can't wait! I just had the worst experience in town. This just made my day!
Doreen
Glad to hear that! It's going to be so good to see you. I'll send you the flight number so you can pick me up.

Anita
Perfect! I feel so much better knowing you'll be here.
Doreen
Of course! We're going to have a great time. And don't worry, we'll figure this out together.
Anita
Can't wait to see you, Doreen!
Doreen
I'll keep you posted if anything changes.

***

Anita parked her car on the Hall's graveled drive and took a deep breath. As she stepped out, she saw Logan approaching from the side of the house. His presence was a welcome sight, grounding her in the reality of the Hall and the work ahead.

"Hey there," Logan greeted her. "Need a hand with those?"

"Sure, thanks," Anita replied, smiling despite the fatigue she felt creeping in. She handed him a few bags and together they made their way to the kitchen. "Guess what? My best friend, Doreen, is flying in some time in the next couple weeks."

"That's great. Can't wait to meet her."

"We've been friends since nursing school." Anita felt a sudden wet blanket douse her excitement. She hoped Doreen's plans didn't mean something had gone wrong for her in LA. She knew the staffing coordinator was not a fan of Doreen. He and HR both had multiple strikes against her.

"Are you sure Harrowsburg can handle two California girls at once?" Anita laughed.

As they entered the kitchen, Logan's eyes widened in surprise. "Wow, you've been busy. What a transformation. It looks amazing!"

Anita beamed with pride. "Thanks. I spent the morning cleaning it up. I wanted to see what it would be like to cook in here, and it looks like it's going to be pretty great."

They set the groceries on the counter, and Anita began unpacking. "I was thinking we could have lunch together. How does bacon-wrapped filet mignon, a side salad, and parmesan roasted asparagus sound?"

Logan's eyebrows shot up. "That sounds fantastic. I didn't realize you were such a chef."

Anita laughed softly. "I like to cook when I have the time. It's relaxing, and it helps me clear my head."

She unpacked the bags and asked, "Could you go trim me some rosemary, basil, and thyme from the garden? And a bulb of garlic if there is one?"

"Yes ma'am," Logan grinned at her. She smiled back and handed him a bowl and some kitchen shears. She watched him through the tall paned windows and wondered if there was anything that man didn't look comfortable doing. He was always so at ease. As he headed back into the house, she tried to busy herself, pretending she hadn't just been ogling him.

"Here you go."

She took the bowl and the shears from him. "Perfect. Thank you."

Anita tried to push the butcher's words from her mind. She didn't want to dwell on it, but she felt she needed to share it with Logan. "I had an interesting encounter at the grocery store," she began, keeping her tone light. "The butcher wasn't exactly welcoming."

Logan's expression darkened slightly. "Dexter can be a real piece of work. What happened?"

Anita shrugged, trimming the asparagus with practiced ease. "He wasn't happy about there being a potential new owner of the Hall. Told me some people in town aren't too thrilled about it."

Logan sighed, leaning against the counter. "I'm not surprised. Not everyone in Harrowsburg feels that way, but there are some who do. It's an old town with a long memory. When one group has money and the other doesn't, there isn't much the first can do without upsetting the second."

Anita nodded, focusing on wrapping the filets in bacon. "He mentioned something about disappearances and blamed the Harrows. What's that about?"

Logan hesitated, then began to explain. "It happened years and years back, when Hyacinth was just a child. There were a few disappearances, and people started pointing fingers. There wasn't much of an investigation because there weren't many clues, as far as I know. But the townspeople blamed the Harrows, thinking they should have done more. It created gossip and bad rumors that have persisted for decades. Some still bring it up, but there's little basis to it."

Anita absorbed his words as she seasoned the filets and prepared the asparagus for roasting. The kitchen filled with the mouthwatering aroma of cooking meat and fresh herbs. "That explains a lot," she said quietly. "It's hard enough moving to a new place without feeling like you're not wanted."

Logan reached out and squeezed her shoulder gently. "Don't let it get to you. There are plenty of people here who will welcome you once they get to know you."

They continued chatting as she cooked, the conversation flowing easily. Logan helped by setting the table, and soon they were sitting down to a beautifully prepared meal. The bacon-wrapped fillets were perfectly cooked, the asparagus tender and flavorful with a crisp center, and the salad a refreshing complement.

"This is incredible," Logan said after taking a bite. "You've outdone yourself."

Anita laughed softly. "Thanks. I'm glad you're enjoying it."

As they ate, Anita felt a sense of normalcy budding. The kitchen was warm and inviting, filled with the sounds of clinking cutlery and light conversation. For a moment, the worries about the townspeople and the Hall's history faded into the background.

She noticed Logan studying her face with a look of concern. "You look exhausted," he said gently. "Did you have another nightmare last night?"

Anita sighed, setting down her fork. "Yes. I woke up before dawn and couldn't get back to sleep. It's starting to take a toll."

Logan nodded thoughtfully. "Are you still planning on making a decision about the estate tomorrow? Or will you wait for Doreen to get here?"

"I want to make the decision tomorrow. If I decide not to stay on, she and I will drive home together."

"Maybe you should try getting away from the Hall for the afternoon. Go somewhere relaxing, get some rest. It might help clear your head."

Anita considered his suggestion. She was hesitant to leave the Hall, but the idea of a change of scenery was appealing. "You might be right," she admitted. "I could use a break."

Logan smiled. "I know just the spot." He reached down to his belt and unhook a set of keys. "It's quiet, and the scenery is almost as good as here. You can make yourself at home and sleep anywhere. There's also a hammock outside in the backyard under a couple giant oaks if you feel like it."

"Your place?" Anita asked surprised.

"Yep. It's a few miles down the road from here, a little out of the way, but the map app will take you right to it. You can spend as much time as you'd like. No one will bother you. I'll be here until early evening, and hopefully, you'll escape the nightmares."

Anita's need for a good nap matched the wave of gratitude she felt for Logan's thoughtfulness. "That sounds perfect."

They finished their meal, lingering at the table as they talked about lighter topics. Logan shared stories about the town and its quirks, making Anita laugh with his dry wit and keen observations. The tension she had felt earlier began to dissipate, replaced by a sense of camaraderie and connection. After lunch, Logan insisted on helping with the dishes, and they worked side by side, cleaning up the kitchen.

The sun was high in the sky by the time they finished, casting a warm glow through the windows.

"Get some rest!" he called as they parted ways in the yard. Anita checked the address he had put into the map app and sure enough it was just a few miles away. She'd just have to go back to the main road on the two-track and then turn away from town. It looked like the property set off the road a bit. There would be no nosy neighbors checking on who Logan had at his house.

Feeling a mix of gratitude and hesitation, she drove away from the Hall. She knew she needed the break and the rest if she truly was going to make her decision the next day. The drive to his house was peaceful, the mid-afternoon sun casting a warm glow over the rolling hills and quaint, rustic rural homes around Harrowsburg.

When she arrived, she found Logan's house nestled among a grove of tall pines, its pastoral charm immediately apparent. The house was small and utilitarian, but it had a warmth and character that spoke volumes about its owner. She parked her car off to the side of the large driveway and approached the front door. She unlocked it with the key Logan had given her.

Inside, the house was immaculately kept. The wooden floors gleamed, and the simple furniture was arranged with a sense of purpose. The living room had a comfortable couch, a sturdy coffee table, and a well-worn armchair. Shelves lined one wall, filled with books and knick-knacks that told the story of a life well-lived. Anita was immediately at ease.

As she explored further, she noticed family pictures on the walls and tables. There were photos of Logan with his parents, and others with a group of friends, laughing and smiling in various settings. More photos with the four siblings Mary and George had mentioned at the coffee shop. She was relieved to see that Vanessa was in none of the frames. It seemed Logan had a close-knit group of people he cared about, and that made her feel even more at ease.

The kitchen was just as pristine as the rest of the house, with clean countertops and neatly organized cabinets. Anita couldn't help but smile at the sight of Logan's meticulousness. It was clear that he took pride in his home, just as he did with his work at the manor. She also wondered if he might be a little OCD.

Eventually, Anita made her way to the bedrooms. She found Logan's room and peeked inside. It was simple and utilitarian, much like the rest of the house. The bed was neatly made, and the room was free of clutter. On the bedside table was a worn Bible with a number of placemarkers and notes sticking out at wayward angles. She felt a pang of guilt at the thought of sleeping in his bed, as if she were intruding on his personal space.

Instead, she chose the guest room across the hall. It was cozy, with a soft mattress, a small dresser, and a nightstand with a lamp. A window overlooked the back garden, where afternoon light created a serene view. She spotted the oversize hammock between the oaks that he had mentioned and could imagine him using it, though he worked so hard, she wondered when he found the time.

Anita set her purse down and sat on the edge of the bed, feeling the fatigue of the past few days catch up with her. She lay down and was asleep within minutes, drifting off into a deep, dreamless slumber.

***

When she awoke, it was almost 8:30 pm. The room was dimly lit by the glow of the moon outside, and she could hear the faint sounds of someone moving about the house. The smell of savory food cooking wafted through the air, making her stomach growl.

Anita stretched and got out of bed, surprisingly refreshed. She tousled her hair and straightened her clothing, hoping she didn't look too unkempt. Following the delicious aroma to the kitchen, she found Logan at the stove, stirring something in a pot. He looked up and smiled when he saw her.

"Hey, you're awake. How was your nap?" he asked, his tone warm and welcoming.

"You mean all six and a half hours of it? It was perfect," Anita purred, her voice still a bit groggy from sleep. "I didn't realize how much I needed it. Thank you for letting me rest here." She yawned and stretched her arms above her head.

Logan waved off her thanks. "No problem at all. I'm glad you could get some sleep. I figured you'd be hungry, so I started making dinner."

Anita's mouth watered as she looked at the food he was preparing. "It smells amazing. What are we having?"

"Just a simple stew," Logan said, "and you're just in time." He ladled some into a bowl and handed it to her. "It's one of my go-to recipes."

Anita took the bowl and moved to sit at the small table, inhaling the savory aroma. "Not so fast," he said, stepping over to the sliding door with his own bowl of stew. He opened it with his free hand and motioned with his head. "Let's sit out here."

She followed him outside to a gorgeous patio space, a tranquil haven of warmth and light, a perfect blend of rustic charm and modern comfort. Nestled at the back of his quaint home, the patio was an inviting retreat where Anita imagined evenings could be transformed into magical experiences. The structure itself was a testament to craftsmanship, with its sturdy wooden beams supporting a beautifully designed roof that provided both shelter and a sense of openness. Twinkling string lights crisscrossed above, casting a soft, enchanting glow that created a cozy ambiance reminiscent of starry nights.

"Did you build all this?" She trailed her fingers over the rough brickwork of a grill area.

"Just a little side project."

At the center of this outdoor sanctuary was a meticulously crafted stone fire pit, its flames dancing with a life of their own. Surrounded by comfortable Adirondack chairs adorned with colorful, plush pillows and one large chaise, it was a place that invited relaxation and deep conversation. The warmth from the fire was not just physical but also emotional, fostering a sense of intimacy. It was easy to imagine Logan and his friends or family gathered around, sharing stories and laughter as the night wore on.

The patio seamlessly extended from the house, with steps leading up to a higher platform that housed a seating area and a table for alfresco dining. The surrounding greenery, well-tended and lush of course, framed the space, adding to the feeling of being in a secluded, personal retreat.

She followed him over to the Adirondak chairs next to the fire pit and moved close to the flames with an audible sigh. "Finally! Heat!"

He laughed at her, as he opened a nearby cabinet and punched a button. Soft music filled the space around them.

She took a bite of the stew before she sat down and closed her eyes in delight. "This is delicious, Logan. You're a great cook."

He chuckled and took the seat next to her. "I do my best. It's a family recipe. My mom taught me how to make it when I was a kid."

They ate in comfortable silence for a while, the warmth of the stew and the gorgeous space filling Anita with a sense of contentment and peace.

"You've got a lovely home," she said, setting her empty bowl on the table. "It's so cozy and welcoming."

"Thanks," he replied, a hint of pride in his voice. "I've put a lot of work into it over the years. It's not much, but it's mine."

She nodded, feeling a deep appreciation for the man sitting next to her. "I can see that. It's got so much character, just like you."

Logan smiled, his eyes twinkling with amusement. "Well, I try."

They chatted for a while longer, sharing stories about their lives and the town of Harrowsburg. Logan opened up about his family, telling her about his parents and the close bond he shared with them despite being adopted.

Anita turned, propping herself on her elbow to look at him, surprised. "You were?"

He nodded and his gaze shifted to the patio lights above. "I don't remember anything before I was three years old. My parents have always just been my parents, my brother and sisters have always been my siblings."

"Do you ever wonder about your biological family?" Anita asked gently, her curiosity piqued by his acceptance and the serene way he spoke of his past.

Logan paused, considering her question. "Sometimes, I do. But I've had a wonderful life, a really loving family. I guess I've always felt that it would be disrespectful to my parents to go digging around for what happened before they came into my life. By the grace of God, they gave me everything that matters, you know?"

Anita nodded, understanding his loyalty and the depth of his gratitude. "That makes sense," she said softly. "Family isn't always about blood. It's about who's there for you."

"Exactly," He replied, his voice firm. "And my family has been there for me through everything. That's what really matters."

They sat in silence for a moment, each lost in their own thoughts. She felt a profound respect for Logan, for the way he embraced his life and the people in it with such wholeheartedness.

Finally, he spoke again, his voice reflective. "If they are ever ready to tell me more, they will. Otherwise, I am who I am because of them and the things I've done in my life, not because of where I came from."

Anita reached out, taking his hand in hers, feeling the strength of his grip and the truth in his words. Logan's identity was shaped by the love and life he knew, not by the mysteries of his early years. In him, she saw the power of nurture over nature, a testament to the family that raised him rather than the one that gave him life. She looked over at him, seeing him not in a new light, but an even better defined one.

He squeezed her hand and stood up. The warm glow of the firepit cast flickering shadows across the patio as the stars above shimmered brightly in the clear night sky, a beautiful backdrop to their evening. Anita realized the only way she could describe it was intimate—not in a sexual sense, but in a deeper, more profound way. She also realized just how easily their time together may have turned awkward had he—or had she—pushed to address the attraction between them. She turned her gaze from the stars to him, and he gave her a look heavy with longing. She had never before judged the strength of a man in what he didn't do.

"I have to head to bed," his voice tinged with regret. "I've got an early morning tomorrow. Some special-order supplies for the orchard finally arrived in Hartford, and I need to go pick them up."

She smiled, though she felt a pang of disappointment.

He returned her smile, his eyes soft with affection. "Do you want to stay out here a little bit longer?"

She nodded.

He laid the fire pit poker against his chair. "Just stir the fire well and then douse it with that watering can in the corner when you're ready to come in. You can stay as late as you want in the morning. Make yourself at home. I'll be back at the Hall around noon."

"Thank you." She laid her head back against her chair and hoped that he could read the layers of sincerity under her words.

"No problem. Good night."

"Good night." She watched him as he walked back into the house. There was something about Logan that made her feel safe and cherished.

The first, she'd been missing for a long time. The second, she wasn't sure she'd ever truly felt before. The warmth of his presence lingered even after he had disappeared inside, leaving her alone on the patio with her thoughts.

Anita remained on the chaise lounge, her mind a whirl of emotions and decisions. The attraction she felt for him was undeniable, but so were the complexities of her current situation. The Hall, with its rich history and the extensive work it needed, loomed large in her thoughts. It was a daunting undertaking, but also an opportunity for a fresh start, a chance to build something meaningful.

The soft sounds of the night filled the silence, the gentle chirping of crickets and the occasional rustle of leaves in the breeze. Anita let herself relax, sinking deeper into the comfort of the chaise. Her thoughts turned to the Hall and the legacy it held. The nightmares she'd been having, the eerie sense of being watched, and the whispered secrets of the past all weighed heavily on her mind.

The realization that Vance had hidden so much from her, that he had led a life she knew nothing about, was a bitter pill to swallow. Yet, despite the turmoil, she felt an inexplicable pull toward the Hall, a sense that it was where she was meant to be.

As the night grew darker and the air cooler, Anita finally decided to head inside. She doused the fire and made her way to the guest room, feeling fatigue settle over her. She slipped into bed, pulling the covers up around her, and closed her eyes, hoping for a peaceful night's sleep.

Chapter Seven

*A*nita found herself once again in the dimly lit room within Harrow Hall for a third time. Only now, the room was in disrepair. The wallpaper peeled away in places, and cobwebs hung from the corners, adding to the eerie atmosphere.

Instead of the two children or the pregnant maid in the chair, a young man in his 20s with bright red curly hair and freckles languished drowsily in the huge chair. He seemed to drift in and out of sleep as if he had been drugged.

Anita's attention was drawn to a teenage boy of sixteen or seventeen standing near a seat at the table, his face etched with a look of terror. **Vance!** His grandmother Hyacinth sat across the table from where he stood.

"Roll the dice, Victor," Hyacinth ordered, her voice cold and unyielding, ringing out over the chanting that was echoing through the room. It rose and fell, disembodied, as if replaying voices through dead centuries.

Victor shook his head, stepping back from the table. "I can't," he whispered, his voice trembling. "I don't want to."

The dolls' eyes glowed in the dim light, and the ghost of Victoria Harrow materialized beside Hyacinth. Victoria's presence was both ethereal and terrifying, her translucent form radiating a cold, supernatural energy. Her visage wavered between different ages, all melding into one and staying unique at the same time.

"You must," Victoria said, her voice echoing with a ghostly resonance. "The ritual cannot be stopped. The Harrow will not allow it."

Vance's hesitation grew, but as he stood frozen in fear, the dolls and

Victoria exerted unseen power. The dolls' eyes gleamed brighter, and an invisible force began to move Vance's hands toward the dice. He struggled against it, straining to pull away, but his efforts were futile as the supernatural power compelled him toward the table.

"No! I won't do it!" Vance cried, his teenage voice breaking as he fought against the invisible force. His resistance was strong, his body trembling with the effort, but the unseen power was stronger.

He finally grasped the bone dice. The chanting fell silent, the tension thick in the air. Vance's eyes were wide with fear as he cast the dice onto the table. They clattered across the surface, coming to a stop with symbols that seemed to pulse with a weak, smoky blue light.

One of the seated dolls calls out the roll, "Light meets light, the Harrow will take the results of the Blight."

The smoky, blue haze was much weaker than in the previous dreams, barely illuminating the intricate carvings on the table. However, as the light crept across the table, it snaked its way toward the red-haired man in the chair. The moment the light touched him, it surged and seemed to gather energy, glowing with an intense, eerie brilliance.

The young man's body convulsed as the light enveloped him; he awoke from his drugged stupor with cries of pain and fear. The chanting grew louder, filling the room with a haunting melody.

Anita watched in horror, unable to move or speak. The air was thick with malevolent energy, and the chanting's crescendo soon drowned out the young man's cries. The smoky blue light pulsed and throbbed, its eerie glow filling the room and casting long, flickering shadows on the walls. The ritual continued, the light growing ever brighter and more intense as it fed off the young man's agony.

Vance fell to his knees with repulsed shock and awe as he watched the young man suffer. Hyacinth and Victoria looked on with calm faces.

***

The peace Anita sought eluded her. The nightmare came, more vivid and more terrifying than the ones before. The pain was even worse this time, and the dull thrum of the chanting sent an ache through her bones she wouldn't wish on her worst enemy. The sense of dread was overwhelming, a suffocating presence that made her feel utterly helpless.

Anita jolted awake, her heart pounding in her chest. Light spilled in from the hallway, and she could hear Logan's voice. It took her a moment to realize that he was kneeling beside her bed in a T-shirt and boxers, shaking her and calling her name.

She shot off the mattress, wrapping her arms around his neck. Her heart galloped as she gasped for breaths between sobs. He pulled her close and held her, sitting down on the bed.

"The nightmare...Vance! What did they make him do?"

"Tell me about it." Logan leaned up against the headboard and Anita curled into him.

Anita took a shaky breath, then began to recount the dream in detail. As she spoke, Logan listened intently, his brow furrowed in concentration.

"I'm no expert, but it sounds like something in the Hall's history is weighing heavily on you for some reason."

"History? As it those dreams really happened?"

"Anita, you and I are living proof that something...some kind of power...whatever you want to call it—supernatural, other worldly—can go on at the Hall."

"What am I supposed to do with it though?"

"You keep seeing that same room? Three times now?"

She nodded.

"Well, I think something is trying to tell you to figure out what happened there. What did the Harrow family do to those people through the years?"

"And until I do, I'll keep having the nightmares?"

"Like I said, I'm not an expert, but it could be logical to think so."

"There's nothing logical about this. If you could just see them or that room or those dolls or Vance..." Anita shivered, and Logan tightened his hold on her. "Even if I go back to California, I'm afraid the nightmares will keep coming."

Logan put a gentle hand under her chin and lifted her gaze up to his, his eyes filled with a mix of concern and admiration. "You're stronger than you realize, Anita. Whatever the Hall holds—the nightmares, the stuff about your husband—I believe you can handle it." He brushed a strand of hair from her face. "You're not alone in this. I'm here with you, every step of the way."

The intensity of the moment hung between them, charged with unspoken emotions. Anita felt a surge of gratitude and affection for Logan, a sense that he was the missing piece in her tumultuous puzzle.

A sense of calm washed over her. The nightmare still lingered in her mind, but its power over her had diminished. She felt he was right. It was part of the Hall's story, a story that seemed to be her responsibility to uncover and possibly set right.

"Will you stay with me, Logan? Just for a little while?"

In answer, he eased off the headboard from their seated position, settling them down against the pillows, still holding her close. She pulled the comforter up around them. He took his free arm and rested it behind his head. Anita admired the definition of his triceps and the way the sleeve of his t-shirt seemed hard pressed to contain the hulk of his upper arm.

She nestled into the hollow of his chest and listened to the steady beat of his heart, feeling her own slow and her muscles relax. "You're some kind of a saint," she murmured.

He gave a quiet snort as he ran his hand gently through her hair. "Not hardly."

As Anita drifted back to sleep, her thoughts were filled with visions of the Hall's potential. It could become a place of warmth, love, and new beginnings. And in those dreams, Logan was always by her side, a steadfast partner in their shared journey.

The next morning, Anita awoke to the soft light of morning filtering through the window. She hadn't heard Logan leave, but she was alone in the guest bedroom. A sense of clarity and purpose that had been missing for so long infused her. "I've made my decision," she said out loud to make it official even if no one else was listening. "I'm going to stay and take on Harrow Hall. For good."

A chill hit her and made the hair on the back of her neck stand on end. Perhaps someone had heard her after all.

***

Logan's pickup rumbled down the highway toward Hartford, the early morning sun casting long shadows on the road. He had a list of supplies to pick up for the orchard at Harrow Hall, and the drive gave him plenty of time to think. Lately, his thoughts seemed to circle back to one person: Anita.

She was different. There was a strength in her, a quiet resilience that drew him in. She was dealing with her own grief and challenges, yet she faced each day with a grace that Logan admired. More than anything, he wanted to be there for her, to help her find peace and happiness in

Harrow Hall.

As the miles rolled by, Logan found himself smiling at the memory of the night. Her nightmares worried him, but he seemed to truly be able to calm her down from the terror. There was a connection between them, something deep and real. He hadn't felt this way in a long time, and the realization that he was starting to fall in love with Anita filled him with both excitement and a touch of anxiety.

Logan switched his line of thought to the task at hand as he pulled into the parking lot of the nursery in Hartford. Even at this early hour, the place was bustling with activity, landscapers and homeowners alike loading up their trucks with plants, soil, and various gardening supplies. Logan parked his pickup and headed inside, his mind still occupied with thoughts of Anita, no matter how hard he tried to set them aside.

He was in the middle of selecting some black cherry tree saplings when a familiar voice called out to him. "Logan! Long time no see!"

Logan turned to see Bill Hansen, the owner of a Marionville landscaping company, headquartered a town over from Harrowsburg. Bill was a large man with a friendly demeanor, and he approached Logan with a broad smile. "How's it going?"

"Hey, Bill," Logan replied, shaking his hand. "I'm good. Just picking up some supplies for the estate. How's your work going?"

Bill's smile faltered slightly. He sighed, scratching the back of his head. "I hate to say it, but we've got some issues. That Vanessa of yours put some restrictions on our small business loan. Any work with the Harrow estate is now off the table. I've got work lined up on the acres that Jansens rent from the estate. It was supposed to be a heck of a project, and they've put half down already for a deposit."

Logan's eyes widened in surprise. "Vanessa did that? I didn't even know she could."

Bill nodded grimly. "The power of money I guess. I don't know how you handle her."

Logan shook his head. "We broke up. It's over."

A look of relief crossed Bill's face. "Well, that's a good thing if you ask me. She was always too hoity-toity for my tastes. High maintenance, that one."

Logan forced a smile, though inside he was seething. Vanessa's actions were petty and vindictive, a move clearly meant to hurt him, Anita, and future work at Harrow Hall. "Thanks for letting me know, Bill. I'll talk to Charlton and Dodd. See if something can be figured out."

Bill clapped him on the shoulder. "I'd sure appreciate it, Logan. Just keep doing what you're doing. And if you need anything, you know where to find me."

Logan nodded. As he finished up his purchases and loaded the truck, his mind raced with worry. Vanessa's vindictiveness was unsettling, and he couldn't help but think about how it might affect Anita. The last thing she needed was more trouble, especially from someone as spiteful as Vanessa.

The drive back to Harrow Hall was filled with a mix of anger and concern. Logan gripped the steering wheel tightly, his knuckles white. He needed to protect Anita, to make sure she wasn't caught in the crossfire of Vanessa's spite. He knew Vanessa well enough to understand that she wouldn't stop at just causing financial trouble. She could make life difficult in many ways, and Logan needed to be prepared.

As he approached Harrow Hall, the sight of the grand estate calmed him somewhat. The Hall stood tall and proud, a symbol of resilience and history. Logan parked his truck and began unloading the supplies, his mind still churning with thoughts of Vanessa and Anita.

***

Hyacinth Harrow's Diary

October 13, 19__

It has been a harrowing day, one that will be etched into my memory for as long as I live. Today, my daughter, Collette, returned to Harrow Hall, bringing with her a storm of emotions, a little boy of three, and another child ready to be born at any moment. The air around the Hall thickened with anticipation and an underlying sense of foreboding, as if the house itself knew what was about to unfold.

Collette's arrival was unexpected, yet not entirely surprising. She has written to me only once in the past year, a brief letter that hinted at the trials she was facing, but it appears she withheld many details. When she arrived today, I saw the exhaustion etched into her face, her eyes shadowed with worry and fatigue. Her little boy, Victor, clung to her skirts, wide-eyed and silent, taking in the vastness of Harrow Hall with a mixture of awe and fear.

We have not seen each other in years, and the reunion was bittersweet. I embraced her, feeling the swell of her pregnant belly pressing against me, and I could sense the urgency in her movements.

She had traveled far and under duress, that much was clear. She barely had time to catch her breath before the first pains of labor began.

I led her to the room that had been hers as a child, thinking it would bring her comfort. But as soon as we crossed the threshold, a chill enveloped us. The temperature dropped noticeably, and I saw my breath mist in the air. Collette shivered, and Victor began to cry, his wails echoing eerily off the walls.

The Hall has always had its quirks—doors that open and close on their own, whispers in the corridors, shadows that move without a source—but today, it felt different. Malevolent. As if the very walls were rejecting us. I tried to calm Collette, to ease her into the bed, but the room seemed to close in around us, the shadows deepening, the whispers growing louder.

Collette's labor pains intensified quickly. It was clear that the child was eager to enter the world, but the Hall seemed determined to prevent it. The lights flickered and went out, plunging us into darkness. The air grew thick with a suffocating presence, and the whispers turned to low, menacing growls. Collette was frightened, and so was I, though I tried not to show it.

I gathered my wits and decided we could not stay in that room. With great difficulty, I helped Collette to her feet and guided her out of the oppressive atmosphere and into the hallway. Victor clung to his mother's skirt, his little face pale with fear. As we moved, the very structure of the Hall seemed to protest our passage—doors slammed shut, windows rattled violently, and an unearthly howl echoed through the halls.

We made our way to the kitchen, hoping to find some refuge there. But as we entered, the stove erupted in flames, and the room filled with acrid smoke. Coughing and gasping for breath, we fled again, this time towards the only place I could think of that might be safe—the orchard.

The orchard had always been a place of peace, a sanctuary from the manor's darkness. As we stepped outside, the oppressive atmosphere lifted slightly, and I could feel the fresh air filling my lungs, giving me strength. Collette's contractions were coming faster now, and she could barely walk. We reached the edge of the orchard, and I helped her down to the ground, under the shade of the old apple trees.

The labor was swift and intense. Collette screamed in pain, and I did my best to soothe her, but the house's influence was still palpable, even out here. The wind picked up, howling through the trees, and the branches swayed and creaked ominously. It was as if the manor's dark presence was trying to reach us, but it was weaker, less focused.

Victor sat nearby, watching with wide, frightened eyes. I prayed silently, begging for strength and protection. And then, with one final, wrenching scream, Collette gave birth to a beautiful baby boy. The child's cries pierced the air, strong and defiant, and I felt a surge of relief wash over me.

We wrapped the baby in a blanket, and I held him close, feeling his warmth against my skin. Collette was exhausted, but she smiled weakly, her eyes filled with tears of both joy and sorrow. The wind died down, and a strange calm settled over the orchard, as if the house had finally relented, accepting the new life it had tried so hard to reject.

As we sat there, catching our breath and marveling at the new arrival, Collette whispered something to me that I could hardly believe. The father of her new baby, she confessed, was a priest. My shock must have shown on my face, but Collette continued, her voice trembling.

"He was kind to me, Mother. He showed me compassion when I had nowhere else to turn. We fell in love, but he couldn't leave the church, and I couldn't stay with him. It was impossible, but we found solace in each other, even if only for a short time."

I held her hand, squeezing it gently. "You've been through so much, my dear. We will get through this together."

As we sat in the orchard, the shadows of Harrow Hall looming in the distance, I felt a sense of hope amidst the darkness. The manor had tried to prevent this birth, to assert its malevolent will, but it had failed. Collette's son had been born, and with his arrival, a glimmer of light had pierced the gloom.

This day will be remembered as a turning point, a moment when we defied the blight of Harrow Hall—perhaps the only time I've stood against it my life long. And though the road ahead will be fraught with challenges, I believe we have the strength to face them. For the sake of Collette, her children, and the future of our family, we must hold on to that hope and never let it fade.

Hyacinth Harrow

***

Anita
Hey Doreen! I have some big news.
Doreen
Hey Anita! What's up?
Anita
I've decided to stay in Connecticut and not come back to California.
Doreen
Wow, that's huge! What made you decide?
Anita
I have a strange connection to the Hall. I'll explain more when you're here. Plus I really think I can make a difference here with the money I'll be in charge of. There's so much potential here, and I feel like I'm meant to be a part of it.
Doreen
That sounds amazing, Anita. I know how much you care about making an impact.
Anita
And there's another reason too. Logan. I feel so close to him, and I want to give whatever we have a real chance to develop.
Doreen
Are you sure? Is it too soon after Vance?
Anita
No. I'm sure this is my new start.
Doreen
I can't imagine the locals are too welcoming.
Anita
Well not yet. But it's still early.
Doreen
I was hoping we would pack you up when I got there and bring you back to LA.
Anita
I thought you'd be happy for me.
Doreen
I am but it's complicated.
Anita
Why? Are you having some trouble again?
Doreen
No of course not. But I just want the best for you.

Anita
Well, I think I'm going to have that.
Doreen
I miss you. Can't wait to be there in person with you. Just be careful, please.
Anita
Don't worry. I will.

***

Anita stepped out of Charlton and Dodd's Law Office feeling like it was the first time she was able to take a full breath of Connecticut air. Mr. Charlton hadn't been exactly surprised at her decision. He hadn't seen any other path forward for the estate or the Hall without her acceptance of the inheritance.

She wanted to tell Logan in person that she was staying, but he wouldn't be back for another couple of hours. She decided it was time to delve deeper into the history of Harrow Hall and the Harrow family. Although she thought the trunks in the attic, stacks of letters, and the photo albums would be perfect sources, she knew the local library would be the best place to give her some context and to start her research. Then she would at least know more about the major players of the family, in addition to Victoria Harrow, and she would be able to connect whatever personal items she found to a person and time period.

First, Anita walked to the hardware store in the hopes they might have a notebook and pen. She was still not ready to return to the grocery store after the butcher's outburst. She perused the store, which was relatively well stocked with lots of variety, and she was happy to see it. She imagined she would become a regular customer with all the work she was taking on.

Anita had just found a stack of notebooks and some basic office supplies when the clack of stilettos approaching drew her focus. Vanessa's presence in the store was like a predator on the hunt. Impeccably dressed in a black pencil skirt, blazer, flowing red blouse, and towering heels, she stood out against the backdrop of dusty shelves and supplies. Her hair was pulled back into a severe bun, and her eyes were fixed on Anita with a fiery glare.

Vanessa came to a halt in front of her. Anita was not going to be the one to speak first. Vanessa was obviously geared for a fight, and Anita hadn't been the one to seek it out.

"Stay away from Logan," Vanessa finally said, crossing her arms over her chest, each word laced with venom. She took a step closer, invading Anita's personal space.

"No." Anita said it with cold disdain, steeling her posture.

Vanessa blinked rapidly. Obviously, she hadn't accepted pushback. "He has no business associating with someone like you."

Anita's eyes narrowed. "Someone like me? What exactly do you mean by that?"

"A greedy California bimbo trying and failing to pose as someone who matters. You have no business at Harrow Hall. Go back to LA before you drive another man to shoot himself."

Anita's stomach hit the floor, and she took an involuntary step back as if she'd been struck.

Vanessa took advantage of the effect of her blow. "Vic was miserable with you, and you couldn't see it. You were so wrapped up in your own little world that you didn't even notice his pain."

Anita felt a wave of guilt wash over her, but she pushed it aside. "You don't know what you're talking about, Vanessa. You weren't there. You have no idea."

"I know enough." Vanessa took a step closer, her voice low and vicious. "Las Vegas. Last October. He told me everything." She drew out the last word.

Anita remembered Vance had attended a tech convention last fall. He had left the day before Halloween. Dressing up, handing out candy to trick-or-treaters for a few hours, and then hitting one or more wild costume parties was one of their favorite holiday rituals. He had never missed it before, but he had insisted that he be early to the convention in order to be ready for an important pitch of a new system he'd been the lead on.

"Then you're the one who told Charlton that he was still alive."

Vanessa ignored her. "Face it, Anita. You're nothing but a selfish, delusional woman who destroys everything she touches. Vic couldn't handle it, and Logan won't be able to either. Do him a favor and leave him alone before you ruin his life, too."

She turned on her heel and stormed off, leaving Anita standing there, shaking with the intensity of the confrontation. As she watched Vanessa disappear around the corner of the aisle, Anita finally took a deep breath in. The panic hit her with terrible force. She grabbed for the nearest shelf to steady her as the sobs came. She shoved her free hand against her mouth trying to muffle them.

What if what Vanessa had said was true? God! Anita had had no indication at all that Vance was miserable or depressed before his suicide. Vanessa had been right about his presence at the tech convention in Las Vegas. Had he really confided things in her?

Anita felt like she was going to vomit. She removed her hand from her mouth trying to take deep breaths through the sobs.

"Oh my dear! What's wrong?" Martha, Logan's mother, turned the corner of the aisle with a small cart half filled with miscellaneous items. She left the cart and rushed to Anita's side.

Anita tried to regain her composure. She was embarrassed about her breakdown in public. But the waterworks would not turn off, and she couldn't catch her breath. Martha guided her by the shoulders toward the back of the store and into the women's bathroom.

Somehow, Martha managed to form a few paper towels into a makeshift bag that she instructed Anita to breathe into. "There you are now. Just like that. Deep breaths." Martha rubbed her back as Anita leaned against the sink counter. Martha deftly drew another paper towel, dampened it with cool water, and wiped it across Anita's forehead and then the nape of her neck. The motion was so gentle and kind that Anita lost it again.

"Oh, you're just beside yourself, hon." Martha gathered her into her arms and hugged her, holding her tight, letting Anita cry herself out like a child.

When Anita's sobs finally settled, and her labored breathing returned to near normal, she leaned back out of the embrace. "I am so sorry, Mrs. Emmerich." She said through the sniffles that remained. Martha handed her a dry paper towel, and she wiped her face.

"No apology needed, dearie. And it's Martha."

"Thank you, Martha," Anita said, pulling a paper towel for herself and blowing her nose.

"What could have you so worked up? Anything I can help with?"

"Not unless you'd consider poisoning Vanessa's next coffee order."

Martha laughed. "Oh my dear, you wouldn't be the first to wish that sort of thing on that willful woman."

"She is horrible." Anita blew her nose again. "What in the world can Logan see in her?"

"Didn't he tell you?"

Anita shook her head.

"They broke up a few days ago."

"Really?"

"Yes and weren't we glad to hear it." Martha adjusted her purse on her shoulder. "The troubles she put our dear Logan through." She let out a huff. "She, of course, has already taken the rumors by the horns and made herself the victim of the story, but I know my son. His torch had fizzled out for her a while ago. It was only a matter of time really."

Martha pulled out a tube of lipstick from her purse and turned to the mirror to apply it. "There. Nothing like a touchup." She smacked her lips. "Now you, my dear, are coming to our house for dinner tonight, and I won't take no for an answer. You are in dire need of some home cooked comfort food, if I do say so myself."

Anita considered refusing for just a moment, but Martha had such a calming presence and had been so kind to her. "That would be wonderful."

"Good. It's the large green house with the white gingerbread trim on the corner of Flax and Greenhow. You can't miss it." She wrapped her arm around Anita's shoulder giving her a final squeeze. "We'll compare poison recipes for you-know-who," she joked.

Anita laughed. "I'll bring my cauldron."

"Perfect! See you around six?"

Anita nodded. "Thank you, Martha."

She blew a quick kiss and pushed out the swinging door. Anita composed herself and returned to the aisle to pick up the notebook and pens. She completed her purchase and left the hardware store without any further drama. If the employees had witnessed any part of her meltdown, they gave no indication.

As she walked down the street, trying to remember where she had seen the library sign, her mind began to buzz with the news about Logan and Vanessa. Martha had said a few days ago. She wondered exactly when it had transpired and what had triggered it. After they had discovered that their dream meeting was somehow real, did he feel obligated to tell Vanessa they had been together—perhaps sparing the unusual details. He was certainly the type to have that kind of honor. But if they truly weren't going to act on things right now, and since the situation was such a one-of-a-kind experience, would it have been more honorable to shoulder the guilt and save Vanessa the pain of being cheated on? Could someone really even consider their encounter cheating? They had both believed it to be a dream while it happened. Could that be held against someone?

Anita arrived at the library. She knew no matter how much she pondered the situation, she wouldn't know the truth of it until she spoke to Logan. For now, she could be thankful that such a kind and generous man was free of that horrible woman.

Anita turned her curiosity to what she might discover in the library about the Harrows. The library was a squat red-brick building with large windows that let in plenty of natural light. The smell of old books and polished wood greeted her as she stepped inside. Anita approached the librarian, a middle-aged woman with kind eyes and a warm smile.

"Good morning," Anita said. "I'm looking for information about Harrow Hall and the Harrow family. Can you help me?"

"Of course," the librarian replied. "We have quite a collection of local history archives. Follow me."

She led Anita to a special section in the back, where rows of neatly organized binders and books awaited. The librarian pulled out several volumes and placed them on a large oak table in the center.

"These should be a good start. Let me know if you need anything else," she said before returning to her desk.

Anita sat down and opened the first volume, which contained records and copies of documents dating back to the 18th century. She quickly found the entry for Oswald Harrow and his wife, Victoria. The Harrows had immigrated from Scotland in 1790, bringing with them a lineage that could be traced back centuries. The name "Harrow" itself was steeped in history, stemming from both early agricultural workers who *harrowed*, or worked, the land but also from the word *hearg* which referred to a pagan shrine. Looking deeper into the word, Anita even found references to writings from early Christian monks in ancient Scotland whose writings translated *hearg* to heathen shrine.

Oswald and Victoria Harrow were visionaries, determined to build a grand estate that would reflect their ambitions and secure their family's future in America. They purchased a vast tract of land in Connecticut and began constructing Harrow Hall. The Hall was completed in 1794, a grand structure with stately columns and expansive gardens. The couple's hard work and determination paid off, and the estate became a symbol of their success and influence.

As Anita continued to read, she came across entries for notable members of the Harrow family. Aldous Harrow, Oswald and Victoria's eldest son, took over the estate after his father died. He was known for his shrewd business acumen and played a significant role in expanding the family's wealth through various enterprises, including mines and tobacco crops that Logan had mentioned.

Emmiline Harrow, Aldous's daughter, was another important player. Born in 1832, she was known for her charitable works and involvement in social causes, though her efforts were often overshadowed by the family's more controversial activities. Emmiline was a complex character, balancing her desire to help the less fortunate with the ruthless business practices that had become synonymous with the Harrow name.

Gabbert David Harrow, Emmiline's grandson, also stood out. He was a businessman and politician who wielded considerable influence in Connecticut during the late 19th and early 20th centuries. Gabbert was instrumental in securing lucrative contracts for the family's enterprises, but his methods were often questioned, and he was known to use underhanded tactics to maintain the Harrows' dominance.

Melusine Harrow, Gabbert's niece, was a woman of mystery. Born on New Year's Eve 1899, she was known for her beauty and intelligence. Melusine never married, and rumors about her love affairs and possible involvement in the disappearances that plagued the Harrow estate swirled around her. She maintained a reclusive lifestyle, and her death in the mid-1900s was shrouded in secrecy. A grainy newspaper clipping copy caught Anita's attention. Melusine in a feathered and pearl headband looked over her shoulder at an intrusive camera. *Melusine was the second woman from her dream that first night.* She had guided Anita to Logan in the orchard.

Anita found herself engrossed in the stories, each page revealing more about the Harrows and their complex legacy. The final entry was about Hyacinth Harrow, the last of the Harrow lineage to live her full life at the estate and manage the Hall. Born in 1922, Hyacinth grew up during a tumultuous time, but her early years seemed untouched by the woes of the Great Depression. A photograph of her as a young girl in the 1930s caught Anita's eye. Hyacinth was petite and beautiful, with an air of innocence and grace that seemed at odds with the dark history of her family.

As she studied the photograph, Anita couldn't help but feel a deep sense of connection to Hyacinth. Despite the family's troubled past, there was something about the young girl's expression that spoke of resilience and hope. She wondered what Hyacinth's life had been like and what had led to her being the last of the Harrows to reside at the Hall.

In so many of the pictorial references, Anita could see Vance's likeness. Strong jawlines, dark eyes and hair, as well as expressions seemed to be coded well in Harrow genes.

Anita continued to pour over the documents, piecing together the history of the estate and its inhabitants. She learned about the grandeur of the early days, the scandals and tragedies that had befallen the family, and the efforts of the more recent generations to rebuild not only grandeur but goodwill with the town. The more she read, the more she understood the weight of the legacy she had inherited.

Closing the final volume, Anita leaned back in her chair, her mind swirling with the stories she had uncovered. The history of Harrow Hall was rich and complicated, filled with moments of triumph and deep shadows. She felt a renewed sense of responsibility to honor this history, to acknowledge the darkness while also seeking to bring light and new life to the estate.

"Excuse me, Mrs. Harrow," the librarian softly padded into the local history room. "We're closing for the lunch hour."

"Oh! I didn't realize. Thank you so much for your help. I've found what I need for now."

"Glad to hear it. You can leave the volumes out. I'll reshelve them when I return."

Anita thanked her again and gathered up her notebook, numerous pages filled with facts and theories, and made her way for the exit. She felt a mixture of emotions—gratitude for the opportunity to learn more about the Harrows and their legacy but also a deep sense of sadness for the lives touched by the family's actions. She knew that her task ahead was not just about restoring a grand old house, but also about addressing the history it carried and finding a way to create a positive future for Harrow Hall. She had the basics, but there was still much more to uncover, more to understand about the place that had become her home. She was ready to face the challenges ahead, to honor the legacy of the Harrow family, and to forge a new path for Harrow Hall.

As Anita returned to her car, she allowed herself a smile in anticipation of seeing Logan at the manor soon. She did her best to shove down the razor-sharp scratches that still lingered from Vanessa's attack. Anita believed she could address it all in time. She was beginning a new chapter in her life, but its details would help to fill in so many blanks in the last one.

***

Anita pulled into the driveway of Harrow Hall, feeling a renewed sense of purpose and determination. The afternoon sun cast bright, compelling light over the sprawling grounds, highlighting the grandeur of the Hall. As she parked her car and stepped out, she saw Logan's pickup already there, its bed filled with new trees and bags of landscaping supplies. He was busy unloading them into one of the outbuildings, his strong, capable hands moving with practiced efficiency.

She walked over to him, her stomach fluttering at the sight of him. "Good morning," she called out, her voice carrying a hint of excitement.

Logan looked up and smiled, his face lighting up with genuine pleasure. "Morning." He set down the load he was carrying on the edge of the pickup box. They shared a loaded gaze with one another. Neither spoke for a moment, but the silence was not awkward.

Anita took a deep breath, feeling a surge of confidence. "I've decided to stay in Harrowsburg and take over the Hall." For some reason, the announcement finally felt official.

Logan's smile widened. "Good. The Hall needs someone like you, and I'm sure you'll do an amazing job."

Anita felt a warm glow of satisfaction at his words. "Thank you." Anita jumped in and began to help him unload.

His eyes filled with warmth. "You've got it, Anita. Whatever you need, I'm here to help."

As they worked together to unload the supplies, she decided to leave out the details of her encounter with Vanessa. There was no need to burden Logan with that negativity. Instead, she focused on the positive developments.

"By the way," she said, lifting a small tree from the pickup bed, "I've been invited to your parents' house for supper this evening."

Logan's expression brightened further. "That's great! I'm sure they'll be thrilled to have you. I can give you a ride into town if you'd like."

"I'd appreciate that," Anita replied, grateful for his offer. "Thank you."

They continued working side by side, the physical labor providing a comfortable backdrop for their conversation. As they moved bags of mulch and young trees, Anita felt the familiar sense of intimacy with Logan that had grown stronger over the past week.

"I've also found out quite a bit of information about the Harrow family at the library," she said, setting down a bag of soil. "I plan on going through a few chests in the attic this afternoon to see what else I can uncover."

Logan's eyes lit up with interest. "I'd love to help you with that, if you don't mind. We need to get to the bottom of those nightmares as fast as we can. I'm concerned about you."

She felt a surge of gratitude. "That would be great."

He gave her a reassuring smile. "It will take me about 45 minutes to finish up out here, and then I'll join you in the house."

"Sounds good," Anita replied, feeling a sense of anticipation for the afternoon's work.

Logan returned to unloading the supplies, and Anita took the opportunity to walk back to the Hall. She found a quiet spot in the sitting room, where she started a list of the cleaning and repairs she wanted to tackle first in the house. As she wrote, her mind wandered to the romantic tension that seemed to hum in the air whenever she and Logan were together. It was an undeniable presence, but she knew they had to focus on the tasks at hand.

She listed the rooms that needed immediate attention: the grand foyer with its dusty chandeliers, the library with its towering shelves and scattered books, the kitchen that, despite her initial efforts, still required a thorough overhaul. The list grew longer with each passing minute, but instead of feeling overwhelmed, Anita felt a sense of purpose.

Time passed quickly, and before she knew it, Logan appeared in the doorway, wiping his hands on a rag. "All done out there. Ready to tackle the attic?"

She looked up and smiled. "Absolutely. Let's see what we can find."

***

Anita stood in the attic, breathing in air filled with the scent of old wood and dust. Logan was beside her, his presence comforting in the vast, dimly lit space. The attic was a treasure trove of the past, filled with trunks and boxes that had likely not been touched in decades.

"Let's start with that trunk. It looks like it might be the oldest," Anita suggested, pointing to a large, ornate chest in the corner. "Maybe it belonged to Victoria Harrow."

Logan nodded, and they carefully moved some boxes out of the way to get to the trunk. It was heavy and intricately carved, showing signs of age but still sturdy. Together, they lifted the lid, revealing a collection of items from the 18th century.

Anita gasped as she gently lifted a portion of Victoria's faded blue silk gown. The brocade fabric was extremely delicate. Some of the golden tobacco leaves were still intact but large sections of the silk gown were crumbling to a fine dust.

Logan picked up a book of pressed flowers, its pages yellowed but the flowers still detailed and colorful. "She must have loved the gardens," he said softly. "It's incredible to think she helped design the Hall and the grounds."

Anita continued to sift through the contents, finding more clothing, a few letters written in script so elegant as to be almost illegible, and a small, ornate box.

They carefully repacked Victoria's trunk, ensuring everything was returned to its rightful place before closing the lid. Next, they moved on to a trunk marked with the initials G.D.H.

"This must have belonged to Victoria's great-great-grandson, Gabbert David," Anita said, opening it with a sense of anticipation.

Inside, they found notebooks filled with accounting figures written in faded ink. Logan flipped through one of them, marveling at the meticulous records.

"Gabbert was known for his business acumen," Logan said. "These must be some of his ledgers."

Anita pulled out a relatively fine top hat, still in good condition despite its age. "I think this would look nice in the foyer," she said, setting it aside.

They continued to explore Gabbert's trunk, finding more 19th-century items, including a walking cane with a silver handle and a few personal letters. The trunk was a testament to Gabbert's role in expanding the family's wealth and influence.

Moving on, they opened a trunk filled with toys from the early 1900s. Anita's eyes lit up as she picked up a small, intricately painted toy horse.

"These must have belonged to Hyacinth's generation," she said, examining the toys with a smile. "Maybe she even played with some of these."

As they surveyed the attic, Logan spotted another trunk tucked away behind a couple of dress forms and some old quilts and drapes. They had to move several items out of the way to reach it, but finally, they pulled it into the light.

"This one belonged to Melusine," Anita said, reading the label in the corner, her voice tinged with excitement and curiosity. "She was the one who led me to you in the orchard that night."

Logan knelt down next to her. "I don't remember Hyacinth talking about her."

"The little bit I read about her today painted her as kind of a black sheep."

Opening the trunk, they were greeted with the sight of gorgeous gowns made of rich fabrics and adorned with intricate beadwork. Logan held one up, marveling at its beauty.

The dazzling dresses evoked the opulence and audacity of the Jazz Age. The first, a shimmering silver sheath, was intricately adorned with swirling beadwork that caught the light, creating a hypnotic dance with every movement. The fringed hemline would have daringly skimmed the knee line, adding a playfulness to the ensemble, while long black gloves and a string of pearls completed the look, exuding an air of sophisticated mystery. Delicate headpieces matched each dress. Melusine would have played the part at a Gatsby soirée, ready to revel in the night's decadence.

Another dress, in a rich crimson hue, exuded a fiery passion tempered by its geometric patterns of gleaming sequins and beads. The V-shaped neckline was framed by sheer, draping sleeves that lent an air of ethereal grace, cascading like soft flames down the arms. The beaded fringes below would sway with each step, creating an entrancing rhythm for a sultry femme fatale dancing in the speakeasies of yesteryear.

"These are incredible," he said. "Melusine must have been quite the fashionista."

Anita carefully lifted out a jewelry box and opened it, revealing an array of expensive jewelry—necklaces, rings, and brooches that sparkled even in the dim attic light. She decided to set the jewelry aside with the intention of putting it into a vault or a safe deposit box.

At the bottom of the trunk, they found an album of old photographs. As Anita flipped through the pages, she was struck by the haunting beauty of the images. The photographs would have been considered risqué in the 1920s and 30s, with Melusine posing in various states of undress, her expression bold and defiant.

"Look at her eyes," Anita said, pointing to one of the photographs. "They're so piercing and intense. It's as if she's demanding to be seen, to be acknowledged."

Logan nodded, his unease growing as he looked at the photos. "There's something about her... a mix of vulnerability and power. It's like she's inviting you into her world but also warning you to keep your distance."

Anita closed the album, feeling a deep connection to the woman in the photographs. Melusine's life had been shrouded in mystery, and these images were a rare glimpse into her private world.

"We should keep these safe," Anita said, adding the photo album to the pile of items to be taken downstairs. "There's so much history here, so many stories waiting to be uncovered."

Logan and Anita continued to explore the attic, finding more trunks and boxes, each filled with relics of the past. They discovered letters, diaries, and more personal items, each piece adding to the tapestry of the Harrow family's history. She certainly felt like she knew the family better, but nothing explained the events of her nightmare.

"I wonder what's in this one." Logan pulled a strange looking chest out from under a pile of old curtains. It was sturdier than the others, almost like it was armor coated, and it was locked. "Have you come across any keys in the house yet?"

Anita shook her head coming to kneel beside him. He examined the hinges on the trunk. "I think I could pop these off with a few tools. I'll be right back."

Anita looked through stacks of letters and journals while he was away. Returning with his tools, he made short work of the hinges. He lifted the lid, back to front, only to find four dolls, eerily lifelike, nestled inside.

Anita's blood ran cold. "Logan," she whispered, her voice trembling, "these dolls... I've seen them before. In my nightmares." Her eyes widened with a mix of fear and realization. "Three times now, they were around the table, doing things that felt... powerful, almost as if they were possessed."

Logan's brow furrowed in concern, but he tried to reassure her. "They're just dolls, Anita. Old and creepy, sure, but just dolls." But the unease running through Anita was palpable, and Logan couldn't shake the feeling that there was something more to her words.

Anita's dreams had been disturbingly vivid. In the first, the dolls had moved of their own accord, their lifeless eyes following her every step. In the second dream, they had spoken to her in hushed, sinister tones, whispering secrets that made her blood run cold. But it was the third dream that had left her truly terrified. The dolls had seemingly come to life, their porcelain and wooden faces twisted into expressions of malevolent glee as they orchestrated events around her. Each time, she had awoken with a sense of dread about them that lingered long after the nightmare had ended.

Logan, though skeptical, couldn't deny the genuine fear in Anita's eyes. "Alright," he said, "we'll make sure they stay in the trunk." He looked at the hinges he had removed to open it. They were old and fragile, but he would replace them with stronger ones to ensure the trunk remained sealed. As he worked, Anita watched anxiously, feeling a strange mix of relief and apprehension. She couldn't shake the feeling that the dolls were watching her, even now, their silent presence a constant reminder of the nightmares that plagued her.

Once the new hinges were in place and the trunk securely locked, Logan stood back, wiping the sweat from his brow. "There," he said, "they won't be getting out now." But Anita remained uneasy, her eyes lingering on the trunk. "We need to keep it that way," she insisted, her voice firm despite the fear that lingered beneath. "I don't know what those dolls are capable of, but I do know I never want to see them again." Logan nodded, wrapping an arm around her shoulders.

As the afternoon turned late, they finally descended from the attic, their arms filled with treasures. Anita felt a sense of fulfillment, knowing that she was beginning to understand the legacy of Harrow Hall and the people who had lived there.

"We've barely scratched the surface," Logan said as they placed the items on a table in the study. "There's still so much more to discover."

Anita nodded, her mind racing with thoughts of the future. "I know. But I feel like we're on the right track."

They spent the next forty-five minutes cataloging their finds, making notes of their discoveries, and reviewing her research from the library. A silence filled the room broken only by the rustle of the old letters as they both read intently. The words on the yellowed paper were a window into a past filled with loss and longing, each line more heartbreaking than the last. Anita's throat tightened with emotion as she read the final, sorrowful words of correspondence between a Civil War era mother and her soldier son. A tear slipped down Anita's cheek, and she wiped it away. She felt the weight of the Hall's history pressing down on her, a centuries-old sadness that seemed to seep into her soul. Just as the ache in her chest began to feel unbearable, she felt the warmth of Logan's presence behind her, grounding her in the here and now.

His hand came to rest gently on her shoulder, a simple gesture of comfort that spoke volumes. The tenderness of his touch seeped through her, chasing away the chill that had settled in her bones. She reached up and covered his hand with her own, her fingers curling around his. When she looked up, their eyes met, and the intensity of his dark gaze made her heart skip a beat. For a long, breathless moment, the world outside the Hall ceased to exist, and it was just the two of them, connected in a way that went beyond words.

"It seems like it always went wrong for them," she said, her voice heavy. "The wealth kept coming, but that wasn't what they needed. Just like Vance. He couldn't find what he needed here, and for some reason he chose a complete escape."

Logan nodded with understanding. Sorrow lingered in the air, her own melding with that of the Hall's and its history, but in Logan's eyes, she found something that made the weight of it all a little easier to bear—a quiet strength, a deep understanding and something more that neither of them was ready to name.

Logan squeezed her shoulder and glanced at his watch, clearing his throat. "I need to clean up a bit before we head to my parents' place."

Anita nodded, removing her hand from his. "I could use a little time to freshen up too. I'll meet you back here in about an hour?"

"Sounds like a plan," Logan agreed, giving her a reassuring smile.

Anita made her way to her room when he left, feeling a mix of excitement and nervousness about the evening ahead.

***

When she returned to the foyer, Logan was already waiting. He smiled appreciatively when he saw her. "You look great, Anita."

She had chosen a light, playful dress, its soft lavender fabric adorned with delicate purple butterflies and scattered yellow daisies. The dress, with its cinched waist and flowing skirt, hugged her figure in all the right places, accentuating her silhouette while maintaining a sense of effortless grace. The long sleeves puffed slightly at the wrists, giving it a charmingly retro touch, and the lightweight material had moved gently with every step she took, making her feel as if she were floating. The dress seemed to brighten the mood around her, a stark contrast to the heaviness she felt.

"Thanks," she replied, feeling a blush creep up her cheeks. "You clean up nicely too." Anita's eyes were irresistibly drawn to Logan, his casual confidence apparent in every move. He wore a crisp white shirt, the top few buttons undone, revealing a hint of tanned skin beneath. The sleeves were rolled up just below his elbows, showcasing his strong forearms, and the shirt was tucked neatly into a pair of well-worn jeans that fit him perfectly. The leather belt cinched at his waist added a rugged touch. He held one hand behind his back, and a silver watch glinted on his other wrist, catching the light as he moved. His effortless style and the way he carried himself held her attention, making her heart skip a beat.

He brought his hidden hand forward and presented her with a pale yellow flower. The single whorled bloom with delicately furled petals offered a fragrance sweet and heady that filled the small space between them. Anita's breath caught as he stepped closer, his warm brown eyes never leaving hers.

"This is a gardenia. Normally they only grow much farther south, but I've been testing some new varieties that are hardier."

With a tenderness that made her heart flutter, he tucked the stem behind her ear, his warm fingers brushing lightly against her cheek.

"It's one of the most delicate flowers. The petals can actually bruise when touched, and they don't last long once you've cut them."

For a moment, time seemed to slow, the world narrowing to just the two of them once again. The gesture was deep, a quiet acknowledgment of the growing bond between them as they prepared to meet his family together. Anita marveled at how something as small as a gardenia could make her feel so cherished.

"It's an evergreen plant actually, but you have to protect it well during the winter."

"Kind of like a California girl, then," Anita joked quietly.

Logan grinned, catching her hand in his. "Exactly like a certain California girl I know."

They shared a laugh, the easy familiarity between them easing her nerves. Logan led her to his pickup, and they set off for his parents' house. The drive was pleasant, and the early evening sun cast a warm glow over the landscape.

As they drove, Anita couldn't help but reflect on the day's events. Despite the tension with Vanessa, she felt a deep sense of satisfaction and clarity. She had made her decision to stay, and with Logan's support, she felt ready to face whatever challenges lay ahead.

Logan's parents' house was a charming, well-kept home nestled in a quiet neighborhood. As they pulled into the driveway, Anita felt a flutter of nerves. Logan sensed her apprehension and reached over to give her hand a reassuring squeeze.

Dinner was delightful. Martha and George welcomed Anita with open arms, their warm hospitality immediately putting her at ease. Logan's pregnant sister Susan and her seven-year-old daughter Grace were also there, adding a lively and cheerful dynamic to the evening.

As they sat around the dinner table, Anita found herself engaging easily with Susan, discovering they had many shared interests. Grace, with her boundless energy and infectious laughter, quickly won Anita over. The meal was filled with delicious food and lively conversation, punctuated by laughter and stories.

After dinner, they moved to the living room for a game of charades. Grace insisted on being on Anita's team, and they quickly became a formidable duo, their synergy leading to several winning rounds. The room was filled with laughter and playful banter, everyone enjoying the lighthearted competition.

At one point, Susan mentioned Vanessa in passing. "She was always terrible at charades," Susan said with a chuckle. "She was so concerned with her appearance that she would never act silly like we are now."

Anita felt a pang but kept her smile. Susan turned to her. "Anita, I heard that Vanessa was quite rude to you at the hardware store. I'm so sorry you had to deal with that."

Logan's surprise was evident. He eased next to Anita on the sofa. "What happened?"

She hesitated, but the concern in his eyes compelled her to speak. "It was nothing, really. Just some accusations she made about Vance."

"Gracie, why don't you go see if grandpa will make us some root beer floats?" Susan sent Gracie to the kitchen. As soon as she was out of sight, Susan said, "Vanessa is a snake. I'm so happy you're rid of her Logan." Susan grimaced and adjusted her position in the overstuffed chair she occupied. "Oof. I swear this kid kicks more than the Olympic swim team."

Logan's voice was gentle but firm. "Tell me what she said."

Anita sighed, feeling the weight of the confrontation. "Vanessa claims to have seen and talked to Vance in Las Vegas last fall. She claims that I…well, that I destroyed him, and that you…She was just trying to get to me, but I'm not to let it."

Logan's expression darkened with concern. "She has no right to say those things to you. I'll talk to her about it."

Anita placed a hand on his arm, trying to reassure him. "I appreciate that, Logan, but I'd rather just put it behind me. The important thing is that you're not with her anymore."

Logan's eyes softened as he looked at her and he squeezed her knee. "The morning after you arrived in Harrowsburg, I ended things with Vanessa. I'd been considering it for a while, and meeting you confirmed it was the right decision."

They shared a moment of understanding before Martha, George, and Grace returned from the kitchen with tall crystal glasses bubbling with creamy floats.

As they enjoyed the treat, Anita turned to Martha and George, expressing her gratitude. "Thank you so much for a wonderful supper and evening. I had an amazing time."

Martha bustled over from the love seat and gave her a quick hug. "I'm so glad. You're always welcome here, Anita."

Logan drove Anita home, the ride filled with a comfortable silence and the beauty of the setting sun. She scooted over on the bench seat, and he put his arm around her. She bathed in the warmth of him. They drove slowly, taking in the picturesque countryside bathed in the soft glow of twilight.

When they arrived at the Hall, Logan walked her to the door.

Anita felt playful. "I have one more charade clue for you."

"Okay." Logan raised his eyebrows.

Anita played the air guitar.

"Song title."

She nodded and held up two fingers.

"Two words."

She nodded and held up two fingers again.

"Second word."

She pointed to herself.

"You...I...me."

At the last Anita touched her nose.

"Okay. Me."

Then Anita grasped Logan's shirt and stood on her tiptoes, pulling his lips to hers. He slipped his arms around her waist. "Kiss Me." He said against her lips and tugged her close against him. "The 90s hit from Sixpence None the Richer. I'm one for one. Let's go again."

She laughed.

"That is a beautiful sound. You should make it more often."

"With you around, I think I will."

"Mmm," he leaned down and nuzzled her neck. "I am known for my comedic side."

Anita laughed again, so happy to be seeing Logan's playful side.

The glow of the porch light cast a warm halo around them. He eased back from her, his eyes soft and filled with unspoken emotions. The night settled around them, and he took her hand gently, his touch lingering, and smiled.

"Goodnight, Anita," he said, raising the back of her hand to his lips. His voice was steady but tender, revealing the depth of his feelings. "Sleep well."

Anita experienced more than a pang of disappointment, but she knew that Logan's gentlemanly behavior was part of what made him so special. He respected her and the boundary they had set for, even if it meant denying the powerful draw they both felt. She smiled back at him, trying to hide the yearning in her heart.

"Goodnight, Logan," she replied softly, her eyes meeting his with a mixture of warmth and wistfulness. "Thank you for today. And for everything you've done."

Logan squeezed her hand gently before letting it go, the absence of his touch immediately noticeable. He stepped back, his gaze never leaving hers, as if committing every detail of her face to memory. Anita watched him, her heart aching yet filled with admiration for his restraint and respect. She knew that their bond was strong, and that taking things slowly was the right choice, even if it meant moments like this—moments of quiet longing and unfulfilled desire.

Standing alone on the porch, Anita wrapped her arms around herself, feeling the cool breeze brush against her skin. She watched Logan's pickup until it disappeared into the night. Despite her disappointment, she felt a profound sense of peace. Love was best built on a foundation of mutual respect and understanding. She knew that when the time was right, they would come together again, and that the wait would make their connection all the more meaningful. For now, she was content with the knowledge that their feelings were true, and that sometimes, doing the right thing meant holding back, even when every fiber of her being urged her to reach out and pull closer.

***

Hyacinth Harrow's Diary

November 3, 19__

 I feel the weight of extra years pressing down on me. Harrow Hall, with its ancient stones and hallowed halls, has been my life's anchor, a testament to our family's enduring legacy. Yet today, as I look out upon the twilight landscape, I am struck by the realization that the power we have guarded so jealously is slipping through our fingers. The Covenant of Shadows, that dark pact that has defined us for generations, may be nearing its end.

 Victor, my dear grandson, has always been a gentle soul. From the moment he arrived after Collette's death, I knew he lacked the hardness, the ruthless determination required to sustain our family's power. He is kind, compassionate, and wholly unsuited to the demands of the Covenant. As much as it pains me to admit it, Victor is not capable of continuing the legacy that has been entrusted to us.

 I have tried to prepare him, to instill in him the importance of our role and the responsibilities that come with it. But his heart is not in it. He recoils from the rituals, shies away from the shadows, and questions the very foundation of our family's power. He is more interested in the arts, literature, and music than in the dark arts that have kept us strong.

 The Hall itself seems to sense Victor's reluctance. The once vibrant and pulsating energy of Harrow Hall has begun to wane. The walls, which used to hum with the power of the Covenant, are now silent. The whispers that once guided and protected us grow faint. It is as if the house is mourning the loss of its future, knowing that the line of succession is failing.

 In Victor's absence, the Hall's power diminishes, and I find myself turning my thoughts to Logan, the child born of forbidden love, his parentage a constant reminder of the fracture within our family. His father, a priest, represented everything the Covenant stands against—purity, faith, and light. Yet, despite his parentage, Logan has shown a strength and resilience that Victor lacks.

 Logan possesses a natural charisma, a quiet intensity that draws people to him. He has an innate understanding of the darkness, an ability to navigate its currents that Victor could never muster. As the Hall's power wanes, I cannot help but wonder if Logan could be the one to take over, to restore the strength of the Covenant. But deep down, I know the truth. Logan, for all his potential, would never embrace the shadows fully. His father's influence, even though absent, runs too deep, and Logan, too, would question the morality of our legacy.

This realization fills me with a profound sense of loss. The great power that our family has wielded for centuries is destined to end with me. I mourn not only for myself but for all those who came before me, who sacrificed so much to maintain the Covenant. Our ancestors, whose blood and toil built Harrow Hall and cemented our pact, would be devastated to see their legacy fade.

As the last matriarch of the Harrow family who truly understands and embraces the Covenant of Shadows, I feel a responsibility to ensure that the next generation, even if it is the last, carries some semblance of our legacy. I think of the next Mrs. Harrow, the woman who will marry into our family, and the burden she will bear. She will inherit a legacy steeped in power and darkness, a history that demands sacrifice and strength.

To the next Mrs. Harrow, whoever she may be, I offer my blessing. She will need it. The task she faces is monumental, and she will need all the strength and resolve she can muster. The weight of our family's history, the expectations, and the Covenant itself will rest upon her shoulders. She must understand the importance of our legacy, even as it fades, and strive to preserve what little remains.

I pray that she will have the fortitude to stand against the inevitable challenges, to face the shadows with courage and determination. She must be prepared to make difficult choices, to sacrifice for the greater good of our family. The Covenant of Shadows is not for the faint of heart, and she must be as unwavering as the stone walls of Harrow Hall.

In my heart, I know that the true power of the Covenant will die with me. But perhaps, in some small way, the next Mrs. Harrow can keep the memory of it alive. She can pass down the stories, the lessons, and the warnings to her children, ensuring that our family's legacy is never forgotten, even if it can no longer be sustained. The walls of Harrow Hall are stained with the weight of our history, a history that I must now accept is coming to an end.

As I write these words, I can hear the distant echoes of those who came before me. Their voices, once so strong and commanding, are now faint whispers. They remind me of the duty I have carried and the legacy I will leave behind. I am not alone in my sorrow, for they too mourn the loss of what we have built.

To Victor, my beloved grandson, I leave a different legacy. He may not be capable of continuing the Covenant, but he has his own path to *follow. I hope he will find happiness and fulfillment in his passions, that he will build a life free from the shadows that have haunted our family. He deserves to live without the weight of our past pressing down upon him.*

And to Logan, the child of light and darkness, I offer my hope. He has the potential to bridge the gap between our world and the world beyond, to find a balance that neither Victor nor I could achieve. His journey will be difficult, but I believe he has the strength to find his way.

The sun is setting now across the grounds of Harrow Hall. As the light fades, I am reminded that even the darkest night is followed by the dawn. Our family's power may be ending, but new beginnings are on the horizon. The legacy of the Harrows will live on in memory, if not in practice, and that is enough.

In these final days of my life, I will cherish the moments I have left, the beauty of this ancient manor, and the love of my family. I will continue to guide Victor and Logan as best I can, preparing them for a future that no longer includes the Covenant of Shadows.

To the next Mrs. Harrow, I leave not only my blessing but also my gratitude. She will be the custodian of our history, the keeper of our stories, and the protector of our memory. I trust that she will honor our family and uphold the values that have defined us for so long.

And so, as I close this diary for the night, I do so with a heart full of both sorrow and hope. The shadows may be receding, but the light of our legacy will never fade. Harrow Hall will stand as a testament to our strength, our sacrifices, and the enduring power of our name.

Hyacinth Harrow

Chapter Eight

Logan had always prided himself on his self-control, but lately, it seemed to be slipping away like a shadow. Anita had become a constant presence in his mind, a figure who occupied his thoughts day and night. He found himself drawn to her in an exhilarating and unsettling way with a magnetic pull. There were moments when he worried that this growing obsession might lead him to cross the boundaries they had both agreed to respect. It wasn't just physical attraction, though there was certainly that; it was something deeper, something more insistent as if an invisible thread connected them.

At times, this connection felt pure and natural, like the gentle breeze that rustled through the trees surrounding Harrow Hall. When he thought of Anita in those moments, it was with a sense of warmth and peace, as if the very earth beneath his feet was whispering that this was right, that they were meant to find solace in one another. He recalled how her laughter would ring out across the garden, or her eyes would soften when she talked about her plans for Hall's future. In these moments, Logan felt a profound sense of contentment, a belief that he could build something real and lasting with Anita, something as enduring as the ancient charter oaks that dotted the estate.

But then there were other times, darker times when that connection felt like a vice tightening around his chest. It was as if the Hall itself, with its long history of secrets and sorrow, was feeding into his emotions, twisting them into something almost evil. He would catch himself brooding over her in the quiet of the night, unable to sleep, his thoughts spiraling into a dark abyss. It was as though the shadows of the past were reaching out to him, whispering that Anita was his in a way that went beyond love, beyond affection—something possessive and consuming.

Those were the moments when Hall's influence felt strongest when he wondered if he was truly in control of his feelings or if something more sinister was at play.

Logan shook his head, trying to dispel the unease that clung to him like a second skin. He knew he needed to distance himself to regain his clarity of mind. Anita had enough on her plate without him complicating things further. She was trying to restore Harrow Hall to its former glory, and Vanessa's vindictive interference with the local businesses had only made her job harder. Contractors and suppliers were suddenly unavailable, and those who agreed to work seemed nervous, as if they feared falling into a trap. Logan hated to think that his past with Vanessa was now casting a shadow over Anita's work, but it was clear that his ex was determined to make things difficult.

The more Logan thought about it, the more he realized that the best way to help Anita might be to keep his distance for a while. He could see how much she was struggling, the weight of her responsibilities pressing down on her. She didn't need the added pressure of his presence, especially when he wasn't sure if he could fully trust himself around her. The last thing he wanted was to push her away by coming on too strong and by allowing his emotions to overtake his judgment.

And so, Logan decided to pull back. It wasn't easy—every instinct in him wanted to be near her, offer his support, and share in her burdens—but he knew it was the right thing to do. He started working more time on the far grounds, tending to the orchards and gardens, and keeping himself busy with tasks that required his full attention. It was therapeutic in a way, losing himself in the physical labor, feeling the earth beneath his hands, the sun on his back. It reminded him of the simpler things in life, the things that had always brought him peace.

Still, even as he worked, his thoughts would stray to Anita. He would imagine her walking through the gardens, her hands brushing against the flowers, her face lit up with that determined expression she wore when she was deep in thought. He would picture her sitting on the porch swing, sipping tea as she pored over restoration plans, her brow furrowed in concentration. He wondered if she ever thought of him as often as he thought of her if she felt the same strange pull that he did.

He had to remind himself that Anita was different from Vanessa. She wasn't someone who would manipulate or control, who would use her emotions as a weapon. She had her own wounds and grief, and she was trying to navigate through them with a grace that Logan deeply admired.

He didn't want to be the one to disrupt that, to impose his own turmoil on her when she was already carrying so much.

The days passed slowly, each blending into the next as Logan immersed himself in his work. He spoke with Anita only when necessary, keeping their interactions brief and to the point. It was difficult, especially when she would look at him with those clear, searching eyes as if she knew there was something he wasn't telling her. But Logan held firm, knowing that his resolve was necessary for both of their sakes.

The Hall seemed to loom larger in the evenings as he retreated to his home, its presence almost oppressive, as if it was watching him, judging him. There were moments when he could almost feel it breathing, the very walls pulsing with a life of their own.

He didn't like its hold over him, the way it amplified his emotions, turning his thoughts into something twisted and unnatural. He had heard the stories, of course—stories of how the Hall had driven people to madness, how it had a way of getting inside your head and distorting your reality. Logan had only half believed those tales, but now, after everything he had experienced, he knew there was some truth.

He wasn't sure how long he could keep his distance, though. The more time he spent away from Anita, the more he realized how deeply he cared for her. It wasn't just infatuation; it was something far more profound. He wanted to protect her, be there for her in every way possible, and help her find happiness in a place that had seen so much sorrow.

***

Anita stepped into the cool, air-conditioned interior of the local bank, a sense of determination set in her stride. She had spent the past week meticulously gathering every piece of paperwork necessary to be added to the Harrow Hall Legacy accounts, and now, with her documents neatly organized in a leather portfolio, she was ready to complete this task.

As she approached the reception desk, she noticed a gruff security guard with a name tag that said Atkins watching her with unusual suspicion. He was a large, burly man, standing tall and imposing near the entrance.

A young woman at the reception greeted Anita with a professional smile. "Good morning, ma'am. How can I assist you today?"

"I'm here to be added to the Harrow Hall Legacy accounts," Anita replied confidently. "Mr. Charlton has looked everything over and said I have all the necessary paperwork."

The receptionist's eyebrows rose, recognition in her eyes at the mention of the Hall. "Of course, ma'am. Please have a seat for a moment, and I'll get someone to assist you."

Anita nodded and took a seat in the waiting area. She watched the receptionist make a phone call, speaking in hushed tones. Atkins' eyes never left her, his presence a constant reminder of the bank's scrutiny. Within minutes, a young banker appeared, his nervous demeanor evident despite his attempt at a welcoming smile.

"Mrs. Harrow? I'm David. If you'll follow me, we can take care of everything in my office."

Anita followed David through the labyrinthine corridors of the bank, finally arriving at a small, sparsely furnished office. She took a seat across from him, placing her portfolio on the desk between them.

David's eyes widened slightly as he scanned through the documents Anita presented. He cleared his throat, shifting uncomfortably in his chair. "It seems everything is in order, but there are a few additional identification documents we'll need to complete the process."

Anita's brow furrowed. "Additional identification documents? I've already provided my passport, driver's license, and several utility bills. What more could you possibly need?"

David hesitated, clearly uncomfortable. "I'm sorry, Mrs. Harrow, but we require a secondary form of identification, such as a certified birth certificate, as well as a notarized statement of identity from a local official who has known you for at least three years. Then there is the necessity of a statement from a financial official familiar with your banking for the past ten years as well as a financial portfolio dating at least seven years."

Anita's eyes narrowed. She had been through enough banking procedures to know this was definitely not standard policy. "Who mandated these additional requirements?"

David shifted again, glancing towards the door as if expecting someone to walk in. "These are very special accounts—"

"—yes, I am aware of that. However, I am also aware that all of these documents from the law office give me absolute right over those accounts."

David stared down at his desk. "These stipulations come from my manager, Vanessa Briggs. She's very particular about high-value accounts."

"All high-value accounts or these accounts in particular?"

David glanced up at her. His face paled, but he didn't respond.

Anita felt a surge of irritation but managed to keep her voice calm. "I see. Thank you for letting me know, David. I will obtain the documents you need and return as soon as possible."

As she left the office, she could feel Atkins' eyes boring into her back. His disdain was almost palpable. Ignoring him, she walked briskly out of the bank and, as soon as she got to her car, called Doreen in California, explaining the situation. Doreen promised to hustle and overnight the necessary documents. Anita hung up, feeling a sense of resolve. She would not let Atkins, David, Vanessa, or anyone else at the bank intimidate her. She was determined to secure her rightful place in the Harrow Hall Legacy accounts.

***

Late the next morning, Anita returned to the bank, additional identification documents in hand. As she entered, she noticed the gruff security guard, Atkins, glaring at her from his post near the entrance.

David's eyes widened in surprise when he saw her. "You managed to get everything so quickly?"

"I did," Anita replied coolly, handing over the documents. "I trust this will suffice."

David examined the papers, his nervousness returning. "Actually, Mrs. Harrow, it appears we also need a recent medical bill or insurance statement."

Anita's patience snapped. "This is absurd. I demand to speak to the president of the bank."

David paled, clearly distressed. "Please, Mrs. Harrow, there's no need for that."

But Anita was already on her feet, her portfolio clutched tightly in her hand. As she marched to the receptionist, she caught Atkins' disapproving scowl. Ignoring him, she demanded an immediate meeting with the president. Within minutes, she was escorted to a large, opulent office.

The bank president, a distinguished man in his sixties, rose to greet her. "Mrs. Harrow, what seems to be the problem?"

Anita quickly explained the situation, detailing the unreasonable demands made by David at the behest of his manager, Vanessa. The president listened attentively, his expression growing grimmer by the minute.

"I'm so sorry for the inconvenience, Mrs. Harrow," he said finally. "I assure you, this is not our standard policy. You have my deepest apologies. Please, let me take care of this personally."

He pressed a button on his desk, summoning David. When the young banker entered, he looked as though he was about to face a firing squad. "David, Mrs. Harrow has informed me of the difficulties she has encountered. Is it true that these additional requirements came from Vanessa?"

David nodded, clearly terrified. "Yes, sir. She insisted on it."

The president turned back to Anita, his expression contrite. "Mrs. Harrow, please rest assured that your paperwork will be processed immediately."

Anita felt a pang of sympathy for David. "Sir, if I may," she interjected. "David was only following instructions. I don't believe he should be punished for this."

The president nodded thoughtfully. "Very well. Thank you for your understanding, Mrs. Harrow. David, you're dismissed for now. I'll speak with Vanessa personally."

David left the office, looking immensely relieved. Anita could see Atkins outside the office through the glass door, his stern gaze still fixed on her. The president picked up the phone, summoning Vanessa. Moments later, the tall, impeccably dressed woman entered the room with an air of authority.

"Vanessa, we need to discuss your handling of the Harrow Hall Legacy accounts," the president began, his tone icy.

Vanessa's eyes flicked to Anita, a calculating look in her eyes. "Of course, sir. There must have been some miscommunication. I only wanted to ensure the utmost security for such a prestigious account."

"Security is one thing, but making unreasonable demands is another," the president retorted. "Mrs. Harrow has been subjected to unnecessary stress and inconvenience. I expect better judgment in the future."

Vanessa's demeanor shifted, a charming smile replacing her earlier coolness. "I understand completely, sir. It won't happen again."

Anita watched, knowing Vanessa was adept at using her charm to diffuse situations. Despite the president's stern words, it was clear

Vanessa would face no real consequences. As the meeting concluded, Vanessa's smile never faltered.

"I apologize for any inconvenience...Mrs. Harrow. I hope we can move forward without any further issues."

Anita maintained her own smile, equally polite but with a steely edge.

As they left the president's office and turned in separate directions, the tension between the women was palpable. Anita knew Vanessa saw her as a threat, and she hoped Vanessa realized that Anita wouldn't back down. She was determined to ensure that next time Vanessa wouldn't escape unscathed. As Anita exited, she couldn't help but notice Atkins' narrowed eyes following her every move. She gave him a curt nod, knowing she had one more adversary within the bank's walls.

***

Anita stood at the grand entrance of Harrow Hall, a place that had become both sanctuary and enigma. The morning sun cast a soft glow over the sprawling estate, highlighting the gardens and the ivy-covered façade. She took a deep breath, feeling a mixture of excitement and trepidation. Today marked the beginning of her ambitious project to renovate Harrow Hall, to breathe new life into its ancient walls while uncovering the secrets it held.

With a clipboard in hand, Anita began her inspection of the exterior. The stone walls, though sturdy, showed signs of age and neglect. Cracks snaked up from the foundation, and the once-grand windows were clouded with years of grime. She made a note to contact a stonemason and a window specialist, imagining the hall restored to its former glory with sunlight streaming through sparkling panes.

Her thoughts drifted to the history of Harrow Hall, a place steeped in mystery and tragedy. She had pieced together stories from old journals, local legends, and her own unsettling, unending dreams. The Harrow family had been prominent landowners, known for their wealth and influence since colonial times. However, their legacy was marred by whispers of dark rituals, ghostly apparitions, and a series of unexplained disappearances.

Anita's own research had revealed that several members of the Harrow family and many townspeople had vanished without a trace over the decades. These disappearances were often attributed to the Harrow family, but no bodies were ever found on the grounds despite numerous searches allowed through the years. She couldn't shake the sense that the past was alive within the walls of the Hall, that the spirits of those who had lived—and died—there were trying to communicate with her.

Moving to the interior, Anita's steps echoed through the grand foyer. The hall's opulence was still evident despite the dust and decay. Marble floors, intricate woodwork, and towering ceilings hinted at a time when Harrow Hall was the epitome of elegance. But now, it was a shadow of its former self. She imagined refurbishing the space, restoring the wood to its rich luster and the marble to its original gleam. She envisioned chandeliers sparkling once more and the air filled with the warmth of a roaring fireplace.

As she wandered through the vast rooms, Anita's thoughts turned to Logan. Since their dinner at his parents' house, he had been somewhat distant. At first, she attributed it to the sheer amount of work required to tame the grounds. Logan was often outside, hacking away at the dense foliage, repairing fences, and tending to the gardens. He seemed absorbed in his tasks, barely taking a break to join her for meals or conversations. While she admired his dedication, she couldn't help but wonder if there was more to his distance than just hard work.

In the drawing-room, Anita paused by the large bay window that overlooked the gardens. She watched Logan from afar, his figure hunched over a wheelbarrow, his movements mechanical and purposeful. He had been her rock, steady and reliable since she arrived in Harrowsburg, but lately, she felt there was a gulf opening between them. She wondered if he was purposely adding distance, and if so, why. Had the house, with all its dark history and eerie atmosphere, begun to affect him as it had her?

Shaking off her concerns for the moment, Anita focused on the task at hand. The drawing room needed extensive work. The wallpaper was peeling, and the ceiling had water damage from a long-neglected leak. She jotted down notes about finding a restoration specialist for the wallpaper and a contractor to repair the roof. Her mind was a whirl of fabric swatches, paint samples, and furniture catalogs, but beneath it, all was a growing sense of unease.

Anita moved on to the library, her favorite room despite its current state of disarray. Dusty shelves lined the walls, filled with leather-bound volumes that had seen better days. The air was thick with the scent of aged paper and wood. She could almost hear the whispers of the past, the hushed conversations of the Harrow family as they sat by the fire, lost in their books or perhaps plotting their next move. The library held many secrets, and she was determined to uncover them.

She had already found several journals and letters hidden among the books, documents that hinted at the darker side of the Harrow legacy. There were references to secret meetings, coded messages, and cryptic symbols that matched the carvings on the mahogany table in her dreams. The more she read, the more she felt drawn into the web of the Harrow family's past, a past that seemed to bleed into the present.

Despite the chilling revelations, Anita was resolute in her mission. She wanted to honor the history of Harrow Hall while making it her own. She envisioned the library as a cozy retreat, with comfortable chairs, restored bookshelves, and perhaps a new fireplace. It would be a place of learning and reflection, a sanctuary from the haunted memories that lingered in the shadows.

Her thoughts were interrupted by a sudden chill that swept through the room. The temperature seemed to drop inexplicably, and the flickering light from the single bulb overhead cast long, dancing shadows. Anita shivered, feeling the unmistakable presence of something—or someone—watching her. She turned slowly, her eyes scanning the dimly lit room, but there was no one there. The feeling lingered, a reminder that Harrow Hall was far from an ordinary house.

Determined not to let fear dictate her actions, Anita moved on to the dining room. The long table was once the site of lavish dinners and family gatherings. The cleaning crews she had hired to work double shifts had cleared the Hall of most of its cobwebs, grime, and dust from the carpets and major surfaces. She imagined the table fully restored, the silverware gleaming, the crystal glasses sparkling under the light of a chandelier. She could almost hear the echoes of laughter and conversation, but those echoes were overshadowed by the darker whispers of the past.

As she made her way through the rest of the house, Anita's mind was a jumble of renovation plans and historical puzzles. She wanted to bring life back to Harrow Hall, but she also felt a responsibility to understand the events that had transpired within its walls. The disappearances, the rituals, the ghostly apparitions – they were all pieces of a larger puzzle, one that she was determined to solve.

Later that evening, as Anita sat in her temporary study surrounded by blueprints and historical texts, she couldn't shake the feeling of being watched. The house seemed to creak and groan around her, as if it were alive and aware of her presence. She glanced out the window and saw Logan working tirelessly, his figure silhouetted against the fading light. She missed their easy conversations and the sense of partnership that had started to burgeon. The distance between them was growing, and she feared it might have something to do with the house and its dark influence.

Despite her concerns, Anita was resolute. Harrow Hall was a place of mystery and history, but it was also her home now. She would face whatever challenges came her way, whether they were supernatural or simply the trials of renovation. She would uncover the secrets of the past and build a future within these walls. And perhaps, in doing so, she could bridge the gap that had formed between her and Logan.

***

Vanessa
Hey Logan, I have some important information I need to share with you.
Logan
What could you possibly have to say to me?
Vanessa
A lot if you would just listen. You used to be good at that. It was my favorite thing about you.
Logan
Come off it V.
Vanessa
I miss you. Don't even miss me a little bit?
Logan
No.
Vanessa
Well, that's disappointing.
Logan
What's disappointing is the awful things you said to Anita at the hardware store and the way you've been meddling with contractors for the estate. You're way out of line. There's nothing you can tell me that I need to hear anymore.
Vanessa
Logan, this is serious. It has to do with old Hyacinth Harrow and Vic. You need to hear this.

Logan

Whatever it is, Vanessa, I don't care. Our relationship is over, and there's nothing you can say that will change that.

Vanessa

Are you sleeping with Anita?

Logan

What happens between Anita and me is absolutely none of your business.

Vanessa

I'm not trying to interfere with your personal life. This is about the estate and some information that could impact both you and Anita.

Logan

I find that hard to believe. You've done nothing but cause trouble since we broke up. Why should I trust you now?

Vanessa

Because this isn't about us. Like I said, it's about Hyacinth and Vic. It's something you absolutely need to know. If you don't agree to see me, I'll find Anita and tell her. And believe me, the news will probably hurt her if it comes from me.

Logan

You really know how to twist the knife, don't you? Fine. Where and when?

Vanessa

How about the diner on Main Street? Tomorrow afternoon at 2.

Logan

Alright. But this better be real V.

Vanessa

I'll see you tomorrow, Logan. You won't regret it.

Logan

We'll see about that.

Vanessa

Goodnight, Logan. I'll be missing you. all. night. long.

***

Anita stood in the main dining room of Harrow Hall, a faint smile playing on her lips as she examined the side tables she was refinishing. The wood was rich and dark, with intricate carvings that spoke of a bygone era of craftsmanship. She had spent the morning carefully sanding and applying the first coat of varnish, the air thick with the scent of the chemicals. Now, as the sun streamed in through the large windows, she debated whether she should attempt to refinish the exquisite buffet that stood at the far end of the room.

It had been a magnificent piece with a surface adorned with delicate inlays and ornate handles. It had seen better days. Now the wood was scratched and dulled by years of neglect. Anita felt a pang of hesitation—was it too great a piece to be maligned by her amateur hands? She stretched her arms above her head, trying to shake off the uncertainty.

Checking her phone again, hoping to have a call back from a local mason that she had contacted last week, her gaze caught something in the reflection of the buffet's polished surface. She froze, her breath catching in her throat. There, in the reflection seated at the dining table behind her, was the doll in mourning clothes from the attic.

Anita whipped around, her heart pounding. The chair was empty. She blinked, her mind racing to rationalize what she had seen. It must have been the varnish fumes, she thought, shaking her head. The chemicals were playing tricks on her eyes.

She turned back to the table, but her breath caught in her throat once more. The doll was now sitting on top of the matching side table, its glassy eyes staring directly at her. She let out a short, startled scream, dropping the cloth she had been holding. The doll's presence was impossible to ignore—it was as if it had appeared out of thin air.

Anita picked up the doll, its porcelain skin surprisingly warm to the touch. Cloaked in a somber black cape, it exuded a gothic air of mystery and foreboding. Its pale face was framed by a bonnet that cast shadows over its eerily serene features, lending an aura of secretive melancholy. The meticulous craftsmanship of its attire, detailed with dark lace and brocade, added to the haunting elegance that surrounded it. Its eyes, dark and deep, seemed to follow you with an unspoken knowledge, a silent witness to unspeakable secrets buried within the folds of its antique garment.

Anita's mind raced, trying to make sense of how it had gotten there. Logan wasn't planning to come in today; it was the weekend. She distinctly remembered their work on the trunk in the attic to replace the worn hinges and shut the lid securely on the eerie dolls.

"It had to have been Logan," she muttered to herself, her voice shaking slightly. "Only he knew where they were and how much they bothered me. But why would he do something so cruel?"

Determined to solve the mystery, she marched up to the attic, the doll still clutched in her hand. When she reached the top, she found the trunk open not by the hinges as they had done, but by the lock. All four dolls were gone. A chill ran down her spine. Someone had deliberately moved the dolls.

She placed the doll from the dining room back into the trunk and set off to find the others. As she searched through the mansion, anger simmered beneath her confusion. This was out of character for Logan; he had always been respectful and kind. Why would he do something like this?

As she moved through the grand hallways, she began to notice other things out of place. The top hat she had set aside in the foyer was now perched on one of the dolls in the library, giving it a disturbingly jaunty appearance. With an almost angelic countenance, the doll's cherubic face was a chilling juxtaposition to the eerie stillness it exuded. Its big, blue eyes were unnervingly lifelike, staring into an unknown void, as if they could suddenly blink and reveal a hidden soul. The delicate lace dress, immaculate and white, seemed oddly pristine, contrasting with the unsettling aura that surrounded the doll. Its golden curls framed a face that seemed to silently scream, a frozen mask of innocence forever trapped in a nightmarish tableau.

"What the hell is going on?" she whispered, her voice barely audible in the vast silence of the house.

She continued her search, the unsettling feeling growing with each step. In one of the guest bedrooms, she found one more doll, leaning over Melusine's photo album from the attic as if engrossed in its contents. The sight was eerie, its tiny hands resting on the pages, its eyes fixed on the images.

The doll was draped in a gown that once spoke of grandeur now tarnished by time. Its porcelain face, pale and pristine, bore an unsettlingly perfect expression, as if trapped in a perpetual moment of poised anticipation. The elaborate curls of its hair framed a visage that felt almost too human, and its glassy eyes reflected a haunting emptiness. The elaborate attire, reminiscent of bygone eras, suggested stories of opulence and decline, leaving an unsettling feeling of a past that refused to fade away.

Anita picked up the doll, her hands trembling. The photographs of Melusine stared back at her from the album on the bed. She quickly closed the album and gathered the two dolls, feeling warmed porcelain against her skin.

She could hear something now, faint and distant at first, but growing steadily louder—the sound of bagpipes. The mournful, eerie tune filled the air, sending a wave of unease through her. It was unintelligible at first, a background noise that seemed to come from nowhere and everywhere at once.

Anita hurried back to the attic, replacing the two additional dolls in the trunk. She slammed the lid shut, her heart pounding in her chest. She then grabbed the photo album and headed to her room, locking it in her suitcase. She felt she needed to keep it safe, away from whatever strange force was at work in the house.

The bagpipes continued to play, their sound now echoing through the halls with an unsettling clarity. Anita followed the noise, her fear mounting with each step. She descended into the wine cellar, the cool, damp air wrapping around her like a shroud.

There, in the corner of the cellar, she found an old-time radio. It was blasting the frightening music, the bagpipes wailing a tune that seeped into her very bones. The radio was not hooked up to a power source and its inside wiring was pulled out. Tools were strewn about as if someone had been interrupted in the act of fixing it.

The fourth doll, the oldest made of straw, sat next to the radio. With lifeless eyes and a tattered dress, she exuded an air of forgotten despair. The fabric of its clothes, yellowed with age, was marked by small, meticulous stitches that hinted at long-forgotten hands painstakingly mending its wounds. Its face, barely discernible through the grime of decades, was a haunting canvas of faded features, an eerie testament to the innocence long lost. The doll's wiry hair, thin and brittle, whispered ghostly secrets of abandoned playrooms and the quiet, creeping dread of solitude.

Anita's breath came in short gasps. This was too much. She left the doll and radio where they sat, turned and ran. Her footsteps echoed in the empty halls. She burst out of the house, the oppressive atmosphere lifting as she stepped into the sunlight. She jumped into her car and her hands shook as she fumbled with the keys.

She drove into town, the Hall's stone silhouette receding in her rearview mirror. Her mind raced, trying to process what had just happened. Pulling into the parking lot of a small café, Anita took a few deep breaths to steady herself. She needed to clear her head, to think rationally about what to do next. She entered the café, the warmth and chatter of other patrons a welcome contrast to the eerie silence of the mansion.

She ordered a coffee and found a quiet corner to sit and gather her thoughts. The waitress gave her a concerned look as she handed over the steaming cup.

"Rough day?" the waitress asked kindly.

"You have no idea," Anita replied, managing a weak smile.

As she sipped her coffee, her mind began to clear. She needed to figure out what was happening at Harrow Hall. The incidents with the dolls and the music couldn't be mere coincidences. There had to be an explanation, something grounded in reality. Anita picked up the menu the waitress had left. Though she wasn't hungry, she knew she should eat something.

Glancing over the top of the laminated folder toward the back of the restaurant, she spied Logan and Vanessa. They were on opposite sides of a table, looking over some pieces of copy paper. Vanessa was animated, her hands moving expressively as she talked, while Logan sat back, his face serious and attentive. Anita felt a jolt of surprise and an uneasy twist in her stomach. She couldn't hear what they were saying, and it didn't feel right to move closer.

Anita froze for a moment, staring over the top of the menu. Her initial shock was followed by a rush of questions. Why were they meeting here? What were they discussing so intently? The scene didn't immediately strike her as romantic—there was no hand-holding, no leaning in, no intimate gestures. But the fact that they were even together, left Anita feeling unsettled.

She eased down in her seat, trying to remain inconspicuous as she peered around her menu. Vanessa seemed to be asking Logan something, her expression expectant as she waited for his response. Logan didn't say anything. Instead, he suddenly stood up and strode out of the restaurant, his movements brisk and purposeful. Vanessa hesitated for a moment, then quickly gathered the papers and ran after him. Neither one seemed to notice Anita across the room, for which she was thankful. Her heart raced as she watched them through the main window for a couple of moments before they disappeared around the corner. She debated whether to follow them but decided against it.

She laid down her menu, her mind reeling. It didn't look like Logan and Vanessa were back together as a couple, but what if that was the reason for Logan's recent distance? She shook her head, trying to dispel the spiraling thoughts. If they were back together, even as friends, he might have shared the information about the dolls with Vanessa. She would have been a more likely culprit than Logan for the terrible trick of placing them around the Hall. And what was on those papers that Logan seemed to strongly dislike?

Anita had no appetite. She finished her coffee, laid a few bills on the table and left the restaurant. As she stepped out onto the sidewalk, she nearly ran into Vanessa returning alone. Anita saw a look of concerned alarm cross the blonde's face, but she shoved it down quickly.

"Anita, what a coincidence," Vanessa said, her tone dripping with false sweetness.

Anita forced a polite smile. "Vanessa. Yes, quite the surprise."

Vanessa's eyes glinted with a mischievous light. "I couldn't help but notice you've been working tirelessly on Harrow Hall. Must be quite the project."

"It is," Anita replied, trying to keep her voice steady. "But it's coming along."

Vanessa stepped closer, her smile widening. "I expect you're utilizing local businesses for the work?"

Anita felt a cold knot form in her stomach. "Yes, I am."

Vanessa's smile turned into a smirk. "If I were you, I wouldn't hold my breath on Rob with Mason and Stone. In fact, you might not hear back from Devest's Plumbing or Myron's Flooring either."

Anita's eyes narrowed. "What do you mean?"

Vanessa's expression was one of feigned innocence. "Oh, just that sometimes our local businesses get...persuaded to avoid certain high-risk clients. Especially when those clients are involved with properties that carry certain reputations. It really could hurt their financing."

Realization dawned on Anita. Vanessa was using her influence at the bank to manipulate local businesses, ensuring they wouldn't work with her. The implications were infuriating.

"You're doing this," Anita said, her voice low and accusatory. "You're making sure they won't work with me. Why?"

Vanessa laughed softly. "Harrow Hall is more than just an old Hall, Anita. It's a legacy. A legacy that people like you don't deserve to be a part of."

Anita's anger flared. "You have no right to interfere with my work. Harrow Hall is my home now, and I will restore it, no matter your interference."

Vanessa's eyes hardened. "You're in over your head, Anita. As for your renovations, without the proper resources, you won't get very far."

Anita's mind raced, thinking of all the phone calls and meetings she had lined up. If Vanessa had her way, all those contacts would be useless. But Anita wasn't about to back down.

"I'll find a way," she said, her voice steely. "You can try to block me, but I will find a way."

Vanessa's smirk returned as she waltzed back into the cafe, her step light as the bell above the door rang. "Good luck with that. You'll need it."

Anita watched Vanessa's triumphant posture, and fury burned within her, but so did a fierce determination. She wouldn't let Vanessa's schemes derail her plans.

As she walked to her car, Anita pulled out her phone and began making a list of alternative contacts. She'd find independent contractors if she had to, people outside of Vanessa's influence. She'd use social media, local forums, whatever it took to connect with the right people.

Vanessa might have her claws in the local businesses, but Harrow Hall was Anita's now. She wouldn't let anyone else, especially Vanessa, dictate its future. The renovation would continue, and the Hall's secrets would be uncovered. Anita was more determined than ever to succeed, despite the obstacles Vanessa threw in her path.

With a renewed sense of purpose, Anita started her car and drove back to Harrow Hall, her mind already formulating new plans. She'd overcome this challenge like she had so many others. Harrow Hall's restoration would not be stopped.

Chapter Nine

Logan stood in the dim pre-dawn light of his kitchen, his hands trembling as he stared at the photocopied pages of Hyacinth Harrow's diary. He hadn't been able to sleep. The room seemed to close in around him, the walls pressing down with the weight of the words. Each line of the diary seared into his mind, tearing apart the fabric of the reality he had known his entire life.

He was Hyacinth Harrow's second grandson, the product of a hidden affair between Collette Harrow and a New Orleans priest that had been carefully concealed from the world—and from him. But now, all those barriers were shattered, and Logan felt as if he were standing on the edge of a precipice, looking down into an abyss of uncertainty and fear.

"How could she?" he muttered, his voice hoarse with anger and disbelief. He grabbed the pages, crumpling them into a tight ball, and chucking them at the garbage can. Vanessa had no right to dig up these secrets, to throw them in his face as if they were some kind of twisted gift. She had done this to manipulate him, to sow doubt and discord in his mind. But it wasn't just Vanessa who had wronged him—Hyacinth and his parents had kept this from him. They had to have known the details, didn't they?

He talked a big game, didn't he? Claiming to Anita to not place stock in where he came from, only in who raised him. His fists clenched, knuckles whitening as the fury coursed through him. Hyacinth had been the last living link to that part of his past, and now that she was gone, all he had left were these pages filled with confessions she had never intended for him to read. She'd had every opportunity to tell him these things, and she chose not to.

He had always felt a strange connection, a sense that he belonged to the grounds, to the earth that surrounded the old estate. It was a bond he had never fully understood, but now it made sense. It was in his blood and birth.

He cursed under his breath, pacing the kitchen as he tried to grapple with the flood of emotions surging through him. Anger at Vanessa for interfering, anger at Hyacinth for never telling him the truth—but more than anything, fear. The fear that now everything he had with Anita would be destroyed. How could he look her in the eyes and tell her what he had learned? How could he confess that he was Vance's half-brother, that he was connected to the Harrows in a way he had never imagined?

Would she run? Would she see him as a threat, someone who might challenge her for ownership of the Hall, or worse, someone who was only with her to get to the estate and the money? The very thought made his stomach churn. He loved Anita, truly and deeply, and the idea that she might think he was using her was unbearable.

Logan stopped pacing and ran a hand through his hair, his mind racing. He had to tell her, but how? How could he explain something so complicated, so tangled in the twisted history of the Harrow family, without driving her away? The last thing he wanted was to lose her, to see the love in her eyes turn to suspicion or fear.

He had never felt this way about anyone before. Anita was so different. She was real, honest, and he had fallen hard for her. The estate, the money—none of that mattered to him. What mattered was her smile, the way she laughed, the way she made him feel complete.

But how could he make her see that? How could he convince her that his feelings for her had nothing to do with Harrow Hall, that he would love her just as much if she were penniless and living in a tiny apartment somewhere far away from this cursed place?

***

Anita stood outside Logan's house on the bright Sunday morning, her heart pounding with a mix of determination and trepidation. She was here to confront him, to get answers to the questions that had been gnawing at her all night. Between fitful stretches of sleep filled with the haunting presence of the four dolls, she couldn't stop thinking about Vanessa and Logan in the booth at the cafe.

Anita took a deep breath and marched up the driveway, just as Logan stepped out the front door. He was dressed sharply, his usual casual attire replaced by a crisp button-down shirt and slacks. He looked up, surprised to see her, and she was startled to see circles under his eyes.

"Anita, hi." he greeted her cautiously. "What brings you here so early?"

"We need to talk," she said, her voice firm.

Logan nodded, fumbling with his keys and not meeting her gaze. "Sure, but can it wait until later? I'm on my way to meet my parents for church."

Anita blinked. She hadn't expected that. She could count the number of times she'd been to church on one hand, and most of those were for weddings or funerals. "Church?" she repeated, trying to mask her discomfort.

"Yes, church," Logan said with a small smile. "Why don't you come with me? We can talk on the way and afterward."

Anita hesitated. The idea of going to church made her uneasy, but she was determined to get her questions answered. "Alright," she agreed. "I'll come."

Logan stifled a yawn. "Great. Let's go."

They climbed into his pickup, and as they drove toward town, Anita turned to him, her mind racing with questions. "Did you move those dolls out of the attic to scare me?" she asked, her voice tense.

Logan frowned, genuinely puzzled. "Dolls? The ones from the trunk with the hinges I replaced?"

"Yes," Anita pressed. "They were moved all over the house and arranged in creepy ways like someone was trying to scare the crap out of me. And it worked."

Logan shook his head. "I swear I wouldn't do that kind of thing. Anita, that sounds awful. "

"What about Vanessa? Did you tell her about the dolls?"

"No, I haven't mentioned the dolls to anyone. And why would Vanessa do something like that?"

Anita's frustration bubbled to the surface. "She's been scheming against me, threatening me, delaying my access to the Legacy accounts, intimidating the local contractors. And that horrifying trick with the dolls. It has to stop."

Logan sighed, scrubbing a hand over his face and through his hair. "Anita, I knew about the contractors. I heard it from one over in Marionville, and I've brought it to Charlton and Dodd's attention. But I had no idea Vanessa might be pulling other crap like that."

Anita studied his face, looking for any sign of deception, but he seemed sincere. "What about your meeting with her? I saw you with her yesterday at the cafe."

Logan frowned, his expression troubled. "Vanessa was trying to convince me of some ridiculous story. She wants to interfere with my life, and I told her I wanted nothing to do with her anymore. I promise you, Anita, there's nothing going on between us. She and I are done."

Anita felt a mix of relief and uncertainty. She wanted to believe him, but there was still a nagging doubt in her mind. She felt there was something Logan was holding back. Before she could say anything else, they arrived at the church. It was a beautiful stone building with intricate, bright stained glass windows that gleamed in the morning sunlight.

Logan's parents were waiting outside, and they greeted Anita warmly. She was glad she had opted for a sundress this morning with a warm sweater buttoned overtop. Though nervousness clawed at her stomach as they made their way inside, Logan's reassuring presence beside her helped to calm her nerves. The Emmerichs walked to a pew near the front where Susan, her husband Brad, and Grace were already sitting. Anita glanced around, taking in the serene atmosphere.

The service began, and Anita was surprised to find herself enjoying it. The congregation was friendly and welcoming, and the church itself was stunning. The stained glass windows cast colorful patterns of light across the pews, and the priest's low, quiet voice was soothing. When the homily began, Anita found herself drawn into his words. His message was one of hope and kindness, and there was a sincerity in his voice that resonated with her. She glanced at Logan, who was listening intently, and she felt a warmth spread through her.

Anita felt a sense of peace. The questions that had plagued her seemed to fade away, replaced by a quiet contentment. As the priest continued his homily, she closed her eyes for a moment, letting his words wash over her. She wasn't sure what the future held, but for now, she felt a renewed sense of hope and possibility.

Anita opened her eyes as the priest stopped speaking and moved to sit in his chair. The deep tones of an organ began to fill the sanctuary. Anita sighed and was surprised to see her breath puff in a cloudy pocket of steam as the air chilled around her. The organ ground to a halt, and everyone and everything around her froze.

The world darkened and the people in the pews faded until they were there but weren't at the same time, degrading to shimmering mists that only formed when the light, fading fast through the windows, hit them just right. A younger version of the priest stood from his chair beside the altar and moved forward. The door of the sanctuary flung open wide, revealing night outside, and Anita watched a young woman in a 1940s dress with a matching clutch run up the center aisle. The hard heels of her shoes beat against the stone floor.

Her entry drew the attention of the young priest as well. He met the woman, who moved with a familiar stride Anita thought.

"Father, please!" the woman gasped. "Please you have to stop them. They're at it again." She fell to her knees on the steps to the chancel.

The priest looked concerned, but slightly irritated as well, Anita thought.

"Melusine," he said calmly, "We've been through this before. These visions that plague you are not real. Your brother and sister-in-law are good people. They—"

Melusine sobbed at his feet. "No! It's the widow Carson and her son this time. They are the pawns the Covenant demands. You have to help me stop them!"

The priest knelt next to Melusine, patting her head. "I wonder if my lack of action on this has been detrimental to you. I thought allowing you to confess your demons would be enough to open them to the action of prayer and the Almighty."

Melusine looked up at him sharply. "*My* demons?"

The priest was no longer listening to her. He took her upper arm firmly in his grasp. "Come now. Let's find a comfortable place for you to rest, and we'll get this whole matter settled."

Melusine allowed herself to be drawn to her feet, but she resisted his pull away from the railing. "How are you planning to settle it?"

"Now don't you worry. I'm sure Mr. and Mrs. Harrow will choose an institution with the best psychiatrists and treatments available."

Melusine attempted to wrench her arm from his grasp. "I am not crazy, Father. I am telling you the truth. The widow Carson and her little boy are in grave danger. We need to act now! Before the game steals their lives."

"We've been through this, Melusine. It is not possible to steal life from someone and give it to another. Not even God himself—Oof!"

Melusine kicked the priest in the shin, and he released his grip on her. She backed away quickly, out of his reach. "Father, please. I know of no one else who could fight the evil behind this. You said you believed me!

I'm begging you one last time."

He lunged for her, and she dodged him. He landed face first into the side of a pew, and Melusine turned for the door. She sprinted away as quickly as she had come.

The strains of the organ returning to life made Anita jump in her seat. Logan gave her a glance and squeezed her hand. Anita looked frantically around, rubbing her eyes. She was back in the Sunday morning service, and the priest was back to his elderly self. He stood and with his hands, bid the congregation to stand as well. Dazedly, Anita rose. Melusine's ghost or memory was gone as quickly as it had come. Anita's heart raced in her chest and she gripped the back of the pew in front of her with white knuckles.

What had it all meant? Why had she been the one chosen to see the exchange between Melusine and the priest years ago? Obviously, Melusine had found no assistance. No one to help her fight against whatever it was that plagued her and the Hall. She had come to the church with high hopes. What had she expected the priest to do? An intervention with her brother and sister-in-law? An exorcism?

Anita finished the service in contemplative silence, only half listening and going through the motions. She had to find out more about Melusine, what exactly she had tried to fight back against, and if she had ever succeeded.

After the service, the priest stood on the steps, greeting the parishioners as they exited. "Good morning, Martha. George." The elderly, white haired man shook their hands. "Good to see you, Logan. And who might this be?"

"Anita Miran. Anita, this is Father Shane Dougherty." Logan introduced them.

"Uncle Logan, look at this!" Grace tugged Logan away from Anita's side and down the steps.

Anita reached out and shook the priest's proffered hand. As she did so, she felt a supernatural surge of anger. "I've inherited Harrow Hall," Anita said.

"Is that so? Well, congratulations and welcome to our little community. Your predecessors certainly were great supporters of Our Lady of the Light. As a matter of fact, we wouldn't have our fine facility here if it wasn't for their generosity."

Anita held tight to his hand. "You have a long history in Harrowsburg, Father Shane."

"Yes, sixty-three years this November." His gaze wandered nervously as he smiled at the last few passing parishioners, and Anita refused to let go of his hand.

"Do you remember Melusine Harrow?"

Father Shane's gaze snapped back to hers, and she thought he paled a little. "That's an unusual name. Hmm…let me think."

Anita felt unnatural rage surging through her, and she cocked her head to one side, leaning forward, her voice dropping with an icy bite. "She begged you for help, Father. You were her last hope, and instead of giving her what she needed, you wanted to have her committed. Is that because you were afraid the 'generosity' would dry up?"

The priest stepped backwards and wrenched his grasp from Anita's. With the loss of touch, she felt the rage drain from her body, leaving her unsteady, her head spinning. She pressed a palm to her temple.

Logan climbed back up the stairs, his smile fading as he took in the looks on Anita and the priest's faces.

"I'm sorry. I don't know what came over me." Anita leaned against the cool stone of the building.

"Yes, well, more things in heaven and earth, as they say." The priest pushed passed her and reentered the church.

"That's Shakespeare, not God," Anita mumbled as her head spun. "Oh boy."

Logan caught her as her knees buckled. "What happened?" he asked as he steadied her.

"I just need to sit down, I think."

He helped her down the steps, and they made their way over to a stone bench on the path.

"I had the strangest vision…or memory…or something in the church during the service. Melusine Harrow was begging Father Shane for help—years and years ago when he was a young man."

"Help for what?"

She looked pleadingly into Logan's eyes. "I think she wanted to stop the Harrows from doing what I've seen in my nightmares."

"Did he help her?"

Anita shook her head. "He thought she was crazy and wanted to help her brother and sister-in-law commit her to a mental institution."

Susan and Grace approached the bench. "Let's go, Uncle Logan!"

"All set?" Susan asked.

"No, uh…" Logan looked to Anita. "Susan and Brad are having their end of summer party this afternoon. It's kind of become a yearly thing. Would you come with me? If you're feeling up to it?"

Anita felt an urge to accompany Logan, to put herself far away from the strange anger that had infused her earlier and the odd occurrences at the Hall. She still wasn't fully convinced that Vanessa would have had the means or opportunity to create the doll trick. If it hadn't been her, and Anita was sure now that it was not Logan, what was the explanation? Or was there a good explanation? Maybe it was the same forces that had given her witness Melusine's memory with the priest and that had brought her and Logan together that first night. She had to put more of the pieces together.

"I saw online that the historical society was open for a couple of hours on Sundays. I'd like to see what more I can find out about Melusine and the rest of the Harrows."

Logan nodded. "I could come with you. That's over in Marionville."

"I don't want to take you away from your family." She cast an anxious glance at Susan and Grace. Logan definitely seemed torn, and that was the last position Anita wanted to put him in. "Why don't I go by myself, and then as soon as the historical society building closes, I will come over to Susan and Brad's."

Logan looked unsure. He tossed a glance at the church, and Anita felt sure he was attempting to decide if she was safe from the strange power that had connected with her there. She was wondering the same thing, but to Logan, she said quietly, "Look, I'm fine now. No need to worry about me. Go with your family, and I promise I'll be there soon."

"Okay but keep me updated." They stood from the bench. "I'll give you a ride back to your car."

On the ride back to Logan's house, Anita explained everything she could remember from the vision in the church. He asked questions but never made her feel crazy, and for that she was extremely grateful. She couldn't quite admit how real everything felt to her.

"So, this game Melusine told Father Shane about was some way to steal life from people?"

"That's the impression I got. And it does fit with my nightmares. The people who seem to be the ones getting hurt are never the Harrows. They're the ones rolling the dice—or the men are, at least. The women seem to be in some kind of command position."

Logan parked next to Anita's car and pulled out his phone. "I'm texting you the address for Brad and Susan's. Promise me you'll call me when you leave Marionville."

"Yes, I will."

He set his phone down on the dash and turned toward her, catching her hand. "Anita this is getting stranger and stranger. I don't really want to believe in this supernatural covenant or demons or whatever seems to be going on with the Harrow history, but I don't think we can deny any longer that there's some kind of power underneath all this."

"More things in heaven and earth, like the priest said."

"Yes, and more dangerous things, I think. Maybe you shouldn't be at the Hall alone."

"I won't be for much longer. Doreen flies in at the end of the week."

"Until then, would you just maybe consider staying here with me instead? I don't want to put you in an uncomfortable spot, but I'm worried that, um—"

Anita watched a blush climb his neck.

"—I just want you to be safe is all. Or I could stay there with you. In one of the guest rooms." He scrubbed a hand through his hair.

She felt a surge of joy. He really was worried about her, but he was doing his best not to push the boundary they'd placed. That had been the reason for his reticence lately. She, on the other hand, suddenly felt ready to shatter that damn boundary.

"Well, just how close would you say we need to be to keep me safe?" She asked, her tone slightly flirtatious. She slid a couple inches over on the bench seat. "Like this maybe?"

His brows rose with surprise, and a grin twitched at the corners of his mouth.

"Or this?" She slid closer until her left foot rested against the shifter case on the floor.

"Not quite close enough," Logan said, and he edged over toward her.

"Ah," she said. "I think I understand now." She eased herself toward him, twisting her torso against his and slid her free hand across his chest. "Yes, this does feel safer. Definitely."

He drew a deep breath. "Are you sure?" His breath was husky.

She nodded, gazing into his eyes. "How about you?"

His answer was in the press of his lips against hers, and the firm grasp of his arms around her body. She sighed as he trailed his kisses over her jaw and down her neck. She ran her fingers through his hair. Logan's phone rang, and she pulled away slightly.

"Nope." He caught her hips and hooked a hand around the back of her thigh, lifting her onto his lap, facing him. She laughed, and he continued kissing her. The phone kept ringing. She glanced over her shoulder and caught sight of Susan's name on the caller ID. "It's your sister." As soon as the ringing ended, two texts came through.

Anita adjusted and bumped the small of her back against the steering wheel. "Oof." Logan moved and his elbow hit the horn. She laughed again. "I don't think this is going work right now."

Logan's phone started ringing again.

He buried his forehead against her collarbone with a heavy sigh. She reached behind her to the dash and grabbed his phone. He answered it.

"Hello."

Anita eased back over to the middle of the bench seat.

"Yes, I can...Okay, I'll tell her...No...Twenty minutes...Okay. Bye." He jabbed the end call button. "She desperately needs ice. Brad's handling a grill emergency. And she wanted me to tell you to bring a swimsuit."

Anita perked up. "They have a pool?"

"Yes, and we usually play water volleyball."

"My suits are still in California," she said with disappointment. She sincerely missed the water. "But maybe I can find somewhere open in Harrowsburg or Marionville to get one."

Logan scrunched his face. "Doubtful on a Sunday."

"Well, I can help Brad with the grilling then. I've been known to wield a mean set of tongs." Anita slid to the passenger door and opened it.

Logan laughed as he got out of the pickup as well. "I'll bet."

She dug in her purse and came up with her keys.

He eased her back against her car, hands firmly on her hips.

"Logan," she murmured as he kissed her some more with a smile. He ignored her, and she shivered at the full press of his body against hers. "You told your sister 20 minutes," she said.

He sighed and eased back, but still held her tightly. "Are you sure you have to go to Marionville today?"

She nodded. "I really feel like I should for some reason."

"Okay."

His last kiss sincerely made her want to change her mind. He paused for a moment, a smug look on his face as if he knew it. She playfully punched his arm. "Ice," she said breathlessly. "Your sister is desperate for ice."

He finally released her. "That may be my only solution for the moment, too," he grumbled with a grin. She laughed, and he opened her car door.

"Call me," he insisted.

She nodded, and he closed her door, sauntering back to his pickup. With a wave, she drove away. Butterflies tickled her stomach, high on hope and happiness that she had feared she might never feel again.

***

Much of the local history that Anita had perused at the library had been published by the area historical society. The group was headquartered two towns over, about a 45-minute drive and housed in a small, unassuming building near the center of Marionville. Anita entered, greeted by the musty scent of old books and documents. An elderly woman behind the front desk looked up and smiled.

"Good afternoon. How can I help you?" she asked.

"I'm looking for information about Harrow Hall and the Harrow family," Anita said. "Anything you have would be helpful."

The woman's smile faded slightly. "Harrow Hall, you say? That place has quite a history. Follow me."

She led Anita to a back room filled with filing cabinets and shelves lined with binders. "We have a lot of records here. Feel free to take your time. If you have any questions, just let me know."

Anita thanked her and began to sift through the documents. She found old photographs, newspaper clippings, and personal letters, all painting a picture of the Harrow family's influence and notoriety. There were mentions of Oswald and Victoria Harrow, their descendants, and the various enterprises that had contributed to the family's wealth—and infamy.

As she delved deeper, Anita stumbled upon a journal that belonged to Melusine Harrow. It was filled with entries that ranged from mundane daily activities to cryptic references about the house and its secrets. One passage in particular caught her eye. "Look at this," she muttered to herself, holding the book close so she could read the entry clearly.

"June 12, 1932—The dolls are restless tonight. I can hear them moving, whispering secrets I can barely understand. There is power in them, a connection to something ancient and unfathomable. I fear what they might do, what they might reveal."

Anita's heart raced as she read the words. The dolls, the strange occurrences—they were not new. Melusine had experienced them too. She flipped the page and continued reading, hoping to find more clues.

"August 4, 1933—The bagpipes played again last night. The music is haunting, calling from the past. There is a spirit in this house that seeks to communicate through these objects."

Anita felt a chill run down her spine. The nightmares, the dolls, the music—it was all connected. She was lost in a world of dusty tomes and yellowed photographs spread out before her on the long, wooden table of the local historical society. She searched for any documents that might shed more light on the dark past of Harrow Hall, her hands carefully turning each delicate page. The musty smell of aged paper filled the air, mingling with the scent of old wood that creaked softly underfoot.

As she sifted through another box of pictures, a voice startled her from her concentration. "I hear that you are our new Mrs. Harrow."

Anita whirled around, slightly taken aback, to see an elderly man with a kind face and bright, curious eyes. He leaned on a wooden cane and regarded her with a warm smile that crinkled the corners of his eyes.

"Well, I inherited and live at the Hall, but you don't have to call me that. I'm Anita," she replied, extending her hand in greeting.

The man shook her hand, his grip firm despite his age. "Samuel Prendergast," he introduced himself. "I've lived here all my life. Never a dull moment with the Harrows."

Anita chuckled softly, brushing a strand of hair from her face. "No, certainly not dull," she agreed.

"I'm here trying to piece together some of the history," she explained.

"Ah, a noble endeavor," Samuel nodded sagely. "That place has a lot of history, much of it steeped in shadow. Not all are brave enough to stir those echoes."

They shared a moment of understanding, the weight of the Hall's history hanging between them. Samuel's expression changed, and he leaned in slightly.

"You know, I have something that might interest you. When I was younger, I corresponded with one of the Harrows—Melusine. She was... different from the rest, to say the least. We were quite close." His eyes clouded with memories. "I've kept a collection of her letters. Never felt quite right about donating them to the historical society. They're quite personal, you see."

Anita's interest piqued immediately. "Melusine's letters?" she repeated, her pulse quickening with excitement. "I've read about her in the family records. She seemed like a remarkable woman."

"She was," Samuel confirmed with a nod. "And misunderstood, I dare say. Those letters... they shed a different light on the Harrow family and the Hall. I think they could offer you some unique insights for your research."

The prospect of gaining a new perspective on the enigmatic Melusine was intriguing. Anita knew any information could be crucial in unraveling the Hall's mysteries. "I would very much like to see them, Mr. Prendergast," she said earnestly.

Samuel's face brightened. "Then it's settled. Why don't you come over to my house tomorrow? I'll have the letters ready for you to look through."

"Thank you, that would be wonderful," Anita responded, her mind already racing with the possibilities of what the letters could reveal.

They exchanged a few more pleasantries and he explained how to get to his house. Then Anita watched as Samuel slowly walked away, his cane tapping rhythmically on the floor. She turned back to her research, thoughts now buzzing with anticipation for tomorrow's meeting. The possibility of unlocking more secrets of Harrow Hall through Melusine's own words was an unexpected and thrilling prospect.

***

Anita stepped out of the historical society building in Marionville. She clutched a stack of photocopies to her chest. Melusine's diary entries had painted vivid pictures of the past, unveiling secrets and stories that had captivated Anita. Even more thrilling was the appointment she had set up with Mr. Samuel to read his letters, promising even deeper insights into the historical tapestry she was unraveling.

The sun was high in the sky, casting a clean warmth over the quaint streets of Marionville. As Anita walked to her car, her thoughts drifted to Logan. She couldn't help but smile, thinking about the party at his sister Susan's place. The idea of meeting Logan there filled her with a mix of anticipation and warmth.

Her car was parked just down the street. She walked briskly, eager to share her excitement with Logan. Reaching her car, she pulled out her keys and her phone simultaneously, intending to call Logan and tell him she was on her way. But in her excitement, she fumbled, dropping the keys. The phone slipped from her grasp too, bouncing once on the pavement.

"Great," she muttered, crouching down to retrieve them. She was picked up her phone, noticing the connected call behind the cracked screen, when she heard the unmistakable roar of an engine approaching at high speed.

Her heart leaped into her throat as she looked up. A white SUV with tinted windows was barreling toward her. Panic surged through her as the SUV showed no signs of slowing down. She froze for a split second, her mind racing to process what was happening.

Anita dropped everything and dove to the side, her body hitting the pavement hard. She winced as her elbow scraped against the rough ground, but adrenaline drowned out the pain. The SUV's tires screeched as the driver slammed on the brakes, the vehicle swerving violently at the last moment. The front bumper missed her car by inches, narrowly avoiding a collision.

Anita lay there for a moment as the photocopies skittered across the pavement in the breeze, her breath coming in ragged gasps. The SUV's engine revved, and then it sped off, disappearing down the street. Trembling, she pushed herself up to a sitting position and slid her phone with a splintered screen across the blacktop, praying it still worked.

She lifted it up to her ear.

"Anita!"

"Logan," she said, her voice still shaking.

"What happened?" Logan's voice was sharp with alarm. "Are you okay? Where are you?"

"I'm at the historical society building," Anita managed to say, looking around as if the SUV might suddenly reappear. "I was just about to call you when I think..." she paused, looking up and down the empty street. "...I think someone tried to run me over."

"Stay there," Logan instructed. "I'm coming to get you. Get in your car and lock your door."

Anita took a deep breath, trying to calm her racing heart. "Logan, I'm okay," she said, her voice steadying. "I just got scraped up a bit. Maybe it was just a reckless driver."

"Are you sure?" Logan sounded doubtful.

"It didn't feel random," Anita admitted, glancing down the empty street. "But I think I'll be alright to drive to your sister's house. I'll be careful."

"Anita, I don't like this," Logan protested.

"I know, but I don't want to make a big deal out of this if it's nothing," she replied, trying to sound more confident than she felt. "I'll drive slowly and keep an eye out. I'll see you at Susan's."

Logan hesitated, but finally sighed. "Please be careful."

"I will," Anita promised. "Give me some easy directions. My screen is all shattered, and I don't know if I'll be able to get my phone to work again."

Logan talked her through the route to Walnut Grove, another small town near Harrowsburg. Luckily there weren't many turns, and the drive should only take about thirty minutes. Logan insisted that if thirty-one passed, he was coming to look for her.

She took a moment to collect herself. Her hands were still trembling as she climbed into her car, but she forced herself to take deep, steady breaths. She couldn't shake the feeling that the incident was more than just a coincidence, but she pushed that thought aside for now. The important thing was to get to Logan and his family safely.

Anita started the engine and pulled out slowly, her eyes scanning the road for any sign of the SUV. The road to Walnut Grove seemed to stretch out endlessly as she drove more cautiously than ever before. Every car that approached made her heart skip a beat, but none of them matched the white, tinted-window SUV that had almost run her down.

She checked her mirrors constantly, half-expecting the SUV to reappear. The closer she got to Walnut Grove, the more her nerves began to settle. The beautiful scenery of the small town brought a sense of comfort, and she felt a little safer knowing she was nearing Logan's sister's house.

When she finally turned onto Susan's street at the far edge of town, she spotted Logan waiting outside, his expression a mix of relief and concern. He waved as she pulled into an enormous half-moon driveway, packed with parked cars, and she felt a rush of gratitude seeing him there.

Logan was at her door immediately, helping her out of the car. "Are you really okay?" he asked, his eyes scanning her for any signs of injury.

"I'm fine," Anita assured him, showing him her scraped elbow. "Just a little scrape. The driver swerved at the last moment."

Logan looked unconvinced but didn't press further. "Come on, let's get you inside."

They walked together to the front door, where Susan greeted them warmly. "Anita! I'm so glad you could make it. Come in, come in."

Anita smiled, appreciating the warmth and normalcy of Susan's welcome. Inside, the house was filled with laughter and friends and family having fun. It was exactly what she needed to calm her nerves.

Logan stayed close to her, his presence a steadying force. As they mingled with people, Anita felt her anxiety begin to fade. She still couldn't shake the feeling that the SUV incident was more than just bad luck, but for now, she focused on enjoying the afternoon with Logan and the people who mattered to him.

Chapter Ten

Anita sat at the patio table, savoring the last bites of her burger and salad. The warm air was filled with the sound of laughter and the splashes from the pool where kids and adults were enjoying the party. She looked around, feeling a sense of belonging that had been rare for her lately. Logan's family so far had welcomed her with open arms, and she appreciated every moment of it.

Susan approached her with a bright smile. "Hey, Anita! We're about to start a game of water volleyball. Do you want to join in?"

Anita grinned. "I'd love to, but I didn't bring a suit to Connecticut. I looked for somewhere to buy one before I went to Marionville, but I couldn't find anywhere that was open."

Susan waved her hand dismissively. "No problem at all! I have plenty of swimsuits you can borrow. Come on, I'll help you pick one."

Anita followed Susan inside the house. As they walked to the bedroom, Susan started chatting animatedly. "So, how are you liking the party? Have you had a chance to talk to everyone?"

"It's been great," Anita replied. "Everyone is so friendly and welcoming."

"Our two oldest sisters should be here shortly. Then you'll have met everyone except our other brother, Gary. He couldn't come this year." Susan opened a drawer and pulled out a couple of swimsuits, handing them to Anita. "Here, try these on. I think they'll fit you just fine."

Anita took the swimsuits and headed to the en suite bathroom to change. When she came back out, wearing a cute two-piece, she felt a bit self-conscious and grabbed a pair of cut-off shorts that Susan had set out as well.

Susan was sitting on the bed, looking thoughtful. "You know, I never really got back down to size after Grace was born," she said, patting her pregnant belly. "Now I really wonder how I'll do it. I kept all my old clothes, but I feel like the size of a hot air balloon now."

Anita smiled warmly. "You look beautiful, Susan. I don't know how you handle Grace's energy with another baby on the way. You're amazing."

Susan's face lit up with gratitude. "Thank you, Anita." She paused, then took a deep breath. "I have a secret I haven't told Brad yet." She paused, beaming. "We're having twins."

Anita's eyes widened in surprise and delight. "Twins?!" she whisper-squealed. "That's incredible! Congratulations!"

Susan laughed softly. "I know, right? I just had to test out the words aloud on someone. I still can't believe it myself. Brad is going to freak out."

They hugged, and Anita promised to keep the secret. Susan positively glowed. "Thanks, Anita. Now let's get out there and have some fun."

They returned to the pool area, and Anita couldn't help but notice Logan. He was shirtless, wearing swim trunks, and the sight of him made her heart skip a beat. He looked up, saw her, and his face broke into a smile.

Logan walked over to her, his eyes twinkling with mischief. "Ready for some volleyball?" he asked, and before she could respond, he swept her off her feet, pretending to toss her into the pool.

Anita shrieked and laughed, her arms clinging to his neck. "Logan, put me down!"

Logan chuckled and set her down gently on the ground, still dry. Just as he did, Brad and another man exchanged glances and, with a running start, shoved Logan into the pool. Logan hit the water with a splash, and everyone burst into laughter.

Anita, still laughing, jumped into the pool to join the others. The volleyball game was a blast, with two couples on each side. Logan and Anita's team played with great teamwork and enthusiasm, ultimately winning the game.

As they climbed out of the pool, Anita reached for a towel and began to dry off. Logan came over, two women in tow. "Anita, I'd like you to meet my older sisters, Claire and Heather."

The women smiled politely, but there was a distinct lack of warmth compared to Susan and their mother. They were well dressed, Claire in a light green romper and Heather in a flowing sundress the color of her name. Both women wore sunhats to match their outfits. Anita felt a bit self-conscious in her bikini top, especially when Logan leaned in and gave her a searing kiss before heading off to help scoop ice cream for the kids.

The sisters seemed to pounce the moment Logan walked away. "So, Anita," Claire began, her tone curious but with an edge. "How long have you been living at Harrow Hall?"

"Just a few weeks," Anita replied, holding her towel tighter around herself.

"And, goodness, California, you're so far from home." Claire continued.

"And the truth about Victor Harrow." Heather clicked her tongue. "All of the Harrowsburg area has just been abuzz."

"Abuzz." Claire agreed.

Anita nodded, wondering if there would be more questions or if they already thought they knew everything about her.

"And that's how long exactly? Since Victor's unfortunate…death?" Heather added, her gaze stabbing.

"Seven months?" Claire peered just as piercingly.

Anita felt the weight of their judgment. "Eight, almost nine."

Claire exchanged a glance with Heather. "It must be quite the adjustment, moving into such an exquisite place after such a *short* time."

Anita felt a flush of discomfort. "It's been an adjustment, but Logan has been wonderful," she said, trying to keep her tone light.

"Even through his sudden breakup with Vanessa," Heather remarked casually, though her eyes were sharp.

The sisters continued to pepper her with questions that weren't really questions, each comment more invasive than the last. Anita felt her anxiety rising and clutched the towel tighter. Finally, she excused herself, seeking refuge with Grace, who was happily eating an ice cream sundae at a nearby table with half a dozen other children and playing a board game.

Grace looked up and grinned. "Logan makes the best sundaes." she said, her face smeared with chocolate sauce.

Anita smiled, her tension easing.

A little girl sitting next to Grace, about four years old, sighed dreamily. "I want to marry Logan when I grow up."

An older boy rolled his eyes. "You can't. He's Mom's cousin."

The little girl was undeterred. "It doesn't matter. He's a prince, and

I'm a princess, and it always works out in the end."

Anita couldn't help but laugh, feeling the innocence and charm of the children wash over her. She glanced over at Logan, who was busy making sundaes for the kids. He caught her eye and smiled, and she felt a warm glow in her chest.

As she listened to the children debate the logistics of fairy tale marriages, Anita decided she preferred their company to the grilling she'd received from Logan's older sisters. Here, with the kids, everything was simple and straightforward. The world of adults, with its complexities and judgments, seemed far less appealing.

When Logan finally joined her, he sat down next to her with a smile, presenting a huge sundae loaded with chocolate sauce, sprinkles, nuts, and maraschino cherries. Two spoons stuck out of it. "You survived my sisters, I see," he said, his tone light but his eyes concerned.

"Barely," Anita replied with a chuckle. "I think I prefer the kids' company. They have a way of keeping things uncomplicated."

Logan handed her one of the spoons and dug in with the other. Anita caught sight of Claire and Heather sitting at a small table on the other side of the pool, watching them. Feeling petulant, Anita scooped a large spoonful of ice cream and popped it in her mouth. Their tongues started wagging, and Logan followed her gaze.

"They can be a bit much, but they mean well, most of the time, I think. And for what it's worth, I think you handled them perfectly."

Anita watched as Grace frowned at the board game on the table, her cousins winning yet another round with seemingly impossible luck. Her small hands clutched the dice, frustration evident in her eyes. Anita leaned over, a knowing smile playing on her lips. "Want to learn a little trick?" she whispered conspiratorially. Grace nodded eagerly, curiosity replacing her frustration. Anita took the dice and demonstrated how to roll them with a subtle flick of the wrist and a gentle release, ensuring they landed on specific numbers. Grace's eyes widened in amazement as she tried it herself, the dice obeying her newfound technique.

Logan, observing, chuckled softly. "That's quite the parlor trick you've got there, Anita," he said, a twinkle of amusement in his eyes. His tone was playful, but his interest was piqued by the seemingly magical control Anita had over the dice. He watched as Grace's confidence grew with each successful roll.

Anita smiled, her thoughts drifting to memories. "It's something Vance taught me," she explained, her voice tinged with a mix of nostalgia and affection. "He had a knack for these kinds of things—little tricks and skills that seemed like magic but were all about precision and practice." She glanced at Logan, her eyes reflecting the warmth of cherished memories. "He always said it wasn't about cheating, but about understanding the game better than anyone else. And sometimes, a little extra help doesn't hurt," she added with a wink, watching Grace's excitement as she finally started winning against her cousins.

***

The party at Susan and Brad's had begun to wind down, and the sun dipped lower in the sky, casting a soft orange glow over everything. Logan approached Anita, who was talking with some of the kids, her laughter mingling with theirs.

"Hey, Anita," Logan said, smiling. "Want to go for a walk down by the river?"

Anita's eyes lit up. "I'd love to," she replied, slipping her dress back on over her bikini. She hoped they might get to swim some more later. The idea of spending some quiet time with Logan, away from the crowd, was appealing.

They waved goodbye to Susan, promising to be back soon, and headed down a path that led to the river. As they walked, the sounds of the party grew fainter, replaced by the gentle rustling of leaves and the distant murmur of the river.

"Tell me more about what you found out today," Logan said, glancing at her with interest.

Anita smiled, feeling a familiar excitement bubbling up. "Well, I was reading Melusine's diary entries at the historical society. She was such a fascinating woman, and her writings are so vivid. I feel like I'm getting to know her personally."

Logan nodded, encouraging her to continue.

"And I met a man at the historical society named Samual Prendergast. He gave an invitation to read some personal letters he and Melusine wrote to each other," Anita continued. I think they're going to bring us closer to understanding the strange events that have been happening there."

Logan raised an eyebrow. "Strange events? Like the dolls?"

"Exactly," Anita said. "It's all connected somehow. Maybe these letters will give us some answers."

As they reached the riverbank, Logan took off his shirt and laid it down for Anita to sit on. He bent down, picked up a flat stone, and expertly skipped it across the water. The rock danced along the surface before sinking with a soft plunk.

"This river holds a lot of memories for me," Logan said, a nostalgic smile playing on his lips. "Susan and Brad's home used to be our grandparents' place. I spent countless hours here as a kid, swimming, fishing, just hanging out."

Anita watched him skip another stone, intrigued by the glimpse into his past. "It sounds wonderful. You must have so many stories."

Logan sat down next to her, his eyes sparkling with remembered adventures. "I do. We used to come here almost every weekend. It was our little escape from the world. My brother Gary used to bring his dates down here all the time, too."

Anita laughed, nudging him playfully. "And what about you? Did you bring your dates down here?"

Logan shook his head, a shy smile crossing his face. "No, I was always awkward and shy in school. I didn't have the confidence to bring girls here or anywhere really."

"I can't imagine you being shy." Anita teased. "I bet you were adorable."

Logan chuckled, his cheeks tinged with a faint blush. "I was a bit of a nerd, to be honest. Always with my nose in a book or working on some project."

"Well, I wasn't exactly Miss Perfect in school," Anita admitted. "I was the bad girl, the punk type. No one could tell me anything because I knew it all."

Logan grinned. "Really? You, a rebel? I would have loved to see that." He sat down beside her and gathered her back against his chest.

They laughed together, sharing stories of their teenage years, each revelation bringing them closer. Logan picked up another stone and tossed it into the river, watching the ripples spread.

"If I had known then what I know now," Logan mused. "High school would have been different."

Anita smiled, resting her head on his shoulder. "You mean you would have charmed all the girls with your smooth moves?"

Logan chuckled. "Maybe. But I've got you down here now, don't I?"

Anita turned her head to look at him, their faces inches apart. "Yes, you do," she said softly.

Their laughter faded into a comfortable silence as they looked into each other's eyes. Logan leaned in and kissed her gently, a kiss that was sweet and tender. They pulled back slightly, their foreheads touching.

"I think I like this spot," Anita whispered.

"Me too," Logan replied, his voice equally soft.

They spent the next few moments lost in each other, the world around them fading away. The gentle sounds of the river and the warmth of the setting sun created a perfect backdrop for their intimate interlude.

After a while, they lay back on the bank, watching the sky change colors. The river's surface reflected the hues of the sunset, and the air was filled with the gentle hum of nature.

"Do you ever think about what the future holds?" Anita asked, her voice dreamy.

"All the time," Logan replied. "Especially now. I wonder what kind of adventures we'll have together."

Anita smiled at his answer, but it faded. "You know, after Vance…well after he died, thoughts of the future just kind of stopped for me. It's only now that I'm kind of starting to realize there actually is a future."

Logan eased up on her elbows, and she craned her neck to catch his gaze. His eyes were serious but full of warmth. "Anita, I want you to know that I'm here for you. No matter what we find out about Harrow Hall, or what challenges we face, I'm by your side."

Anita felt a rush of emotion, her heart swelling with affection for this man who had become so important to her. "Thank you, Logan. That means more to me than you know."

They shared another kiss, deeper and more passionate this time, a promise of the bond they were forging together. The world seemed to stand still as they held each other, wrapped in the magic of the moment.

Sitting together on the bank of the river, the gentle murmur of the water provided a serene backdrop to their conversation. The sun was setting, casting a warm, golden glow over the landscape, but the tranquility of the scene was in stark contrast to a sudden tension that settled into Logan.

He shifted uncomfortably, his eyes fixed on the rippling water. "Anita, there's something I need to tell you," he began, his voice hesitant. "Vanessa has copies of some kind of journal from Hyacinth. It claims that I'm a Harrow."

Anita sat up and turned to him, her eyes wide with surprise and a growing sense of dread. "A Harrow? How are you related to Vance?"

Logan took a deep breath sitting up as well, still avoiding her gaze. "According to the information Vanessa has, I'm his half-brother."

The revelation hung in the air, heavy and disconcerting. Anita's mouth fell open in shock, her mind racing with implications. "You're Vance's brother? How is that possible? Why—Why did you wait to tell me? Is this what Vanessa was telling you at the diner?"

Logan finally looked at her, his expression a mix of anxiety and frustration. "Yes, it was. In all the years I worked for Hyacinth, she never once brought up this information. I don't understand why she kept it hidden, or why Vanessa has it now, or if it's even true."

Anita struggled to process the information, a knot of worry tightening in her stomach. "But if you're Vance's brother, then don't you have more right to the Hall than I do?"

Logan shook his head vehemently. "No, that's not why I'm telling you this. I don't want the Hall, and this isn't about some claim to power or money. I don't trust Vanessa, and I don't know what her motives are. I just needed you to know the line she's pushing because this affects us both."

Anita's mind raced, trying to piece together the implications of this revelation. "How would Vanessa have this journal? And why would she reveal it now?"

Logan's face darkened. "That's what worries me. Vanessa isn't someone who acts without reason. She must have a plan, and whatever it is, it's not going to be good for us."

Anita felt a chill run down her spine. The peaceful riverbank now seemed like an illusion, hiding the undercurrents of deceit and danger that threatened to engulf them. "What do we do now, Logan? How do we deal with this?"

Logan sighed, running a hand through his hair. "We need to find out more about this journal and what it says. We need to understand why Hyacinth kept this secret and what Vanessa intends to do with it. And most importantly, we need to stick together. Whatever happens, we face it as a team."

Anita nodded, though her mind was still reeling. The idea that Logan, the man she trusted and was really starting to feel for—she wasn't ready to actually consider love yet—was actually Vance's half-brother was almost too much to comprehend. But she knew Logan was right. They had to stay united if they were going to navigate the treacherous waters ahead.

***

Anita and Logan returned to the party, the weight of Vanessa's revelation hanging heavily over them. Anita's mind buzzed with conflicting emotions, and she struggled to maintain a semblance of normalcy. The joyful atmosphere of the gathering felt jarring and out of place given the bombshell that had just been dropped.

"Anita, are you okay?" Logan asked, his concern evident in his eyes.

"I just need a moment," she replied, forcing a weak smile. "I'm going to change out of this swimsuit and get my head together."

Logan nodded, watching her go with a mixture of worry and helplessness. Anita made her way inside, navigating through the throngs of guests until she reached Susan's room. She changed quickly, trying to calm her racing thoughts. As she walked back down the hallway, she heard voices from the kitchen.

"Honestly, I don't know what Logan sees in her." Claire's voice was sharp and disdainful.

"Me neither," Heather agreed. "She's bad news."

Anita froze, her heart sinking. She moved closer to the corner, listening intently despite the tightening knot in her stomach.

"Come on, you two," Susan's voice interjected, defensive. "Anita is good for Logan. She's strong and capable. You don't know her like I do."

"But we know enough," Claire shot back. "She's the type to always be surrounded by drama. Who knows what messes she'll drag Logan into."

Heather chimed in, "Exactly. She's a distraction. Logan needs stability, not someone with a haunted past who's going to play the sad little victim for who knows how long."

Anita's breath caught in her throat. She felt a sharp sting of hurt. She had gathered from the moment she met them that Claire and Heather didn't approve of her, but hearing their harsh words was more painful than she had imagined.

"Susan, you're too nice," Claire continued. "You always see the best in people, but sometimes you have to face reality. Anita is not good for Logan."

Susan sighed, her voice weary but resolute. "You're wrong. Logan loves her, and I believe she's coming to love him, too, in her own time.

That should be enough for you."

"Love isn't always enough," Heather said coldly. "Logan deserves better."

The words pierced Anita's heart. She backed away from the door, her vision blurring with unshed tears. She couldn't bear to hear any more. The judgment, the harshness, the complete lack of understanding from Logan's sisters was too much to take.

Slipping out of the hallway, Anita made her way quietly through the house, avoiding eye contact with anyone. She needed to leave, to get away from the hurtful words and the suffocating judgment. She needed to think, to process everything that had happened.

As she reached her car, fumbling with the keys, Logan appeared, jogging up to her. "Anita, wait!"

She turned to face him, unable to hide her distress. "Logan, I need to go. I can't stay here."

"What's wrong? What happened?" His voice was laced with concern, his eyes searching her face.

"I just—" Her voice trembled. She longed to tell him what she'd heard and receive the comfort she was certain he would offer. But she wasn't going to step between him and his family. "I just need some time to sort things out."

Logan took her hand, his grip firm and reassuring. "After that close call in Marionville this afternoon, I don't want you to be alone, especially at the Hall. What if something happens?"

"I'll be fine," she insisted, pulling her hand away gently. "I promise, if anything happens, I'll call you."

"How? Your phone is busted, and there is nowhere open to replace it today. Let me come with you. We can figure this out together."

She managed a faint smile, touched by his concern. "I need to do this alone. I need to clear my head."

He reluctantly nodded, his worry evident. "Okay, but please be careful. Come over to my place immediately if you need anything. It doesn't matter what. Anything at all."

"I know," she replied softly. "Thank you."

Anita got into her car and started the engine, giving Logan one last look before she drove away. She saw him standing there, his expression a mix of worry and helplessness, and her heart ached. But she knew she needed this time to herself, to process everything and figure out her next steps.

The drive to the Hall was a blur. Anita's mind raced with the events of the evening. Vanessa's revelation, Logan's sisters' harsh words, and the implications of it all swirled in her head like a storm. By the time she reached the Hall, she was emotionally exhausted.

She needed rest. The emotional toll of the evening had left her drained. As she climbed the stairs to her bedroom, she felt a sense of calm settling over her. She would face the challenges ahead, but she would do so on her own terms.

***

Anita found herself in one of the grand, opulent rooms downstairs, the walls lined with ancient books and artifacts. The room held both the terror of her previous nightmares and the wonder of her first amazing encounter with Logan. The feelings fought, and she felt that at any moment one would have to win out.

A woman stood before her, elegant and imposing, with a regal bearing and piercing eyes. Anita recognized her immediately: Victoria Harrow. Her ghostly visage flickered through the years of her life, presenting the woman through all her ages like the choppy flow of a silent movie on the silver screen.

"Welcome, Anita," Victoria said, her voice smooth and commanding despite her appearance. "You are a true Mrs. Harrow. Widow of one and the lover of another."

Anita felt a strange mix of fear and fascination. "Why am I here?" she asked, her voice echoing in the vast room.

Victoria smiled, a cold, calculating smile. "I have been watching you. You possess a strength and determination that is rare. You have the potential for unimaginable power. Power that only I've been able to yield in the history of the Harrows."

Anita felt a shiver run down her spine. "What kind of power?"

"The power to shape your destiny, to bend others to your will," Victoria replied. "All you need to do is bring those who trouble you to the Hall, and I will show you how to deal with them with no consequences. And in return, you will receive a boon from the Harrow."

Anita felt a strange compulsion to agree, the promise of power and retribution intoxicating. She was tired of being on the bottom, tired of being judged and played. "What do I have to do?" she asked, her voice barely a whisper.

"Simply bring them here," Victoria said, her eyes gleaming with an almost predatory light. *"I will take care of the rest."*

In the dream, Anita reached for her cell beside her, Vanessa's image clear in her mind. But just as she was about to wake the phone, the dream began to fade, and she woke with a start, moonlight still filtering through her bedroom window.

Anita sat up, her heart pounding. The dream had felt so real, so vivid. She looked at her phone's shattered screen, half-expecting to see a call log or texts from last night, but there was nothing. Had she really contacted Vanessa, or was it just the influence of the dream?

Shaking off the remnants of sleep, Anita made her way to the kitchen before dawn and brewed a strong pot of coffee. She sat at the table, her mind still buzzing with the details of the dream. The promise of power, the offer from Victoria… it all seemed too surreal, and yet, she couldn't shake the feeling that there was truth to it, just like there was to all the clues of the Harrows' history.

And what of Victoria Harrow's confirmation of Logan's parentage? Hadn't Anita, from their first meeting in the diner, noted Logan's similarities to Vance?

As she sipped her coffee, Anita tried to decide what her next steps should be. She knew she couldn't ignore the dream. The offer of power was a tangible draw that she attempted to set aside, but it kept nipping at her. She knew that she needed to tread carefully. The stakes were high, and one wrong move could have disastrous consequences.

Chapter Eleven

The pale light of dawn filtered through the lace curtains of the Hall's kitchen. Anita cranked open one of the tall windows and was greeted with cool, fresh air, filled with the promise of a respite from the oppressive Hall spirits and gloom. She dressed quickly, laced up the boots Logan had given her, and slipped out the front door. The estate grounds, shrouded in mist, called to her with a whispering allure.

She wandered aimlessly at first, letting her feet guide her along the winding paths. The dew-laden grass kissed her boots as she walked, the autumn earth beneath her soft and yielding. The trees, ancient sentinels, stood tall and proud, their branches intertwining overhead to form a natural canopy. Birds began their morning chorus, their melodies weaving through the leaves in a symphony of nature.

As Anita meandered, she came upon a path she had not noticed before, partially hidden by overgrown vines and wildflowers. Intrigued, she pushed aside the foliage and stepped onto the narrow trail. It twisted and turned, leading her deeper into the heart of the estate. The further she went, the more the air seemed to thicken with an almost tangible sense of history.

Suddenly she realized she stood on the path from her dream where Melusine had pulled her aside toward the orchard. She could barely make out the sharp angles of an iron fence ahead. The path eventually opened up to a clearing, and Anita found herself standing before a gate, its once ornate design now rusted and tangled with ivy. She pushed it open, its hinges groaning in protest, and she stepped inside. Before her lay the Harrow family cemetery, a place both beautiful and haunting.

The space was bathed in the soft light of dawn, casting long shadows that danced among the headstones. Each monument was unique, crafted with a level of artistry that spoke of a bygone era. Marble angels stood watch over the graves, wings drooping, their expressions haunting and sorrowful. Moss and lichens clung to the stones, adding a touch of wildness to the otherwise orderly rows.

Anita walked among the graves, her fingers brushing against cool stone as she read the epitaphs. Each one told a story, a glimpse into the lives of those who had once walked the same paths she now explored. There were headstones adorned with intricate carvings of flowers and vines and weeping willows.

One headstone caught her eye, its surface covered in a delicate pattern of roses. She knelt to read the inscription:

**Charles Harrow
Beloved husband and father. Rest in eternal peace.
1897-1952

Beside Charles' grave was another, smaller and more modest. The name on the stone was almost obscured by time, but Anita could just make out the inscription:

Rose Harrow
Beloved wife and mother.
1903

There was no death date.

Anita frowned and moved to the next grave. It was the same: a man's name, complete with birth and death dates, and beside it, a woman's name with only a birth date. She continued down the row, and each pair of stones told the same story. The men's graves were complete, but the women's were eerily unfinished.

She wandered deeper into the cemetery, drawn by a sense of curiosity and unease. The older graves were even more elaborate, with grand obelisks and statues of mourning figures. One particularly striking monument featured a woman, her face veiled and hands cupped and outstretched. Lichens covered large spots of the statue including obscuring what the woman held in her hands. Anita gently picked away enough to realize the woman was holding a likeness of the dice from her nightmares.

The stone was inscribed with the name:

Victoria Harrow
Beloved daughter, sister, and mother.
1767

Again, no death date.

Anita touched the stone, tracing the delicate lines of the statue. The craftsmanship was exquisite, the artist capturing the folds of the veil and the gentle curve of the woman's face with remarkable skill. But the absence of a death date cast a shadow over the beauty of the monument.

She stood and looked around, her eyes scanning the rows of graves. The realization struck her with a cold clarity: none of the women's stones had death dates. It was as if their stories had been left unfinished, their lives forever suspended in a state of limbo.

The mist began to lift, and the first rays of the sun broke through the trees, casting a golden glow over the cemetery. The light danced on the headstones, illuminating the names and dates etched into the stone.

She continued to explore, her footsteps rustling through vegetation on the soft ground. The cemetery was larger than she had initially thought, with rows upon rows of graves stretching out before her.

As she walked, she came across a small, secluded corner of the cemetery. Here, the graves were newer, the stones not so weathered and worn by time. A small beveled marker stood for Victor Harrow. She remembered Logan told her that he and Hyacinth had buried the urn they'd received from Florida. The newest grave, though, was that for Hyacinth. It was covered with vegetation, but a slight mounding could still be seen. Her stone, like those of the other Harrow women, lacked a death date.

Anita felt a profound dredge in the pit of her stomach as pieces began to fall into place. The dice the woman's statue held, the men rolling them during her nightmares, and the argument between Melusine and the priest.

The missing people through the years connected to the Harrows were sacrifices. The roll of the dice stole the years of their life which were either given to a Harrow woman or to the Harrow itself, that supernatural force behind the menacing blue mist. Though the current Mrs. Harrow would command the game, she didn't roll the dice. That was up to a male Harrow. And it appeared through the years, just as Vance had been, the men had become more resistant to their part.

One thing Anita noticed lacking in the cemetery was the usual iconography of the cross. Even if the Harrows hadn't been devout church goers, they had supported the church throughout the history of Harrowsburg, according to the priest. *Keep your friends close and enemies closer*, Anita thought.

And what of Logan, then? If he truly was a Harrow, why wouldn't Hyacinth have needed to clue him in on his heritage so they could continue the game? She kept him close enough as grounds keeper. Why didn't she reveal Logan as a blood heir after Vance's supposed death?

Anita left the newer corner of the cemetery and wended her way to the far back, returning to Victoria Harrow's grave and statue. Next to Victoria, Oswald Harrow's stone held no death date either. She went on a frantic search of the other graves again. As far as she could tell, Oswald's was the only male grave without a death date.

"And the men are the ones forced to roll the dice in the game," Anita mused out loud. "Why?" She knelt at Oswald's stone, tracing the strange symbols carved around the border, so very reminiscent of those on the mahogany table in her nightmares.

Suddenly the symbols shone with a thick blue shimmer. The first birds of the morning took flight, their wings beating hard against the soft sky. Long shadows danced among the trees. The soft light of dawn had cast an ethereal glow over the Harrow family cemetery, but now the sky darkened abruptly. The clouds gathered with unnatural speed, turning the early morning into a foreboding twilight. A sudden chill swept through the air, raising goosebumps on Anita's arms. She glanced up, her curiosity turning to apprehension as the first rumble of thunder echoed across the sky.

Anita stood from Oswald's grave, her eyes scanning the cemetery for any option for shelter. The ground below her began to tremble, and a loud, crackling noise bounced off the stones.

Before her, the grave of Oswald Harrow was now shaking violently. The earth around the headstone began to fracture, and a skeletal hand burst through the soil. Anita gasped, stumbling backward as she watched in horrified fascination.

The hand clawed its way upward, followed by another, and then a skeletal figure began to emerge from the grave. Its bones were covered in remnants of decayed clothing and dirt, and its empty eye sockets seemed to stare directly at her. Anita's breath came in short, panicked bursts as she took another step back, only to trip over a low footstone. She landed hard on the ground, pain shooting through her ankle, but her eyes remained fixed on the grotesque sight before her.

As Oswald Harrow's skeletal form fully emerged from the grave, the ground around other headstones began to tremble. One by one, the graves of the Harrow family erupted, and more figures began to claw their way out of the earth. The cemetery was soon filled with the sounds of rattling bones and mournful wails of the undead.

Anita's mind raced. At first, she thought they were coming for her, and she scrambled to get up, her eyes darting around for an escape route. But then she noticed something. The undead were not moving toward her. Instead, they seemed to be fixated on one another.

The men, their hollow eyes filled with an inexplicable sorrow, called out mournfully to the women. "Murderers! You've made us murderers!" one of the men cried, his voice a hollow mush-mouth echo that sent shivers down Anita's spine.

The women, their skeletal forms no less terrifying, responded with venomous anger. Cowards! Yellow bellies!" one of them spat, her voice filled with a centuries-old rage. "You left us to suffer the Harrow's wrath while you rotted in peace!"

Anita watched in horror as the men and women, now fully risen from their graves, began to clash. They scratched and clawed at one another with a ferocity that belied their atrophied frames. Gaunt limbs snapped and splintered, but neither side seemed willing to relent. Bony fingers scrabbled against one another, and the air around them began to shimmer the blue mist of the Harrow.

The mist grew thicker, swirling around the combatants as they fought. As Anita watched, horrified, the mist seemed to sap their strength. With each passing moment, the combatants grew weaker, their bones becoming more brittle. Finally, with a weak touch of the blue mist, the haggard bodies began to disintegrate, turning to dust and leaving nothing behind but shimmering blue haze.

Anita pushed herself to her feet, ignoring the pain in her ankle. She had to get out of there. The undead Harrows were too engrossed in their macabre battle to notice her, but she had no intention of sticking around to see how it ended. She turned and ran, her heart pounding in her chest.

The path she had taken earlier seemed to twist and turn more than she remembered, but she forced herself to keep moving. The sounds of the undead battling behind her grew fainter, but the image of their skeletal forms tearing each other apart was seared into her mind.

As she ran, the storm above intensified. Lightning flashed, illuminating the cemetery in brief, blinding bursts of light. Thunder roared, shaking the ground beneath her feet. The wind whipped through the trees, tearing at her clothes and hair.

She stumbled again, this time catching herself before she fell. The iron gate of the cemetery loomed ahead, and with a final burst of speed, she sprinted toward it. She reached the gate, her fingers fumbling with the latch. For a heart-stopping moment, it seemed stuck, but then it gave way, and she pushed the gate open, floundering through, landing at Vance's feet.

***

Anita's breath came in ragged gasps as she stared up at him from her knees. His features shifted mercilessly from the man she remembered through their marriage to the body she had found that horrible day to the young man and child she had seen in photographs. The storm raged above, its fury undiminished, but the immediate threat of the undead was behind her. Even if it hadn't been, she would have braved hell itself to speak to him again. The air was thick with humidity, and the distant roll of thunder added an ominous soundtrack to her racing heart.

"Vance!" she cried out, her voice trembling with a mix of relief and sorrow. She lurched to her feet and reached out to him instinctively, but her hand passed through his form as if he were made of smoke. He was just mist and memory, a ghostly apparition that couldn't be touched.

"'Nita," Vance's voice was soft, almost ethereal, carrying hints of the warmth she remembered so well. He reached out to cup her face in his hand, but it only left a spike of a chill on her skin.

She took a step closer, her eyes filling with tears.

"There's so much you don't know, so much I wish I could have told you. But I was weak... and I thought I could escape it all by starting a new life. I was wrong."

"I know. This legacy of the Harrows. It's awful. I don't blame you for trying to start over. But why didn't you—" She gasped as his form wavered, and he seemed to struggle to maintain his presence. "No! Don't go!" She grabbed at his flickering form even though she knew it was useless.

"I'm weaker near the Hall and Victoria. She... she draws strength from those around her, keeps us tied to this place. But farther away, I have more strength. I can't stay long, but you have to listen."

Anita nodded, her heart aching with every word he spoke. "Tell me what I need to do, Vance."

"You have to destroy the Harrow legacy once and for all," Vance said, his voice urgent. "Find the dice. Hyacinth must have hidden them somewhere. They hold the key to ending this curse. Without them, Victoria's power will remain unchecked."

His ghostly form flickered, his eyes filled with sorrow and regret. "I thought I could protect you by staying away. I thought I could keep you safe. But I was wrong. I should have told you everything. I should have fought harder. I'm so sorry, Anita. I love you."

Vance's form began to fade, the edges blurring into the surrounding mist. "You have to end this for all of us." He gestured toward the cemetery. "The Harrow holds them all here in rage to fuel Victoria."

He was barely visible now. "I'm sorry, 'Nita. I'm so sorry for everything."

"Vance, please!" she cried, desperation lacing her voice. "Don't go! I would have understood. I would have helped you! Why, Vance? Why did you leave me? Why did you kill yourself?"

He shook his head slowly, his form flickering like a candle in the wind. "I didn't kill myself."

His form dissipated into the mist, and Anita was left standing alone, the storm raging around her. His final words echoed in the air long after he was gone. *I didn't kill myself.*

Anita sank back to her knees in the mud, the weight of the revelation crashing down on her. She sobbed uncontrollably, the pain of losing Vance all over again almost too much to bear. But deep inside, a spark of determination began to ignite. She wiped her tears, her mind racing with the new information. Vance didn't take his own life. That meant someone was at fault, and she was certain their motive had something to do with the Harrows.

The dice.

Anita knew she had to find them and put an end to the curse that had plagued the Harrow family for generations. She took a deep breath, forcing herself to stand. The storm showed no signs of abating, but she felt a newfound strength within her. She had to find the dice, and she had to do it soon. She knew in her heart that by stopping the Harrow she would find out the truth of Vance's death.

As she made her way back to the Hall, her mind was a whirlwind of thoughts and emotions. The path seemed longer and more treacherous than she remembered, the shadows deeper and more menacing. But Anita pushed on, her resolve unshakable. Her meeting with Samuel Prendergast that day would open up Melusine's story, and from what she'd learned so far, Anita was sure Melusine had wanted to destroy the

Harrow almost as much as Anita wanted to.

***

Logan's footsteps echoed in the quiet corridors of Our Lady of the Light Church as he made his way to Father Shane's office. The old stone building, with its high arches and stained-glass windows, had always filled him with a sense of awe and peace. Today, his heart pounded with a mix of anticipation and dread. He needed answers—about the Harrow family and about himself.

Father Shane's door was slightly ajar, and Logan knocked softly before entering. The priest, looked up with kind, tired eyes from his desk. He smiled, but it was tinged with weariness.

"Logan, my boy," Father Shane greeted, gesturing for him to sit. "What brings you here today?"

Logan took a seat, trying to gather his thoughts. "Father Shane, I need to know about the Harrows. And...I need to know about my birth."

The priest's face paled, and he shifted uncomfortably in his chair. "The Harrows," he repeated softly, as if the very name weighed heavily on his tongue. "Why now, Logan? Why are you asking about this now?"

"Because I need to understand," Logan said, his voice steady despite the turmoil inside. "There's so much I don't know, so much that's been kept from me. Please, Father. I need to know the truth."

Father Shane sighed deeply, his fingers tapping nervously on the wooden desk. "Very well, Logan. But understand, what I'm about to tell you is not easy for me to speak of. It's... it's a dark part of our town's history."

Logan nodded, leaning forward. "I'm ready."

Father Shane took a deep breath, his eyes clouding with memories. "I was very young when Melusine Harrow came to me for help. She was desperate, scared. She confided in me about the mysterious power of the Harrow family and the terrible game they were playing—a game that involved ancient rituals and a dangerous legacy."

"What did the game do?" Logan asked.

"The Harrows believed they could control fate itself through a set of enchanted dice," Father Shane explained. "These dice held great power, and they used them to manipulate events to their favor. But it came at a cost—an insidious, malevolent force that fed on their souls."

Logan's mind raced as he processed the information. "And you didn't believe Melusine?"

The priest shook his head, regret etched on his face. "No, I didn't. I was young, naive. I thought it was just the ramblings of a frightened, ill young woman. It wasn't until years later that I realized she had spoken the truth. By then, it was too late to help her."

Logan's heart ached for Melusine, and he couldn't help but feel a pang of guilt for doubting the stories he had heard about the Harrows. "And what about me? What do you know about my birth?"

Father Shane's eyes met Logan's, and for a moment, he seemed to struggle with whether to speak. Finally, he nodded. "You deserve to know, Logan. You are... a Harrow."

Logan felt as though the ground had shifted beneath him. Vanessa's accusation was something he could doubt, but he trusted the priest.

Father Shane continued, his voice trembling slightly. "Your mother gave birth to you at Harrow Hall. Hyacinth, your grandmother, arranged for you to be given up for adoption immediately after you were born. She placed you with the Emmerichs to protect you."

Logan's mind reeled. He had always felt out of place, but this revelation was almost too much to bear. "Why? Why would she give me up?"

"Because your father was a priest," Father Shane said softly. "And the Harrow was certain not to like that. Hyacinth wanted you away from the Hall, away from the family's dark legacy."

Logan's breath caught in his throat. "So, she thought the Harrow would what? Kill me?"

Father Shane nodded. "Yes, Logan, or worse. She believed that your connection to a man of faith made you a threat to the Harrow's power. By placing you with the Emmerichs, she hoped to keep you safe."

"But a priest fathering a child—if what I'm understanding about the Harrow is true, wouldn't that fit right into their dark legacy?"

"A priest is still a man, my dear boy. As much as we fight the flesh, we never escape it until our last day. Another thing we never escape is love. We know you were given life through God's love, but if your parents conceived you in a state of love as well...Well, that certainly wouldn't be agreeable with the Harrow Legacy."

Logan's thoughts raced as he tried to process the weight of this revelation. His whole life, he had believed he was someone else, someone ordinary. But now, he understood the true depth of the darkness that had shaped his existence. "Why didn't anyone tell me?"

"Hyacinth swore me to secrecy," Father Shane said. "She believed it was the only way to protect you. And over the years, as I saw the truth of what the Harrow was, and I knew she was right."

Logan leaned back in his chair, staring at the ceiling as he tried to make sense of everything. "And what about Melusine? What happened to her?"

"Melusine disappeared," Father Shane said, his voice heavy with sorrow. "Some say she ran away, others think she took her own life. I don't know. But she was a brave woman, trying to protect her family from a darkness she couldn't escape."

"So, what do I do now?"

Father Shane reached across the desk, placing a comforting hand on Logan's shoulder. "You do what I couldn't for Melusine. You give that Anita every bit of help you are able and rely on God for what you're not able. He will strengthen you in this fight."

Logan nodded, determination hardening his resolve.

The priest's eyes filled with a mixture of sadness and pride. "Be careful, Logan. The Harrow family has always been dangerous, and you carry their blood. But you also have the strength of your father and the love of those who raised you. Use that to guide you."

Logan stood, his heart heavy but his spirit unbroken. "Thank you, Father Shane. For telling me the truth."

"Go with God, Logan," the priest said, his voice barely above a whisper. "May He protect you."

Logan left the church, the weight of his newfound knowledge pressing down on him. He walked through the quiet streets of the town, the clouds overhead beginning to part as the odd morning thunderstorm passed. He felt a sense of purpose he had never known before, a drive to uncover the secrets of his past and put an end to the dark legacy that had haunted the Harrows for generations.

***

Samuel Prendergast lived in a modest house on the outskirts of Marionville. The place had a whimsical charm, with a garden filled with blooming flowers and dozens of gnomes of all colors, sizes, and occupations. A well-maintained path led to the front door. It was barely 9:30 am. They hadn't set a time, but Anita couldn't wait much longer. She knocked and waited.

The door creaked open, revealing the elderly man with kind eyes and a weathered face that spoke of years of wisdom.

"Thanks for having me, Mr. Prendergast," Anita replied, stepping inside the cozy home. The walls were lined with bookshelves, and the air carried the warm scent of freshly brewed coffee.

"Just Samuel is fine," he said with a chuckle, guiding her to a comfortable armchair in the living room. "Would you like some coffee?"

"Yes, please," Anita replied, settling into the chair.

Samuel moved to the kitchen and returned with two steaming cups. He handed one to Anita and took a seat opposite her. "So, you want to know about Melusine," he said, his expression turning nostalgic.

"Yes," Anita said softly. "I'm trying to understand more about her life and the Harrow family."

Samuel nodded, his eyes misting with memories. "Melusine was a special person. She had a heart full of kindness, even though she was surrounded by so much cruelty." He reached for a small, wooden box on the table beside him and opened it, revealing a stack of yellowed letters tied with a delicate red ribbon.

"These are the letters she wrote to me while I was overseas during the 1940s," Samuel said, handing the bundle to Anita. "We were just kids, really. She was a few years older than me, but we shared a bond that transcended age."

Anita untied the ribbon and gently unfolded the first letter, her eyes scanning the elegant handwriting.

October 5, 1943

Dear Samuel,

I hope this letter finds you well and safe. Life at Harrow Hall continues to be a challenge. My family's cruelty knows no bounds. They see me as nothing more than a pawn in their endless games of power and manipulation. I long to leave this place, to run away and find freedom. But the ties that bind me here are strong, and I fear I may never break free.

You are the only one I can confide in, the only one who knows my true heart. Your letters bring me comfort in these dark times. Stay safe, my dear friend.

Yours, Melusine

Anita felt a pang of sadness as she read the words. She could sense the despair and loneliness that Melusine had endured. She carefully unfolded another letter.

March 12, 1944

Dear Samuel,

The days here grow longer and more oppressive. My family's demands are relentless, and their games grow ever more sinister. I often dream of escaping, of finding a place where I can be free of their control. But every attempt I make is thwarted by their watchful eyes.

Sometimes, I feel like a prisoner in my own home. Your letters are my only solace. They remind me that there is goodness in the world, that there is hope beyond these walls. I wish I could leave and be with you, far away from this cursed place.

With all my heart, Melusine

Anita glanced up at Samuel, who was watching her with a mix of sadness and fondness. "She really trusted you," Anita said softly.

Samuel nodded. "She did. I was just a boy, but I loved her deeply. She was like an angel trapped in hell."

Anita continued reading through the letters, each one revealing more about Melusine's struggles and her desire to escape the confines of Harrow Hall. In one of the final letters, Anita found a particularly haunting passage.

July 27, 1945

Dear Samuel,

I fear this may be my last letter to you. My family's games have grown more dangerous, and I am afraid for my life. They are obsessed with their secrets and their power. I have hidden the rules to their twisted game, a game that has caused so much pain, and I swear I will take them to my grave.

If something happens to me, know that I loved you with all my heart. You were my only source of light in these horrid shadows. I pray that one day, the truth will be revealed, and this curse upon the Harrow family will be lifted.

Yours forever, Melusine

Anita's heart raced as she read the letter a second time. "The rules to the game... She said she would take them to her grave," Anita murmured.

Samuel nodded slowly, his eyes filled with tears. "She was so brave, even in the face of such cruelty. She wanted to protect others from the same fate she endured."

Anita set the letters down and looked at Samuel. "I found the Harrow family cemetery this morning." She stifled a shiver. "I didn't see a stone for Melusine. Do you know what happened to her?"

Samuel's expression turned somber, and he took a deep breath before speaking. "Yes, I do. I'd just gotten home from the war, and the official story was that she ran away and got lost in the woods, but I didn't believe it. She knew that land like the back of her hand. Her time outside of the Hall was her only source of peace."

He paused, his voice thick with emotion. "I searched for her through three nights on the Harrow property. I finally found her body by the fruit orchard, hidden away in an apple cart. The townspeople never cared enough to look for her. They preferred to make up stories and rumors about her, rather than see the real her.

"She wasn't..." He took a deep breath and the lines around his eyes creased deeply. "She'd been gone a while, but from what I could tell, she'd been strangled and her neck was broken. By who or what I don't know, but you can bet her family was behind it." Tears streamed down Samuel's face as he continued. "I closed her up in that apple cart with a quilt and gave her a proper burial on the hill by the orchard. I carved an M on the tree next to her grave."

"Wouldn't the authorities have—"

He shook his head vehemently. "Her sister-in-law had had the old sheriff in her pocket for years by then. They'd have done nothing. Worse yet, I was afraid they would have placed the blame on Melusine. They called her crazy, even her own family. I couldn't...I just couldn't let them tell another lie about her."

Anita's heart ached for Samuel and for Melusine. "I'm so sorry," she whispered. "She deserved so much better."

The old man nodded, wiping his tears with a trembling hand. "She did. She was a bright light in a dark world. I've spent my life trying to honor her memory."

Anita reached across and gently squeezed Samuel's hand. "Thank you for sharing this with me. I'll do everything I can to uncover the truth and bring some peace to her memory."

Samuel's eyes filled with gratitude. "Thank you, Anita. It means a lot to know that someone cares about her story."

As Anita left Samuel's home, she felt a renewed sense of purpose. She knew she had to find Melusine's grave and uncover the hidden rules of the Harrow family's game. She was confident that the rules and the dice, as Vance had instructed, would give Anita the tools she needed to stop the Harrow.

Chapter Twelve

The sun was beginning to set as Anita returned from Marionville, her mind a tumult of thoughts and unresolved mysteries. The drive back to Harrow Hall was uneventful, but as she approached the entry to the familiar two-track road leading to the estate, a white SUV with tinted windows pulled onto the highway ahead of her. She narrowed her eyes, trying to get a better look, but the vehicle sped away too quickly for her to see any identifying marks.

A chill ran down her spine. The SUV looked suspiciously like the one that had tried to run her over in Marionville on Sunday. She considered following it, but it was already racing away, and her concern shifted to what they might have done at the Hall. Anxiety gnawed at her as she turned onto the two-track, her car bouncing over the uneven path.

As the Hall came into view, Anita's heart skipped a beat. There, sitting on the front porch swing was Doreen. She was gazing out over the grounds with an air of calm that contrasted starkly with Anita's own frantic state. Relief washed over Anita, mingling with the confusion and worry that had been her constant companions since morning.

"Doreen!" Anita called out, as she jumped out of her car, slamming the door. "What are you doing here? You weren't supposed to fly in until the end of the week. Is everything okay?"

Doreen looked up, a tired smile spreading across her face. "I was worried about you, Anita. You haven't been responding to my messages or calls. So, I found an earlier flight and got a rideshare from the airport in Windsor Locks."

Anita's heart warmed at her friend's concern. "My phone got damaged." She took the porch steps two at a time and enveloped Doreen in a hug. The familiar scent of her perfume and the solidness of her presence were incredibly comforting after the day's supernatural horrors.

"I'm so glad you're here," Anita said, her voice muffled against Doreen's shoulder. "You have no idea what I've been through—today alone."

As their embrace ended and the greeting cooled, Anita couldn't help but glance back toward the road. A niggling suspicion wormed its way into her mind. Could Doreen have been in that SUV? It seemed unlikely, but the coincidence was too glaring to ignore.

"Doreen, did you see a white SUV with tinted windows when you got here?" Anita asked. She couldn't keep the concern verging on panic from her voice.

Doreen blinked in surprise. "A white SUV? No, I didn't see anything like that. Why?"

Anita hesitated, her thoughts racing. "It's just that a white SUV tried to run me over in Marionville yesterday. It seemed odd that the same kind of vehicle would be around here."

Doreen's eyes widened. "Run you over? Oh my God, Anita, are you okay?"

"Yeah, I'm fine. It just shook me up a bit. But are you sure you didn't see anything? How long have you been here?"

Doreen looked thoughtful for a moment before shaking her head. "My rideshare was just a regular car. I don't know anything about an SUV."

Anita was surprised by her friend's reaction. Something nagged at her to push the matter and repeat her unanswered question about how long Doreen had been on the porch, but she decided to brush it aside for now. She attributed the suspicion to the surrealness of her day so far. Maybe the SUV had come in far enough to see that someone was outside and then turned around and left right away. Anita forced a smile. "Okay. Let's get you and your luggage inside."

They gathered Doreen's bags from the porch and made their way into the Hall. The grand foyer, with its dark wood paneling and antique furniture, felt eerily quiet after the events of the morning. Anita couldn't shake the feeling that they were being watched, but she forced herself to focus on Doreen.

Doreen chose a room for her stay, delighted by its blue and white colors and French theme, and she and Anita nicknamed it the Bleu Room. They shared another hug. "I have so much to tell you," Anita said. "You won't believe what has been happening."

The friends lounged on the huge four-poster bed while she attempted to explain the strange events that had happened since she arrived in Connecticut. With Doreen, she held nothing back. She only stopped for Doreen's occasional questions for clarification. When Anita had finished recounting the events, she stood from the bed, tracing the pineapple finial on a post at the foot end.

Doreen lay on her back, staring at the ceiling, taking it all in. After a couple of minutes, she responded, "Holy shit!"

They both burst out laughing, and Anita collapsed back onto the bed. "I know, right? I don't know what to think of it most days myself."

Through the breeze of the open window, Anita heard the crunch of gravel outside. She peered out and saw Logan's pickup pulling up the driveway. Relief flooded through her.

"Logan's here," she announced to Doreen, who followed her down the main stairs. He knocked and let himself inside. His expression was a mix of determination and concern as Anita took the steps two at a time with Doreen behind her.

Logan caught Anita's hand at the base of the stairs, and she appreciated the tug to his side. She melted into the embrace he offered. "Logan, this is my friend Doreen."

He held out his free hand to shake hers, holding Anita close with his other arm. "Nice to meet you. I've heard a lot about you."

"Likewise," Doreen said.

In answer to his questioning gaze, Anita said, "She was worried about me, so she took an earlier flight."

Doreen yawned and stretched. "I've been on night shifts for the past two weeks. The flight wasn't so bad, but the morning is getting to me."

"Why don't you go get some rest, and we'll make some lunch?" Anita suggested.

"Sounds like a plan, 'Nita."

Anita flinched slightly at the nickname coming on the heels of her encounter with Vance's ghost. Doreen gathered her into a big hug and then headed back upstairs.

Anita and Logan walked into the kitchen, the comforting smells of spices and freshly washed vegetables already mingling in the air. The spacious kitchen, with its rustic wooden beams and large windows overlooking the grounds, always felt like a safe haven amid the chaos that seemed to pervade the Hall.

As Logan began to chop vegetables for a salad, he glanced over at Anita, who was busy boiling water for pasta. The silence between them was filled with the unspoken weight of their respective discoveries.

"I went to see Father Shane," Logan began, breaking the silence. His voice was steady, but there was an underlying tension. "He confirmed what Vanessa was pushing. I was born a Harrow."

Anita paused, turning to face him. "What did he say?"

Logan took a deep breath. "He told me about how my mother gave birth to me here at the Hall, and then Hyacinth gave me up to the Emmerichs right away. My birth father...he was a priest. That's why Hyacinth never revealed my parentage. She believed that the Harrow would harm me because of my father's faith."

"And Father Shane believed this from Hyacinth, but didn't believe Melsusine when she had come to him for help?"

"He admitted that later on in life experience showed him his mistake, but by that time it was too late to change it."

Anita absorbed the information, her mind flashing back to her own encounter in the cemetery. "Logan, there's something you need to know. I went to the cemetery this morning, and I saw some strange things."

Logan's knife paused mid-chop. "Strange things?"

Anita nodded, her expression grave. "The women's headstones...none of them had death dates. It was like they never truly died. Oswald's stone was the only male one without a death date. I think it has something to do with the Covenant of Shadows game. It's like it took life from those who went missing over the years, and their fates were never truly sealed.

"The Harrow family—the men and women—their spirits or their essences, I'm not sure what I saw—they are set against each other in some kind of enraged war. The men claim that the women turned them into murderers."

Logan's eyes widened as he listened. "That's...unsettling. But it makes a twisted kind of sense."

Anita hesitated, then continued, "I saw Vance's ghost, Logan. He told me to find the dice used in the game. He said they hold the key to ending the curse."

Logan's reaction surprised her. Instead of shock or disbelief, he nodded thoughtfully. "I know where the dice are."

"What?" Anita asked, taken aback. "How?"

"When we received the cremated remains of what we thought were Victor Harrow, Hyacinth asked me to add some strange dice to the inside of the urn," Logan explained. "I didn't think much of it at the time, but now it makes sense."

Anita's mind raced with the implications. "Then we need to get that urn. But there's something else. I visited Samuel Prendergast. He showed me letters from Melusine. In one of them, she swore to take the rules of the game to her grave."

Logan's expression turned grim. "So, you're saying we might have to dig up two graves? Melusine's and Vic's?"

Anita nodded slowly. "It seems like it."

At that moment, Doreen walked in, her cheerful demeanor a stark contrast to the serious conversation. "Lunch smells amazing!" she exclaimed. "I wasn't able to sleep, so I thought I'd come down and join you." She walked over to the pasta pot and grabbed a noodle, slurping it down. "So, what's this I hear about grave robbing?" she asked nonchalantly as she chewed.

Anita laughed. "I was just filling Logan in about what happened today."

Logan's expression was wary of Doreen. "Oh, Anita caught me up about what's been going on here. Don't worry, I'm all in."

They dished up lunch and sat down at the kitchen island. Anita couldn't shake the feeling that time was running out. She caught Logan's eye across the table, a silent understanding passing between them. They had a daunting task ahead, and every moment counted.

After lunch, Doreen offered to clean up, insisting that Anita and Logan take a break. They stepped out onto the porch and were met with a cool breeze.

"We need to be careful," Logan said quietly. "Digging up those graves...it's not just about breaking the curse. It's about uncovering the truth, no matter how dark."

Anita nodded, her resolve hardening.

They stood in silence for a moment, watching the clouds roll in from the horizon. The storm brewing seemed to reflect the turmoil in their lives. But together, they knew they had the strength to face whatever came next.

Inside, Doreen hummed a tune as she washed the dishes, seemingly oblivious to the storm gathering both outside and within the walls of Harrow Hall. But for Anita and Logan, there was no escaping the shadow of their legacy. They could only move forward, armed with the truth and their unyielding determination.

***

Thunder clapped again as it had been for the last hour, and rain pounded against the windows of the Hall as it had all afternoon. Anita and Logan lay on the couch in each other's arms, both scouring stacks of letters and journals from the attic. Doreen sat sideways in an oversized chair, her legs slung over the arm, scrolling online forums.

"There aren't really any direct mentions to a Covenant of the Shadows, but I'm finding hints of things that might be related. Nothing, though, that specifically explains a dice game."

Anita slapped down the journal she had been reading and sat up. "There's nothing here. We need to find Melusine's grave." Another crack of thunder rattled the Hall, and the electricity went out. "Great!" She threw her hands up.

Doreen turned on the flashlight on her phone. "You know, 'Nita, maybe what you need is a break from all of this. We should head out and see if town still has electricity—find somewhere with a drink."

Despite Anita's pushback, Doreen insisted. Anita thought to herself that Doreen's arrival had come at the worst possible time, but she didn't want to alienate her friend by throwing her into the middle of the chaos they were facing. She could find no easy way to justify how critical she felt the timing was to get to bottom of everything, so when Logan suggested a neighboring town's trendy pub, Anita just went with it.

As they entered the dimly lit establishment, a mix of laughter, clinking glasses, and music enveloped them. The pub was buzzing with life, filled with patrons enjoying their evening.

The trio found a cozy booth near the back, away from the bar's hustle. They ordered drinks and began to unwind, recounting the events of their week. Anita was starting to relax when a man with thick pop-bottle glasses approached their table in the dim light.

"Wow, man! Nothing for 20 years and then twice in one year. What are the odds of that?" he exclaimed.

"Sorry. Do I know you?" Logan asked.

The man startled. "Oh, sorry. I thought you were—Jeez, you sure look like someone else. Sorry."

Anita and Logan exchanged a look. As the stranger turned away, Anita lunged forward to the edge of the booth catching his sleeve. "Wait. Who did you think he was?"

"Oh, it's not important. Just, uh, someone—"

"Was it Vance Miran or Victor Harrow?" Anita asked hurriedly.

The man turned back toward the table and nodded.

"I'm Anita Miran. Vance was my husband."

"Was?" He questioned the tense.

"Yes. He died around eight months ago."

"No! What happened? I just saw him last October in Vegas."

Anita's stomach dropped. Vanessa hadn't been the only one from Vance's earlier life to meet with him at the tech conference in Nevada.

"Please sit down," Anita said, motioning to the spot next to Doreen.

"How did you know Vance?" Doreen asked as she scooted over a bit to give the lanky man some room.

"Well, it sounds like the cat's out of the bag for the whole Victor/Vance thing, then?"

Anita nodded, and Doreen took a long slug of her drink.

"I guess it would be okay then to tell you. I'm Oliver Crane, the one who assisted Victor in becoming Vance, on the paperwork end at least, more than 20 years ago."

"And then you saw him again in Las Vegas in October around Halloween?" Anita questioned.

"Yes. We were both attending a popular technology conference as vendors."

Logan drummed his fingers on the table. "There was another person from this area of Connecticut there also. A tall, slender blond woman, around 35. Probably always in heels and a designer suit."

The man adjusted his glasses. "You mean Vanessa Briggs?"

Anita's mind began racing. "Did you see them together?"

Oliver hesitated, but the intensity in Anita's eyes compelled him to speak. "Yes," he said quietly. "I saw them together. There was a huge blowup between them. They were arguing loudly, and it drew quite a crowd."

"Do you have something to do with Vanessa's work in banking?" Logan asked.

Oliver shifted uncomfortably. "I can't tell you that," he said. "I'm under a non-disclosure agreement. Vanessa is the last person I would want to cross."

Anita's frustration boiled over. She surged forward, leaning over the table toward Oliver. "Vance's death looked like a suicide, but I know someone killed him. I need to know exactly what went on at that conference, and I'll figure it out any way I can!"

Doreen spilled her drink at the outburst, and it poured over the edge of the table onto Oliver's lap. She grabbed for a stack of napkins.

Logan placed a calming hand on Anita's shoulder. "Anita, let's take it easy," he said gently. "Getting angry won't help."

She eased back to a seated position. Taking a deep breath, she tried to regain her composure. "Please, Oliver. We need to know the truth."

Oliver sighed, realizing he had no way out. "My tech company is developing a program for Vanessa and her bank," he admitted. "It assists in hiding accounts and assets from the government."

Anita's eyes widened. "Did Vance know about this?"

Oliver continued to wipe at the spilled drink. "He was aware of it, but with his own history, I don't think he was planning on touching it with a ten-foot pole."

"So, he wasn't trying to stop you?" Doreen asked. "That doesn't seem like the Vance I knew."

Anita was surprised at Doreen's comment. She glanced at her friend sipping a vodka cranberry but returned her focus quickly to Oliver.

"What was his argument about with Vanessa then if not that?" Logan asked. He handed his glass of water and some more napkins to Oliver.

"Thanks. From what I could tell it was the Vic to Vance thing."

Anita looked at Logan. "That would have been enough certainly to make someone even like Vanessa blow up publicly. She thought he'd died long ago."

"We all did," Logan said.

"I knew that he'd had a girlfriend way back when. He'd intended for her to believe the same as everyone else."

Doreen leaned back. "Well maybe you have it then. His secret was finally out. This Vanessa sounds like a piece of work, and I doubt she kept the news quiet for very long. He probably just couldn't bear the truth getting out there. Especially to you, 'Nita."

"Vance did not kill himself," Anita said firmly, furrowing her brow at Doreen.

Doreen gave Anita a pitying look. "Hon, I thought you were past this. For heaven sakes, you're the one who found him like that."

Anita couldn't believe the position her friend was taking. As if sensing her growing anger, Logan caught her hand and gave it a squeeze. Anita took a deep breath.

Oliver held up his hands. "I swear I had nothing to do with his death. I didn't even know he was dead."

"We need to be careful," Logan said. "If Vanessa was somehow involved, we're dealing with things a lot deeper and dangerous than we first realized."

Anita nodded slowly, her resolve hardening. "We'll get to the bottom of this," she said firmly. "For Vance."

The weight of the conversation hung heavy in the air. Oliver stood up and sidled out of the booth. "Look, I'm really sorry to have interrupted your night. It's just that you look so much like him, man."

After Oliver slipped away quietly, clearly relieved to be leaving, Anita, Logan, and Doreen decided it was time to leave the pub, too. Its lively atmosphere seemed distant and surreal compared to the gravity of their conversation. They headed to Logan's pickup, and Anita decided it was time to fill Doreen in on the biggest parts of the hauntings and strange occurrences at the Harrow estate as they drove back. She was convinced that the reason Doreen wasn't being supportive was because she didn't understand everything that was going on.

The winding road seemed longer in the darkness, the headlights casting eerie shadows on the trees lining the path. Doreen listened intently, her eyes wide with a mixture of fear and curiosity.

"I still can't believe you went through all of that alone," Doreen said, shaking her head. "The spirits, the voices...it's like something out of a nightmare."

Anita nodded, her expression grim. "It was, and it still is. But we have to finish what we started. We need to find Melusine's grave and get Victor's urn and the dice. I believe they're the key to stopping all of this."

When they arrived at the Hall, the night was overcast, and a thick blanket of clouds obscured the moon, but the rain had slowed to a drizzle. The house loomed in the darkness, its silhouette imposing and foreboding. They parked near one of the outbuildings. Logan handed out some rain gear, and Anita found flashlights and shovels.

"Doreen, Logan, I need you two to go to the family cemetery and dig up the urn. I don't want to risk reawakening the spirits like I did before," Anita instructed. "I'll find the apple tree where Samuel Prendergast buried Melusine and start digging there."

Logan gave her a reassuring nod. "Be careful. We'll find you as soon as we have the urn."

Doreen held her shovel at arm's length. "Spirits and digging up graves? Are you sure about all this, 'Nita? I mean—"

"—Stop calling me that!" Anita snapped and tried to calm herself. "Yes, I'm sure, and you're my best friend, so it shouldn't even be a question."

Doreen shrugged. "It's just a lot to take in."

Anita tried to be understanding. All of the strange events of the past weeks were so very real to her and also to Logan. Of course, Doreen must be shocked, but she just wasn't acting the way Anita had expected. Hadn't she come early because she was worried about Anita? Well, this was the way to fix what was wrong. Couldn't she see that?

Anita watched as Doreen and Logan made their way toward the cemetery, their flashlight beams bobbing across the darkness. She took a deep breath, steeling herself for the task ahead, and headed towards the apple tree that Samuel Prendergast told her about.

She found it easily, even in the night, feeling as if she'd been led right to it, past the hundreds of other trees in the orchard. It stood tall and twisted, its gnarled branches reaching out like skeletal fingers. Anita's flashlight beam illuminated the M carved into the tree just below the crook of the lowest branch more than half a century ago. She paced off about four feet from the trunk and began to dig. The soil was damp and heavy. As she dug deeper, she couldn't shake the feeling that she was being watched.

Three feet down or so, Anita's shovel struck something solid. Her heart raced as she cleared the dirt away, revealing flat planks of lumber. She dug more fiercely, exposing the perimeter of the apple cart that Samuel had buried. She used the spade to pry the partially rotted wood off the top of the cart's frame.

Inside, tattered cloth from the burial quilt and clothing still clung to bones. Anita gently shifted some of the remains, and her flashlight illuminated a small leather journal nestled near her ribcage. The pages were yellowed with age but surprisingly intact.

She carefully retrieved the small book. Anita felt a chill run down her spine. This journal could hold the answers they desperately needed. As she clutched it to her chest and laid her shovel to the side of the grave, a sharp pain exploded at the back of her head. The world spun and went dark as she crumpled. Her last blurred view before losing consciousness was a fleeting image of Melusine's tortured spirit.

***

When Anita came to, she felt an overwhelming sense of claustrophobia. She was in a confined space, her body curled awkwardly.

She tried to move, but wooden walls pressed against her on all sides. Panic surged through her as she realized she had been buried alive. Melusine's bones poked into her back and sides.

She screamed and thrashed, but the wooden planks of the apple cart that enclosed her were sturdy, bolstered by the packed earth around. The lid she had pried open had been replaced with new wood fastened down tightly. Her cries were muffled by the dirt above. Tears streamed down her face as she pounded on the walls, her mind racing with fear and despair.

Suddenly, a spectral figure appeared before her glowing faintly in the darkness. "Do not panic," a woman's voice whispered, eerily calm and soothing. "Help is coming. You must stay strong."

As Anita lay trapped in the cold, damp grave, her heart pounding, the shadows fled with fear, as a soft, ethereal glow spread. Slowly, a discernible figure emerged. Melusine's ghost was a vision of haunting beauty, her translucent form shimmering with an otherworldly light. Her long, flowing hair cascaded around her like a silken veil, rippling gently as if stirred by an invisible breeze. Her eyes, deep and sorrowful, held a wisdom and sadness that transcended time, yet there was a serene calmness in them that eased Anita's terror. Melusine's delicate features were ethereal, her lips parted in a gentle, understanding smile, as if she knew every fear and every sorrow that plagued Anita's heart.

The spectral figure floated gracefully, her ghostly gown billowing around her like mist, its edges fading into the air. As she drew closer, the chill of the grave seemed to dissipate, replaced by a comforting warmth that radiated from her presence. Melusine's hands, slender and pale, reached out towards Anita, offering solace and protection. Her touch, though ghostly, felt like a soft whisper against Anita's skin, a reminder that even in the darkest moments, beauty and light could be found. The ghost's aura was calming, wrapping around Anita like a protective embrace, and in that moment, the oppressive weight of the grave felt lighter, the shadows less menacing. Melusine, with her haunting elegance and calming presence, became a beacon of hope in the suffocating darkness.

Anita's fear waned. She took a deep breath, trying to calm herself, and, in the moments, reflected on everything that had happened. She thought about Vance and how his death had been falsely ruled a suicide. She had been so close to uncovering the truth and bringing justice to the Harrow family. And Logan—she realized with a pang of fear and affection how much she had come to care for him. What had happened to him and Doreen? Had they been attacked as well?

"Tell me Melusine. What was in your rule book that will help us stop the Harrow?"

"You must share the roll thrice, and it can only end in light."

"The roll of the dice?"

The shimmering woman nodded.

"Share it how?"

"The Harrow was never meant to extend the lives of only the women, but when Victoria and Oswald came to this place, she stole the Harrow from him completely."

Time passed slowly, each second feeling like an eternity. Anita's thoughts swirled as she lay trapped in the apple cart. The weight of the earth above pressed down on her, but she fought to keep her mind clear, focusing on Melusine and her advice.

Finally, she heard scraping sounds above her, followed by muffled voices. Hope surged within her as the noises grew louder. The wood above her splintered and cracked, and she shielded her face as dirt and debris fell in.

"Anita!" Logan's voice was filled with desperation and relief as he ripped the remaining planks away. He reached down and pulled her out, cradling her in his arms. His face was bruised and bloodied, his movements slow and pained.

Within him, the ghost of Vance flickered in and out of view. His spectral form seemed to be infusing Logan with strength, keeping him upright and moving. Logan's eyes were filled with a mixture of anguish and determination as he held Anita close.

"It was Doreen," Logan said, his voice ragged. "Doreen, Vanessa, and the bank security guard, Atkins. They attacked me in the cemetery the minute we found the urn."

Anita's heart ached with betrayal. "Doreen? But why?" She felt a warm wetness coming from Logan's chest. She leaned back, making an inspection in the dark. "Logan is this a gun shot? Oh my God, what did they do to you?"

Logan shook his head, wincing from the pain. "They worked me over pretty good. Vance woke me up. I think he's somehow helping me to stay alive."

Anita watched Vance flicker through Logan, who gave her a solemn nod. "You have to stop them," he said, his voice echoing with an otherworldly resonance. "They have more plans in motion, and they won't stop until they get the Harrow for themselves. It's all that Vanessa has ever wanted."

Anita helped Logan to his feet, her mind racing with the implications of what had happened. "We need to get out of here," she said urgently. "We need to get you medical help and regroup to figure out our next move."

Logan shook his head, leaning heavily on her for support. "We don't have time. We have to stop them."

"Anita," Vance's voice echoed softly, yet with an urgency that cut through the silence. "They're in the covenant room. They are going to try to awaken the Harrow. If they get control of it, it will be all over."

Anita's eyes widened with alarm. "Can you lead me to the room, Vance?" she asked, her voice trembling slightly.

Vance nodded. "Follow me."

They walked along the side of the Hall, catching sight of the malicious white SUV parked at the front. They entered a side door. In the dimly lit Hall, the air was thick with a sense of foreboding. Shadows flickered along the walls as if the house itself was alive, breathing a slow, menacing breath. Anita stood in the hallway, her heart pounding with a mix of fear and determination. The spectral form of Vance appeared to shimmer through Logan's body, casting an odd translucence in the faint light.

Anita followed, her footsteps echoing softly on the wooden floors. They moved through a series of twisting corridors, the Hall's labyrinthine layout becoming even more confusing in the dim light. Finally, they reached a hidden panel in the wall of Anita's room. Logan pressed against a small, inconspicuous spot, and a secret door swung open with a creak.

"This way," Vance whispered, leading her into a narrow, dark corridor.

Anita stepped inside, the darkness enveloping her like a shroud. She felt a chill run down her spine as she followed Vance, his ghostly glow the only source of light. They moved slowly, the sound of their breathing the only noise in the suffocating silence.

As they crept down the corridor, the faint rise and fall of voices reached them. Anita strained to listen, recognizing Vanessa's pleading tone. They approached a heavy wooden door, slightly ajar, from which the voices emanated. Vance paused, his form flickering with tension.

"Be careful," he warned. "We're close."

Anita nodded, peeking through the crack in the door. Inside, she saw Vanessa and Doreen standing near the large, ornate chair. The security guard, Atkins, was bound to the chair, struggling against his restraints. Doreen held a handgun. Nearby, the four dolls were arranged around the carved mahogany table, their glassy eyes reflecting firelight. The ghost of Victoria Harrow stood the table, her spectral form shimmering with an ethereal glimmer.

"Please, Victoria," Vanessa was saying, her voice filled with desperation. "We need to awaken the Harrow to continue the game."

Victoria's ghostly face was impassive, her eyes fixed on Vanessa with a cold, distant gaze. She seemed to be listening, but there was a palpable sense of reluctance in her stance.

On the large table, Melusine's book of rules lay open, and the dice were placed beside it. Anita's heart raced as she realized the significance of the scene. If Vanessa succeeded in awakening the Harrow, the consequences could be catastrophic. She was already corrupt. Anita feared the havoc she would wreak with the Harrow behind her.

Anita took a deep breath, steeling herself. She had to stop them. She crouched low, staying against the wall, creeping into the room on her hands and knees. Her eyes were locked on the dice. She moved slowly, inching closer to the table, her heart pounding in her chest.

Just as she was about to reach the dice, she felt a hot, iron grip on her wrist. She gasped and looked up to see the doll dressed in mourning clothes, holding her hand with an unnaturally strong grip. The touch made Anita's stomach churn.

"Mrs. Harrow has joined us," the doll intoned in a chilling voice, its glassy eyes staring into Anita's.

Anita's blood ran cold. The doll's grip was unyielding, and she struggled to free herself. Vanessa and Doreen turned at the sound, their eyes widening in shock and anger.

Vanessa's face was flushed with a manic determination. She shoved hard at Doreen. "You said you got rid of her."

Anita, feeling the desperation in Vanessa's voice, took a step forward, her gaze shifting to Doreen. She could see the conflict in Doreen's eyes, the way she shifted uncomfortably. Anita seized the moment.

"Doreen," Anita said softly but firmly, "how long have you been involved in this?"

Doreen hesitated, her face pale. Vanessa shot her a warning glance, but Anita pressed on.

"Please, Doreen. If there's any part of you that cares about what's right, you'll tell me. How long?"

Doreen's shoulders slumped, and she let out a shaky breath. "It started shortly before Vance's death," she admitted, her voice barely above a whisper. "Vanessa came to California to try to get Vance to turn the estate over to her. I came over and witnessed them fighting... She promised me a way out, Anita. I just. I owed so many dealers. I..."

Anita's mind reeled. She had trusted Doreen, never suspecting she had been part of this all along. "Why didn't you ask us for help?"

"I never meant for it to go this far," Doreen pleaded, her face crumpling with guilt. "I just wanted a way to escape the life I was trapped in. Vanessa promised she could help."

Vanessa, unable to contain herself any longer, stepped forward, her eyes blazing. "I paid you well enough."

"I didn't want to hurt you." Tears streamed down Doreen's face.

Vanessa whirled on her. "You should have thought of that before you drugged Vic and pulled the trigger."

Anita's vision blurred with shock and red-hot rage. "You *killed* him?" Her voice cracked. "You killed Vance?"

Vanessa smirked, the cruelty in her eyes evident. "Yes, she did. He refused to cooperate, and it was the only way to take control."

Doreen pushed past Vanessa. "I didn't want to, 'Nita. I swear. I just had the drug access. She was supposed to do it, but then she made me."

Anita's fury erupted, and she felt something within her respond. The Harrow, the malevolent force that had haunted her nightmares, awakened by her anger. Blue smoke began to seep from the walls, swirling around Vanessa, Doreen, and the security guard.

Anita's anger transformed into raw power. The Harrow's smoke engulfed the room, its tendrils wrapping around the three figures.

Vanessa's smug expression turned to one of fear. "What is this?" she shrieked.

Doreen screamed and dropped the gun, her voice piercing the air. The security guard struggled, but the smoke tightened its grip. The room filled with the eerie blue light of the Harrow's power.

Logan, or rather Vance in Logan's body, dragged himself into the room, his face contorted with pain. "Anita, stop!" he called out, his voice strained.

Anita, consumed by her rage, barely heard him. The Harrow's power surged, responding to her emotions. It was exactly as Victoria had described—strong, intoxicating. But then, through the chaos, she saw something that made her pause. Victoria Harrow's ghost was smiling, a look of pure delight on her face.

That smile snapped Anita out of her trance. She realized with horror what she was doing. "Stop!" she commanded, her voice trembling.

The Harrow eased, its smoke receding. Anita looked at the symbols on the table, the blue smoke and light infiltrating them just as it had in her nightmares.

"Vance, what do I do?" she whispered desperately.

Vance's voice was faint but clear. "The dice, Anita. You and Logan must roll a light symbol three times in a row. Remember how to roll."

Anita grabbed the dice, her hands shaking. She handed one to Logan, who nodded weakly, understanding what needed to be done. Victoria Harrow's ghost shrieked in fury, and the dolls began to climb over their chairs, coming for them, their eyes glowing with malice.

"Roll!" Anita shouted, her voice cutting through the pandemonium.

Logan, with all the faint strength he could muster, rolled his die. It landed on a light symbol. Anita's heart pounded as she rolled hers, and it too landed on light.

Victoria Harrow screamed, her ghostly form twisting in agony. The dolls lunged at them, but Anita and Logan fought them off, aided by the spirit of Melusine, who appeared beside them, her presence radiating strength.

The second roll was just as tense. Logan's die landed on light, and Anita's followed suit. The room shook with the force of the Harrow's rage, but they pressed on.

"Just one more," Vance whispered, his voice a lifeline amidst the chaos.

Logan, his face pale and sweating, rolled his die for the third time. It teetered on the edge before landing on light. Logan collapsed, his and Vance's collective strength spent. Anita rolled her die, her heart in her throat. It spun and finally settled on light.

A deafening roar filled the room as the Harrow's power was sucked into the table, the symbols glowing brightly. The dolls exploded in a shower of blue dust, their malevolent energy dissipating, and the table split jaggedly along the center, the break shaking the Hall and Anita to the bone.

Anita rushed to Logan's side, her hands shaking. "Logan!" she cried, her voice choked with emotion.

He opened his eyes, a weak smile on his face. "We did it," he whispered.

Anita hugged him tightly, tears streaming down her face. The nightmare was over. The Harrow's power was gone, and the Hall was finally at peace.

She looked around the room, taking in the aftermath of the battle. The security guard was unconscious, but alive. Doreen was sobbing quietly, her face buried in her hands. Vanessa lay still, her expression one of shock and defeat.

Victoria Harrow's ghost lingered for a moment, her form flickering. She looked at Anita with a mix of anger and respect before finally fading away, her presence no longer a threat.

Logan lay in Anita's arms, his breaths shallow and ragged. The room, once filled with chaos, was now eerily quiet. She held him tightly, her tears falling onto his face, mixing with his own. She could feel his life slipping away, and the pain was unbearable.

"Anita..." Logan's voice was weak, barely more than a whisper. "I could feel Vance's love for you. He... he would have never left you."

Anita sobbed, her body shaking with the force of her grief. "Please, Logan. I can't lose you too."

Logan's eyes were filled with sorrow. "I'm so sorry...I wish... I wish I could stay."

Anita clung to him, her heart breaking. "You can't leave me. Not now. Please, Logan, please stay with me."

His breathing grew more labored, and Anita could see the life draining from his eyes. She felt a deep, wrenching pain in her chest as she held him, begging for a miracle.

As Logan took his last, shallow breaths, the room began to glow with a soft, sublime light. Anita looked up through her tears and saw the spirits of Melusine, Hyacinth, and many other Harrow women appearing around them. They stood silently, their presence both comforting and sorrowful.

Melusine, dressed in a 1920s flapper dress with pearls draped elegantly around her, stepped forward. She knelt beside Logan, her celestial form shimmering. She pressed her hand against his chest, her eyes filled with compassion.

Anita watched in awe and desperation as Melusine's hand seemed to transfer a gentle glow into Logan's body. One by one, the spirits of the Harrow women began to fade, their forms dissolving into the light that flowed into Logan. Each ghost gave a part of themselves, their sacrifice a silent act of love and redemption.

The light grew brighter, enveloping Logan completely. Anita felt a surge of hope mixed with fear. She held her breath, praying for a miracle.

Finally, the last of the spirits disappeared. Logan lay still in her arms, not breathing. Anita's heart shattered, and she let out a cry of pure anguish.

But then, Logan's chest rose with a sudden, deep gasp. His eyes flew open, and he inhaled deeply, his body shuddering with the effort. Anita's breath caught in her throat as she watched, hardly daring to believe it.

"Logan?" she whispered, her voice trembling.

He looked at her, and there was no flicker of Vance in his eyes. Logan was alive. He was truly back. The Harrow women had given up all their power to save him.

Anita's tears flowed freely, but now they were tears of joy and relief. She hugged Logan tightly, feeling his warmth, his life. "Oh, Logan," she cried. "You're alive. You're really alive."

Logan, still weak but breathing steadily, held her close. "I'm here, Anita. I'm here."

Anita looked around the room, knowing that the spirits had given up everything to make this possible. The air felt lighter, freer, as if the weight of the past had finally been lifted.

"Thank you," she whispered to the spirits, though they were no longer visible. "Thank you."

In that moment, surrounded by the remnants of the Harrow's legacy, Anita and Logan held each other, their love and the sacrifices of the past binding them together in a way that nothing could ever break.

The blight was cured.

Epilogue

One Year Later

The sun hung low in the sky, casting a golden hue over the sprawling fields surrounding Harrow Hall. Once a place of haunting memories and dark secrets, it now stood as a symbol of resilience and renewal. A year had passed since the tumultuous events that had brought Anita and Logan together, and in that time, they had built a life filled with love, laughter, and the promise of a bright future.

Before Doreen left Connecticut, she had insisted on turning herself in to law enforcement. She told Anita that she couldn't handle what she had done anymore, especially now that Anita knew the truth. It had been a day for the Harrowsburg Sheriff's Office record books when Doreen, Anita, and Logan stepped through the door. Doreen was extradited back to California, and the medical examiner reopened Vance's death investigation. After entering a guilty plea, Doreen was sentenced to twenty-five years. Even though Anita knew they would never reestablish the relationship she had cherished with Doreen prior to the events at Harrow Hall, she was relieved to see that the time behind bars would hopefully allow Doreen to break free of her drug addiction.

Charges had been filed against Vanessa as well. Though she was finally arrested on an outstanding warrant in Florida, she posted the two million dollar bond with the assistance of a business contact. Shortly after, Vanessa disappeared, jumping bail, with what Anita assumed was help from the same business contact. If what Oliver Crane had claimed about Vanessa's project at the tech conference was true, she was involved with dangerous people. Anita was confident that someday, Vanessa would cross the wrong one.

Anita stood on the veranda, her hand resting gently on her growing belly. The gentle breeze played with her hair as she looked out over the fields, feeling a profound sense of peace. Logan's strong, reassuring presence was a constant in her life, and the love they shared had only deepened with each passing day.

"Hey, beautiful," Logan called from the garden, where he was tending to a small hedge of white gardenias. "How are you feeling?"

Anita smiled, turning to face him. "I'm good, just enjoying the view and thinking about how far we've come."

Logan wiped his hands on his jeans and walked over to her, wrapping his arms around her from behind. "It's been quite a journey, hasn't it?"

She leaned into him, savoring the warmth of his embrace. "It has. And I wouldn't change a thing."

They stood in comfortable silence for a moment, the only sounds, the rustling leaves and distant chirping of birds. The tranquility was a stark contrast to the chaos they had faced, but it was a testament to their strength and commitment to each other.

"Have you thought about names yet?" Logan asked, placing a gentle hand on her stomach.

Anita chuckled softly. "I can't seem to settle on anything. There are just so many possibilities."

Logan kissed the top of her head. "Well, we have time. And whatever name we choose, it'll be perfect."

Their conversation was interrupted by the sound of laughter coming from the side of the house. Susan appeared with Grace in tow. The girl ran ahead, her boundless energy infectious.

"Aunt Anita! Uncle Logan!" Grace shouted, racing up to them with a wide grin.

"Hey there, kiddo!" Logan said, scooping her up into his arms. "What's got you so excited?"

Grace giggled. "Mommy said I can help with the baby room today! I want to paint flowers on the walls!"

Anita smiled warmly. "That sounds like a wonderful idea, Grace. We'll make sure the baby's room is the prettiest one in the house."

Susan approached, her own smile mirroring her daughter's. "I hope we're not interrupting anything important."

"Not at all," Anita replied. "We're just enjoying the day and talking about baby names."

Susan's eyes sparkled with excitement. "Oh, names! Have you thought about using a family name? Something that connects the past with the future?"

Anita and Logan exchanged a thoughtful glance. "That's a great idea," Logan said.

Anita nodded. "Melusine, after Melusine Harrow. She was a remarkable woman."

Susan clapped her hands together. "I love it!"

Grace wriggled out of Logan's arms and ran toward the house. "Come on, let's start painting!"

Logan laughed. As they followed her inside, the warmth and love of their family enveloped them. Harrow Hall, once a place of fear, had transformed into a haven of happiness and new beginnings.

That evening, after dinner with Susan and her family, Logan and Anita found themselves alone on the porch once more. The stars twinkled above, and the soft hum of crickets filled the night air.

"Do you ever think about how different our lives would be if we hadn't met?" Anita asked, resting her head on Logan's shoulder.

Logan nodded. "I do. And I'm grateful every day that we found each other. You brought light into my life, Anita."

"And you got rid of the shadows in mine," she replied, her voice filled with emotion.

They sat silently for a while, content in each other's company. The future stretched out before them, filled with endless possibilities and the promise of a life well-lived.

Over the next few months, the preparations for the baby's arrival consumed their days. Friends and family came together to help, filling Harrow Hall with laughter and joy.

On the coldest morning of the winter, Anita went into labor. Logan was by her side every step of the way, his presence a source of strength and comfort. After hours of anticipation and excitement, their baby girl was born.

Holding their daughter for the first time, tears of happiness streamed down Anita's face. "She's perfect, Logan. Absolutely perfect."

Logan kissed her forehead, his own eyes glistening with tears. "She is. Just like her mother."

They named her Melusine Grace, honoring the past and celebrating the future. As they brought her home to Harrow Hall, the Hall seemed to embrace them with open arms, welcoming the new life and the hope she represented.

The years passed, and the Harrow family grew. Logan and Anita's love only deepened, and their bond with their daughter was unbreakable. Melusine grew up surrounded by the beauty of the Hall and the love of her parents and four younger siblings, their laughter filling their spaces, inside and out, with joy.

Over the years, Anita often reflected on their journey, amazed at how far they had come. Harrow Hall, once a place of sorrow, had become a sanctuary of happiness and love. The legacy of the Harrow family had been rewritten and transformed by the power of love and resilience.

***

When Anita had been widowed again for nearly a decade, it was finally her turn to leave the Hall for the last time. She stood in the window of her bedroom late one evening, watching her grandchildren chase fireflies through the garden. The ghost of Melusine Harrow appeared on the path below, shimmering radiantly, the beaded fringe of her dress blowing in the breeze. Anita took the steps of the grand staircase quickly, the arthritis that had been her constant companion for years gone.

With a haunting smile, Melusine took Anita's hand and led her once again to the apple orchard to meet Logan.

* * *

Madeline Quinn is the pen name for a funeral director and embalmer who moonlights as an author in western North Dakota. She finds the same mix of art, science, and dedication required for funeral service to be essential for writing.

Milton Keynes UK
Ingram Content Group UK Ltd.
UKHW041634240924
448733UK00002B/173